THE SMELL OF APRICOTS

And Other Stories

GW00691831

By

Dominic O'Sullivan

Shield Crest

ISBN: 978-1-912505-08-1

A CIP catalogue record for this book
is available from the British Library

MMXVIII

Published by

ShieldCrest
Aylesbury, Buckinghamshire, HP22 5RR
England.

www.shieldcrest.co.uk

To Peter and Mary

The Pomegranate Moment

With a certain amount of elation Mildred Roache closed the front door behind her when she returned that evening. Normally its abrupt click signalled silence, the calmness of an empty house, occasionally punctuated by the gentle buzzing of the fridge. But this evening a sense of euphoria accompanied her through and into the living room.

They had *not* come last, her team! Not been last at the monthly quiz at the Bull and Gate. And the reward on this occasion had been to arrive home empty-handed! The four members of her group, oddly named the Leprechauns – although there had been one Dermot participating at its inception – were habitually and literally carrying home a small wooden spoon, which alternated amongst the various members of the party.

Tonight would have been her turn to carry home the trophy of humiliation, the accolade of dismal progress. The trouble with these quizzes, she thought, was they invariably relied on questions about celebrities and soap operas, of which she and her cohorts knew very little. She had tried to watch one once but it seemed to be set on a surfing beach in the colonies where everyone was in search of his or her long-lost parent, as it so happened they had been fostered out at a tender age. On her friend Elsie's recommendation she had switched to a more gritty soap set in a small housing estate. However, the alarming homicide rate and heady variety of natural disasters meant that the cast was in constant need of renewal. No sooner had she got to know one character, accommodated their gloomy foibles, than they disappeared in a puff of smoke – quite literally – as the gas cooker in number seventeen was always blowing up. She had hoped for a quiz question on the housing estate's most lethal method of despatch but it never materialised.

That night she slept well and strangely dreamed of being shown around some electricity showrooms by a young man in tight-fitting jeans. However, just as he bent down to examine the label on the Manager's Special, an owl hooted from beyond the window and the dream evaporated.

She sighed softly and listened to the night visitor which gave another parting hoot and then fell silent. Mildred was not able to return to the delights of the showroom but instead found herself sitting mysteriously by a pond. She meant to keep a diary at her bedside and jot down the dreams when she first awoke. Sadly, it would be one of those things that never came to fruition, being forgotten, remembered, then forgotten again...

The next morning, Mildred, despite the disappointment of owl-interrupted sleep, found herself oddly upbeat. She rang two of her friends, fellow examiners whom she encountered from time to time on what was called the 'circuit'.

"That's marvellous," enthused Connie on hearing about the wooden spoon. "With a few less soaps you could move swiftly up the ladder."

"Let's hope so," replied Mildred, uncertain in her analytical mind as to whether it should be 'fewer' or 'less' soaps. They were always making this mistake on the Today programme, as pointed out by a Colonel Blundeston, who lived near Bury St. Edmunds. She pictured him sitting by the radio, alert and waiting to pounce.

When she rang Guy Cuthbertson he was far less appreciative of their triumph.

"There's a tomcat keeps weeing on my tagetes," he grumbled. "I've had to change the containers twice."

"How unfortunate!" commiserated Mildred. "I suppose it's some kind of scent-marking perhaps."

She had seen tigers do it on a programme about the wilds of Borneo.

"It's most unpleasant," remarked Guy. "And I'm constantly running out of Brobat!"

"I thought they weren't supposed to like marigolds."

She started telling him about the wooden spoon to cheer him up but he still sounded agitated. Perhaps Guy could be a secret authority on soaps and celebrities and might possibly want to try out an evening in the Bull and Gate. However it seemed that now was not a good time to extend an invitation.

"A water pistol might help," she suggested. "One of those large space-like things that looks like a fire extinguisher."

Guy gave a disgruntled 'Harrumph!' and the conversation began to falter.

Later that morning Mildred breezed around town, skipping nimbly between the library and the large fish stall which offered a tempting deal on sea-bass. She liked the sound of it; dark and mysterious. Was there a freshwater relative maybe? And its French name 'loup de mer' was even more enigmatic. Then she realised she had had a dream which involved sitting by a pond. Was it some kind of premonition, then?

She gathered up the bass, smothered now in sheaths of wrapping paper. Fish, with its beneficial effect on the brain might put her in credit for the Bull and Gate. Stuffing the long slither of bass later with flaked almonds, she placed it under the grill and added a touch of lemon and ginger. It did not disappoint; she let it melt tantalisingly in her mouth.

It was then that the letter-box emitted its usual rasping clunk and she heard something land on the mat. She saw Jimmy the postman nipping past the window to deliver letters to the house next door. She did not begrudge him his momentary trespass – least of all in the summer when he wore those pale khaki shorts. She watched his bulging sack of mail

3

brush momentarily against the glass and resumed her contemplation of the sea-bass.

Perhaps when summer returned she could invite him into the garden for a glass of something. His round was a very long one with unforgiving houses and heartless flights of steps. However, he must possess extremely firm legs if he was obliged to do all that climbing. She saw him leave the house next door and briefly wave from down the garden path. Savouring her last mouthful of fish, she returned the greeting.

Only after a raspberry posset and a herbal tea that was supposed to relieve flatulence did she see what Jimmy had deposited on the mat. There was a glossy magazine from the wine company that kept on sending her brochures. Guy maintained it was the railway line who had passed on details of its railcard holders to a third party. Very likely. She had never requested it. Then there was a large brown rectangular envelope. On closer scrutiny she saw that it was from Hilltop. What could it be? Another meeting perhaps? Or yet more errata from the recently issued set of exam materials?

She slid it open with a wooden paper-knife. Inside lay a brief letter and a copy of her last expenses form. Various boxes had been underscored with a red tick, which for some reason she remembered signalled disapproval in Swedish. A neighbouring asterisk accompanied a terse reminder to 'Herewith provide a breakdown of food consumed'.

She peered again. She was not dreaming – the red ink was as vibrant as heavy lipstick, ominous as spilt blood. What did it mean 'provide a breakdown'?

The letter had rather upset her so she tried to console herself with an Aussie soap, the one where all the men drank beer from the fridge in 'tinnies' and whose wives dutifully bustled about in large kitchens apparently cooking nothing in particular. Yet each time she gazed at the homely domestic interiors replete with bare-chested, ale-consuming spouses, her thoughts wandered back to the living room and the vision that had rudely appeared on the doormat.

Her first recourse was to ring Connie and bathe in sympathy but the line was repeatedly engaged. Maybe Hilltop had struck there too and she was eliciting comfort from another colleague. In desperation she quickly dialled Guy's number.

"I can't stop now!" he yelled, trying to raise his voice over an increasingly crackling line.

"I could pop in, though, after my library visit tomorrow."

It would have to do, thought Mildred gloomily. She tried to ring Connie again but the line was still busy.

Later on in the day, she felt annoyed with herself for having agreed to Guy's suggestion as he had failed to specify what time he was going to the library. It would mean having to wait around for him.

The next morning she busied herself in the garden, keeping an eye and ear open for the front door. Occasionally she went to tap the phone buttons to see if he might have called but the last entry was more than a week ago.

It was then that she saw and picked up the leaflet on the doormat. It was small but brilliantly coloured. Reaching for her glasses she examined it more closely. 'Karma Sutra Exotic Restaurant. Join us on Wednesdays for our *special feast*.' The name sounded oddly familiar. 'First time customers only nine pounds!'

Then she glanced up at the calendar and discovered that next Wednesday she was due to examine at Bonehill Park Community College.

"So am I!" announced Guy when he popped in belatedly at five o'clock. "Sonia's off sick again so they've drafted me in as a last minute replacement."

"We could perhaps go for a meal afterwards at the new oriental restaurant," she suggested. "It's on the way back from Bonehill."

"It's a possibility," said Guy, who seldom liked to commit himself. "What's the name?"

"The Hare Krishna, I think," replied Mildred.

Three days later they were standing outside the restaurant.

"It's a bit dark inside," said Guy.

"In you go," suggested Mildred. "The gentleman always goes in first."

"Does he really?" queried Guy, who was not well versed in any form of etiquette.

The restaurant played a chime to announce their arrival. After a moment or two there was a swish of beads and tassels from long hanging drapes and a slender girl stood in front of them.

"You are two?" she enquired. She seemed surprised to see Mildred.

"I believe so," replied Guy, a touch acidly Mildred thought.

They were shown into a discreet corner where soft music, sounding very much like Pan Pipes, drifted over them.

"I wish I'd brought my glasses," complained Guy.

"Me too," said Mildred. "It's the lighting. Do you think we could get them to shine a torch?"

"I hardly think so," he replied.

They looked around, observing the soft decor of the restaurant.

"The service is a bit slow," said Guy after a while.

"But we've only just got here," Mildred replied.

She hoped he wasn't going to create a scene. Perhaps choosing your eating partners was a bit like going on holiday with someone. A longer than usual period of captivity – almost as soon as you got on the plane, you began to regret it.

"Some drink?" asked a voice behind them.

Out of the shadows stepped a tall young boy with a notepad. He was probably from Goa, Mildred decided, noticing that he had beautiful eyes.

"Er, perhaps a lemonade," she replied.

Guy was scanning the menu for beverages.

"We would like to offer you some cocktail," the waiter replied.

"Oh I couldn't possibly touch alcohol," said Mildred. "It always makes me squiffy."

"We have *with* and without."

"Without what?"

"Without the alcohol. It is very refreshing."

"Sounds like a waste of a drink, then," muttered Guy. "What's in it?"

"It is on the house," answered the waiter, ignoring him.

"What is, dear?" enquired Mildred.

"The drink," replied Guy, a touch testily.

Holiday, thought Mildred. It was like going on holiday – breaking the workplace taboo. But Guy needed a drink and might be all the better for it.

"Yes, please," she said gratefully.

"One with, one without," echoed the waiter, sliding back into darkness.

"I think I'd like to order," Mildred announced brightly. "That last pair of students made me quite hungry."

Guy gazed back at her, trying to work out the connection. Within a few moments the waiter had returned with what looked like Knickerbocker Glory glasses and a long twirly straw.

"Good heavens!" said Mildred. "I'll never drink all that."

The waiter handed her a heavy, plushly-bound menu and then shoved one rather more brusquely to Guy.

"I can't make out these dishes," he complained.

"I think it might be one of those places where you order by numbers," chirruped Mildred helpfully.

She sipped her drink. It had a nice zesty lime taste. By the time the waiter had returned again, Guy was halfway through his.

"Ready to order, madame?"

He placed the emphasis on the second syllable in keeping with the exotic nature of the restaurant decor.

"Er, yes, please," said Mildred bravely. I'd like the Gok Pa Waa. Er, number forty seven," she added just in case the waiter had misunderstood her.

His eyes gave a flutter of a smile and he lifted his pen to speak to Guy.

"For you, sir?"

"Er...I think... Well, what would you suggest?"

Mildred glanced over in amazement. Guy seemed suddenly relaxed, amiable almost.

"I think the starter is nice, sir. We can do for two. It is better."

"Oh," said Mildred, wondering if they would exceed their meal allowance.

"Capital," said Guy. "And I'd like a number forty-nine." He grinned at Mildred. "I couldn't hope to pronounce it."

The waiter took the menus and a spare set of cutlery. Banquo's ghost would not be dining then, thought Mildred as she glanced back at Guy, whose eyes seemed to be following the waiter's path into subdued light.

"It's nice to have something different," she said.

"I think I might have another cocktail," Guy announced, ignoring her and raising an arm to attract the waiter.

"Might I have another one?" he waved.

The waiter swooped to remove the empty glass. Guy was becoming polite, placid even. What *was* in that drink of his?

The waiter turned his attention to Mildred.

"Might I have one, too?" she enquired timidly.

There was a sudden flash of white teeth, a gentle grin. Guy smiled too. He was diligently following the waiter's path again. Was she imagining it, she wondered, but was he surveying the gyrations of his bottom? She turned to look for herself but it had vanished behind a bamboo screen.

"Lovely," said Guy when the drinks arrived.

"I wonder what's in it?" Mildred ventured.

She took a tentative sip. It tasted of subtle fruit, of lime and ginger, with a sudden hefty kick at the end. The waiter swiftly returned with what looked like a plate of salad.

"Enjoy," he exhorted.

Mildred wasn't quite sure what she was supposed to be enjoying. It seemed to be a mixture of pickled cabbage and crispy cut vegetables. Like a spicy Kim Chi, she thought, only...

"It's Kim Chi," she announced to Guy. "Or something like it."

"Kim who?" asked Guy, almost choking on a chilli.

"Like Thai food," she suggested. "Hot!"

"Tai Chi?" answered Guy bewilderedly. He ordered a pint of water to assuage the chilli.

"I'm told a lemon works," Mildred volunteered.

"And another of those cocktails, please." He motioned to the lurking waiter.

By the time dinners forty-nine and forty-seven had appeared at the table, the restaurant had filled up.

"You will stay for belly dancer?" the waiter asked as they were looking down at the dessert menu.

Mildred partly spluttered on her lime juice and inhaled a slice of ginger.

"I don't think so," she replied. "It might spoil the effect of my dinner."

Guy was less willing to agree, she noticed, and was now staring into the waiter's eyes.

"I think I'll have a pineapple organism," he said.

Mildred glanced curiously at him. Were the cocktails affecting his ability to read the menu? The waiter paused for her reply.

"Er, perhaps the pomegranate passion, then."

She saw Guy's eyes dancing at things behind her head.

When the puddings arrived they came in more than ample bowls; almost like miniature baptismal fonts, she thought.

"Very nice," she said after the dessert had vanished in three spoonfuls.

"Excellent," Guy responded. "So fruity and fluffy!"

"Er, could we have *separate* bills, please?" Mildred asked when it came to paying.

The waiter seemed confused. "Separate? Not come together?"

"Yes, please. You see, it's for our exam board. It's the expenses."

"Expensive?" queried the waiter.

"Yes, our board."

"Your board is expensive?"

He brought them two individual till receipts and a saucer full of mints.

"Very thoughtful," said Mildred. "It's probably because of the garlic."

"We'd better leave a tip, then," suggested Guy.

To her surprise she saw him put down a ten-pound note.

"Isn't that a little too much?"

"Not really." He was beginning to slur his words. "Cocktails on the house. Yes, very presentable."

Did he mean the food or the waiter, she wondered?

They were helped on with their coats.

"Lovely," said Guy as the waiter brushed his shoulder in a parting gesture.

To her surprise she saw Guy lean over to give him a hug.

"Thank you, madame," said the waiter, as if the hug had never happened.

"Absolutely dishlishous," slobbered Guy.

"I think we'd better order a taxi," she suggested, fearing for Guy's return journey.

"Well you're the boss, dear," said Guy suddenly linking arms with her.

They stopped at his place first. She watched him lurch out of the cab as he prepared to pay the driver.

"I'll settle it, Guy," she insisted and instructed the taxi man to drive on.

In the mirror she saw him stagger haphazardly down the path.

It was less than ten days after the meal that the letter arrived. Brown, ample, rectangular, familiar.

'In future,' said the crossly-worded letter, 'examiners will *not* be permitted to dine at the Weedon Hill Karma Sutra Restaurant with its famous belly dancers.'

She noticed that the itemised receipt she had hastily placed inside the envelope and without checking had been doubly underlined. The offending items were cited as firstly the 'Pussy Galore' and 'Cucumber Throbber' cocktails. Following this were dinners forty-nine and forty-seven from the 'Viagra' menu. And finally 'Pineapple Orgasm' and 'Pomegranate Passion Sensation' were triply underlined and with double exclamation marks.

Mildred sat down at the breakfast table in a state of shock. If only they had brought their glasses with them, acted less hastily, considered what they might have been ordering! And she was sure it was called the Hare Krishna!

At the bottom of the till receipt, lay the restaurant's gothically inscribed motto.

'Food. The natural aid for rewarding sex. Have a nice day!'

Without thinking she picked up the phone. She was in desperate need of reassurance and sympathy no matter how rough. An almost inaudible voice answered.

"Is that you, Guy?"

But familiar all the same.

"Mr Guy is in kitchen. He helping me with my English."

"Pass me the cocktail shaker, dear," she heard Guy say.

Sunlight

He was one of her favourite writers when she was younger. The stories he wrote were often dark, quirky, sardonic, leading inevitably to their melancholic conclusion. And she always enjoyed the word 'creek' which, she thought, was quintessentially American, until she moved to Suffolk and discovered one near Southwold. In itself the word seemed murky and mysterious, unfamiliar and eerie.

A wind blew in at the porch where she was waiting. Like in the tale of 'Owl Creek Ridge' – the exact title escaped her – it was as if much of her past life was floating before her.

She and Toby would often read on summer evenings, sitting outside till midges buzzed and the skies began to darken. Toby would turn his pages more slowly than she did, as if following the more demanding obligations of the novel whereas Kate's predilection for shorter tales or long short stories gave her the opportunity to mull over and re-read the sentences that she particularly liked.

"Look at this," she would say, and her brother would glance up grudgingly.

"Yeah, not bad. Quite interesting," was the reply after she had recited what had caught her eye, returning quickly to the page where his finger had been impatiently waiting.

Toby invariably wore shorts, the colours varying according to the time of year. Despite his long exposed legs, the mosquitoes never bothered him. Kate, on the other hand, would be surreptitiously bitten, the victim of some sneaky ambush whose trophy would be a large red and white bump.

"You could try garlic," he suggested, wafting a hummus breath in her direction. She noticed the soft stale scent as she tried to duck it. "Or lavender water. They don't like that."

The sun streamed in now at the church door where she stood in the anticipatory pose of someone who was waiting for a signal, a cue. She could see him, though, in the front row, more heavily attired than usual in accordance with the demands and dictates of the ritual. And she, with her fluttering veils and wisps, felt rather like a giant moth or something that had been covered with cobwebs. Why had they both agreed to it all, she and Daniel, and succumbed to the various pressures of his family? Wouldn't it have been better to have done it the way Emma did, just go away, tie the knot and then tell everybody afterwards?

She parted the veil that obscured her vision and gazed out through the church door into the sunshine where the birds were singing. The path with its headstones was only very slightly overgrown and amidst the gleaming grass she could see the shiny beacons of buttercup and dandelion. As she stared at the patchwork quilt of green and yellow, turning her back on the scene within that awaited and expected her, she found herself thinking, trying to recall a quote from the same writer whose tales she so enjoyed. Ambrose Bierce that was the name. She remembered now. She had seen it translated into German and had first encountered it when she used her cousin, Lucy's loo in the house of many bathrooms. There was usually a good supply of reading material placed on a conveniently low shelf in the middle toilet, but her favourite book, whilst indulging in thronal contemplation, was a handy volume of quotes and sayings, one for each day of the year. Three hundred and sixty five 'Sonnengedanken' – although leap years were not catered for in these revelatory thoughts. 'Ein positiver Begleiter durch das Jahr.' And in this helpful yearly companion to lavatory occupation, there was a little piece of advice or homily nestling under each quotation; a fragment of homespun German philosophy.

When she sat in the fragrant peace of Lucy's upstairs loo, she used to imagine acting out the bits of cobbled-together wisdom and anticipating their results. It was perhaps more interesting to fantasise and conjecture than to actually do it. She remembered an odd novel that Toby had lent her once where the main character, for hero was not appropriate, embarked on an imaginary trip to London from his living room or study.

"Not long now," said Uncle Arthur, whose task it was in the unavailability of her remaining parent to give her away.

She smiled as he touched her arm, heard the organ inside rev up a notch or two in volume, and she thought how peculiar it was to be thinking about books of all things on this the most important of days. But it was the quote that formulated at the back of her mind which had started it all and for some reason would not let her go. It was like a tune running round her head, an earworm as they call it. She shuddered.

"I never get bitten," Toby proudly boasted. With his deep-golden hair and olive-toned skin he was a freckle-free zone whereas for Kate...When the autumn days grew chilly they would read upstairs in his room, quietly turning pages into late evening.

And one time a gale was blowing outside, the wind angrily rattling the lattice windows and some of the doors in the passageway. Toby was lying on the bed while Kate was sprawled out on the floor, head propped up against an assortment of pillows. Scuds of rain spattered beyond the half-drawn curtains.

"The wind!" said Toby getting up to draw them and managing to exclude some of the more potent draught.

She had tried to carry on reading but this time the gusts seemed to shake the whole house.

"The wind is scary," she said to him.

He lazily turned over a page. "In the old house the chimney blew down. You probably don't remember it." He had been away that night for a hockey match and had missed the scene of destruction. For some time afterwards the vegetable patch had been out of action as they painstakingly rebuilt the chimney from scratch. "It's unlikely to happen again," he said to her half-reassuringly.

But the damage had been done. She could hear what sounded like the howling of an angry furnace or a tube train entering a tunnel.

"It's okay," he smiled. "Lightning doesn't strike twice."

But it wasn't lightning and it was a different house. The wind shrieked again at the window and she visibly flinched.

"There!" he said, putting an arm round her. He was warm and firm to the touch. "There's no need to worry, is there?"

"No." There was a long pause.

"And if you want, you can stay here. You don't have to go back to yours."

A silence passed over the room as she thought about what he had said. The wind screeched. She went to the bathroom listening to the sounds outside and slowly brushed her teeth. In the mirror she caught a glimpse of her face. Maybe she shouldn't after all. Perhaps brave it out within the confines of her room. The curtains were thicker for a start. But as if to undermine her already frail resolve, the windows clattered and she heard something tumble from the roof.

The lighting was different when she went back to Toby's room. There was only a bedside lamp now which sent out a soft glow. She lifted up the covers and dived in. He was naked beneath the sheets but warm, oh so warm, as he held her.

From that time on she hardly ever slept in her room.

There was a gentle tap on her shoulder. Uncle Arthur was smiling.

"Time to go in," he said.

Time.

The organ struck up a familiar tune. The congregation rose from their seats and she was sailing on his arm down the fully packed aisles, stepping over flagstones towards her partner Daniel. He was over to one side in a pale grey suit with vague long dark stripes. For a moment she thought of some kind of zebra and was tempted to laugh. The beaming faces as she passed by persuaded her otherwise. Smile. Smile. It was a joyous occasion.

And standing next to Daniel was her brother Toby, who had been asked to be best man. She saw his flaxen hair glint in a shaft of light that streamed through the windows. It contrasted with Daniel's immaculately groomed auburn crop.

Smiles, flashes, cameras.

And then as if illuminated by the flash, the darting blue spots that swivelled in front of her eyes, she suddenly remembered the quote that had been teasing her.

The priest was beginning the litany, welcoming the assembled congregation. He was small and avuncular. But somehow she didn't hear the words. Instead she was translating back from that book of quotes, the one that languished in Lucy's upstairs bathroom.

'Die Braut am Hochzeitstag...' began Mr Bierce. She pieced the words back to the original. 'The bride on her wedding day, a woman with radiant expression at the happiness now lying behind her.'

The church was awash with sunshine. It seemed to come through every available window. Dazzling sunlight as Catherine, as she was being referred to now, squinted in the falling beams and smiled ever wider.

In a Spin

"I wonder," said Josephine, her voice wafting over the crackly line, "if you wouldn't mind popping over."

"Of course," said Ernie. "It'll be my pleasure."

"The spin-drier's making that peculiar smell again."

"Spin-drier's playing up," Ernie announced to Angela a little while later. "I said I'd go over."

Angela fixed him with a solid if silent glare of incredulity. The number of things that seemed to go wrong in Josephine's, Ernie's former wife's house was staggering!

"Has she not heard of electricians, dear? Plumbers perhaps? There are some very nice Polish men around."

"Yes," replied Ernie. "But you know how she's always strapped for cash. Just unlucky with her purchases, I suppose."

Or fortunate, thought Angela. Fortunate in that they *always* seemed to go wrong and necessitated the attention of a solicitous Ernie. Over the years, Josephine had become a spectre that had not been entirely dispensed with. Whenever she went away on holiday, Ernie was obliged to travel the all too convenient three miles across town to Josephine's house and water the plants, feed the cat...

"Could she not ask neighbours?" Angela enquired. "I imagine she has those."

"She's fallen out with them," explained Ernie. "Besides, it's never been a friendly block."

It wouldn't be with Josephine there, concluded Angela!

Then at weekends, normally on a Sunday before Desert Island Discs, he felt obliged to make a telephone call to see how she was faring or whether there was anything that needed mending. It was as if Josephine was tapping in on Ernie's feelings of guilt for having moved away and yet it was she *Josephine* with her longings for Italian barber Sergio, who had first fired the parting salvos.

Josephine, as Ernie's then wife, had taken to passing by Sergio's barber shop window regularly and casting an enquiring eye inwards in the hope of meeting his mysterious yet penetrating gaze. Once this had been secured, she felt she could now wave at him as she staggered by, her arms heavily laden with the various fruits of shopping. As the waves grew more flamboyant, she eventually plucked up courage, after a glass of Guinness or two with her friend at the Lamb and Flag, to ask the smiling Sergio whether he did Unisex...

"For you, lady, I do any sex..."

Josephine blushed a little.

And so in the uniquely male barber shop with its twirling, stripy pole outside, she tiptoed in around half past six, after the last customer had vanished, to bathe in Sergio's sole attentions. She'd enjoyed the waft of his breath on the back of her neck, something that sent up a constant array of goose-pimples. She loved the way he washed her hair, almost as if he was wrestling with an elusive fish. And she adored the manner in which she was paraded before his mirror, his swarthy hands as laurels on her shoulders. She was his prize exhibit and *his* creation, the product of careful and expert snipping, as he crouched and leaned in front of her.

One day, in a waft of Brylcreem passion, he had closed the blinds that looked out onto the High Street and they had made love on the very throne where the ritual shearing had taken place. Josephine had yelled so much, he feared for the windows. Thereafter, visits to Sergio's became much more frequent and it was one evening when Ernie was passing that he personally witnessed the lowering of the blinds. The love-bites that subsequently appeared on Josephine's slender shoulders had not helped matters either, imbued as they were with a tinge of aftershave.

The revelation that Sergio also lowered the blinds for Gethyn the paper-boy had brought an abrupt end to Josephine's patronage. She sought to resuscitate her dwindling relationship with Ernie but by then it was too late. He had now met Angela during a rained-on flower festival and her insightful horticultural tendencies had established an immediate bond. They were soon travelling to distant gardening exhibitions together and lodging in small hotels. Josephine had merely become a spent milestone on the long road to Chelsea.

And yet, perhaps, as Ernie had deserted Josephine because of her High Street improprieties, there remained a speck of guilt within, and one that she, Josephine, in all her domestic helplessness, had tapped in on. Around the time of Sergio's impending civil partnership with Gethyn, who was now both university student and early morning paper-boy, it seemed he was needed by his former wife on an almost daily basis.

"The fact that the barber shop is still there with an increase in clientele is a painful reminder for her," Ernie explained to an unsympathetic Angela. "She even stopped having the Daily Mail delivered," he added. "It was part of Gethyn's delivery round!"

The house was silent on Ernie's departure, a temporary if uncertain bereavement, while Ernie would be breezing through Josephine's, and to Angela's, unknown residence, whistling, adjusting taps, moving beds. The image was as uncomfortable as it was disturbing. Yet Angela trusted Ernie and had no wish to pry. He would not want to reacquaint himself with soiled goods, sullied by Italian hairdressers, and oversized paper-boys. She had seen Gethyn once, tall, dark and lanky, delivering the Woodburne Advertiser over on the Whalebone Estate.

"I thought we'd go to the Rose and Nightgown," announced Ernie next morning. He was looking slightly sheepish and compensatory after a four-hour battle with Josephine's erratic spin dryer. In her annoyance, Angela had not waited up.

"Lovely, dear," she said, brightening up slightly.

'What's the occasion?' she nearly blurted out, but then looking at the large squares of the calendar that hung by the fridge, she was reminded of the anniversary from when Ernie had first proposed. He was clearly aware of the date, too, courteous and considerate as always.

"It does Mexican food," he added.

"Lovely," she repeated as though she was not entirely sure what Mexican cuisine was. Her neighbour, Jean, said they mixed chilli with chocolate and they had some unusual biscuits called Machos.

"Didn't it used to be called the Frog and Nightgown, dear?" she enquired, referring to the pub.

"It may have been once."

Angela considered the Rose and Nightgown to be much of an improvement. It seemed more exotic, romantic even, and she pictured a heavily scented Bourbon rose and a woman in a skimpy, loose-fitting nightdress.

"I booked the table," he informed her later. "But I couldn't get one till Monday, though. Booked up solid it was."

Monday, thought Angela. The day *after* he'd proposed. But it would do; the memory lingering on as she would gently sip her Mateus Rose with its mildly erotic fizz and Ernie swill his pint of Boddington's.

On the Sunday evening Angela experienced a peculiar dream in which a Mexican called at the house on horseback. Under his large sombrero, which adequately shielded the two of them from a blazing sun, they sauntered through a housing estate, passed Gethyn emerging from the closed shutters of a barber shop, and ended their spontaneous journey in a supermarket car park. Beyond was the enticing world of seductive BOGOFs and sticky Nectar points, yet oddly enough she was succumbing to something else.

For the next day, she felt uncomfortably guilty as if she herself had fallen prey to the Josephine affliction.

"I'm just getting a shave," Ernie announced as Angela removed out of date chilli powder which had congregated at the back of the cupboard.

She glanced over at the clock. It was only a few minutes after five, nearly an hour away from the time they usually had their tea. But now she thought positively of the Rose and Nightgown, whose blousy Bourbon scent eclipsed the attentions of the nocturnal Mexican...

In half an hour, a dapper, smart and newly-shaven Ernie appeared at the bottom of the stairs. How youthful he looked, she thought! How slim and engaging!

"Shall we make our way, dear?" he suggested.

Angela smiled.

She heard him locking the back door which led out onto the patio, silence the dripping tap over by the sink, and give his customary jangle of house keys. But now suddenly there was a trilling sound, harsh and urgent in its insistency, reverberating around the living room. Ernie went to answer it.

Leave it, she wanted to say. Leave us to the necessity of the moment. They can ring again. But she knew Ernie would never leave an unanswered phone. And now there was the prelude of a familiar conversation.

"What's the matter?" he was saying. "How much water?"

If only he hadn't picked up. Had not, like Orpheus in his voyage to the Underworld, looked back.

Suddenly Angela in a fit of anger was unlocking the securely bolted back door, opening the garden shed, removing an implement.

"I suppose I could pop round," Ernie was saying, "and then we could get a taxi..."

The garden shears were crisp and shiny – they had been a birthday present – and they closed neatly like a crocodile's jaws. Waving them in her arms, Angela made towards what she thought was the telephone wire and severed the umbilical cord that led to Josephine.

There was a blinding flash followed by a brief explosion and Angela had the fleeting sensation of sailing above the fridge, or was she being carried away on horseback?

The room she lay in was small and blue. There was a bedside table with a collection of coloured wires. And there was a tube leading from her arm to a suspended bottle that looked like a saline drip. A blurred face came towards her, gazed anxiously as it came into focus.

"You've had a nasty shock, dear," said the familiar voice. "Quite literally. Ernie said something about garden shears."

Ernie? *Her* Ernie? Where was he? Where was *she*?

"Ernie," she wanted to moan, but the name seemed to merely evaporate.

"He'll be along in a wee while, dear. He's just fixing the thermostat in my kitchen. You know for days now I haven't been able to turn the heating down. 'Can't get the parts', the gas man said. But Ernie knows what to do. He always does."

She was not mistaken. Josephine's lampshade fringe came alarmingly into view.

"But don't worry, dear. Everything's in hand. Of course, it'll take some time to convalesce. Recover fully..."

Angela remembered a bang; a brilliant light; of flying...

"So this is where I fit in. Just my way of saying thank you, of course. You know how good Ernie's been, coming over to fix things. You must think I'm *quite* helpless really. So when you get out of hospital – you're in the P and N, by the way – and need some help with things, well, *I'll* be there. You know some things that are not *suitable* for a man. Till you get back properly on your feet. They say it can take a while to build those muscles up, gather strength. I put it to Ernie and he was about to shake his head, but I said 'No, no, I simply won't take no for an answer.' I can be quite persuasive sometimes and so Ernie agreed. He's such a love!"

Angela, gazing up in horror, met the full force of Josephine's lampshade smile. She wanted to scream the word 'No!', yell it from the painted walls of her cubicle all the way down to the reception desk, but no sound came out.

Josephine only increased the width of her smile.

"Now you just lie back, dear, and relax. It's the least I can do to look after you. And what a happy house it's going to be! Just the two, no, the three of us!"

Elemental

I take people in. Always have done, of course. Ever since…
I need the money. Well look around you. The buildings, the outhouses. The upkeep. And then there are those restrictions you have to follow, preservation orders. Things you can and can't do.

It's been a busy summer. It's always the way. It's when people want to come. Combine language with a slice of Norfolk! That was my slogan for a while but my good friend Trevor persuaded me to give it up. 'Makes you sound like a tea room,' he said.

A tea shop out in the sticks. Wind blowing barley from the nearby fields. The plaintive, echoing sound of sheep. Idyllic? Maybe. But you should try living here in winter.

Anyway, I'd had a couple of Germans and an unsmiling pair from somewhere called Plovdiv. They told me they saved it for when it really matters. Smiling that is. And I thought, oh dear, life must be such a trial. Yet for the Germans I was far more concerned in case there was any unwitting residue in some of the rooms. One year a stray sock found its way under the bed. It's well known that socks have a will of their own. There were repercussions, however. A written complaint to the agency who in turn sent me a 'naughty girl letter.' I subsequently abandoned the agency for fear of further missives. That sock might have been a rat for all the hue and cry that ensued.

But then I get this email. It's slightly broken, disjointed, but comprehensible nevertheless. Could he come under the Scheme? Well not *his* words but mine. Accommodation, tuition and board and in return they do jobs for you around the house. Well, looking at this place it's an ongoing labour of love.

A labour of love.

I remember the day we, Dennis and I, first saw it. Took an unexpected detour off the main road. I was attracted by the name of a nearby village and then when I saw the large pond across the dusty road... As we gazed at it, impressive in its crumbling splendour, Dennis slid his arm around me and squeezed me gently, ever so gently.

I look at the mistakes in the email, seem to hear a staccato, uninflected voice and decide Eastern Europe maybe. He's signed himself Martin so it could be anywhere.

I email back directions and send a picture of the place. He emails in reply 'Lovely' and I arrange to pick him up from the station. I give him the phone number in case he is delayed.

He *is*. I go to the station to meet the train but there are no eligible candidates. A few grungy schoolboys. Surely not? An hour or so later, the phone crackles. 'Are you at the station, I ask?' 'Train,' he says. 'Train.' Is he *on* the train or *getting* the train? It's nearly ten to eight, three hours later than the scheduled arrival time so I drive back along the hedgerow lanes, park by the entrance to the station and wait.

There is a complication with the line. Sections of single track. The trains invariably delay each other with their missed timings. I get out, walk up and down.

Eventually the train slides in like a recalcitrant slug. At first no one alights and then...

Someone's coming towards me. Tall, mid-twenties. 'Martin?' I say.

'Martin,' he replies and smiles.

It's when we're in the car, parallel yet in close proximity, that I realise he knows only very few words of the language which is to be our common bond. My introductory questions are met with incomprehension, silence. He looks out of the window, tall hedges sailing by, obscuring fields and sheds and abattoirs.

'Nice weather,' I say as the sun sinks behind a hedgerow.

He nods and I sort of smile.

He sleeps in late. It was a long journey. Some twenty hours by coach and then two trains up from London. Not that I get the information from him but I look again at the itinerary, guess at the times.

Around midday he emerges.

'Would you like something to eat?' I ask. It's not working so I try again more slowly.

I don't know if you've noticed, but when people are confronted with foreigners they either slow down drastically or invariably shout. I refrain from the latter. Benign incomprehension spreads across his face. I point to my stomach. 'Eat?' I gesture. This seems to work.

And now food becomes our golden moment when we are in simultaneous communication and purpose. Along the way I introduce him to a few kitchen utensils, get him to repeat the names, which he does after a fashion and then promptly forgets.

'Spatula,' I say.

'Ehspatoola.'

Doesn't sound very English. Then to my electric piece de resistance. 'Remoska,' I point.

His eyes light up. 'Ah, Remoska!'

We have a union, a coming together.

'Czech. It is the Czech,' he says, stretching powerfully into a sentence.

'And you?' I enquire. 'Are you Czech?'

'Nie. Nie som česky. Ja slovensky.'

I'm divining that it is the adjacent counterpart, the jilted republic from a pragmatic 'marriage' which lasted over seventy years.

He shows me pictures, pictures of a Slovak town with an unpronounceable name. His fingers point enthusiastically to a telephone which is also a camera.

The next day he starts working. He is efficient and well-organised and despite our failings, our inability to reach mutually comprehensible communication, he seems to know what to do. He gets me to order some new pantiles for the dilapidated barn and then, heroically ascending a ladder, eschewing the need for expensive and superfluous scaffolding, he is up on the roof rearranging the tiles, replacing those that are worn-out and cracked. I feel comforted knowing that the cause of some of those depressing and embarrassing leaks might be averted.

And it's true. The heavy thunderstorm of the following weekend wreaks no damage. Nothing at all.

He is always busy around the house, a restless moth to the flame of work. He puts Bob Stringer, on whom I have relied probably for too long, to shame.

We are eating one of our silent meals now. This morning I taught him a few adjectives. 'Tasty, delicious, moreish and bland.' For some reason he is more focused on the last adjective and I wonder if he is being painfully honest. Somewhere in one of the cupboards there is a recipe for goulash.

And then just as I am wondering in which drawer the cookery book still lives, I hear a clanking, a clunking and a turning of the lock. Martin looks momentarily anxious, assumes the pose of an attentive guard-dog.

'It's only Edmund.'

'Edmund?'

'Edmund, my son.'

He stands before us now, before Martin on introduction, and the two greet each other warily.

'Hello.'

'Hollow.'

Martin offers a hand which, rising from the protective spread of the dining table, looks huge and in which I'm sure Edmund's less spacious offering will disappear. Edmund looks back at me, bewildered, part-accusatory.

'Martin is my new student. He's been fixing things in return. The barn, the roof, *your* room in fact.'

Once a leak sprayed Edmund's books. He was distraught, outraged. Edmund melts slightly at the vanquished leak, says something to Martin which Martin fails to understand.

'His English is not very good,' I whisper diplomatically. 'Progress has been rather slow.'

I can't quite banish Edmund's initial look from my mind, the one in which he made me feel like some kind of tart.

My neighbour, Marcia, drops in from time to time. My vocation in life is to sublimate the lack of a supermarket. Today she is short of clothes pegs.

'This woman no buy nothing,' Martin asserts one morning on seeing Marcia ready to pounce at the gate.

A double negative is normal in most languages. I don't bother to correct it. It caused too much confusion last time. But I hope that Marcia hasn't heard Martin's astute observation as I wonder what I can oblige her with this time. Coriander leaves, a pork chop, some balsamic vinegar, a day trip to Bruges?

'How's your, er…man getting on?' Marcia asks as a prelude to her inevitable request.

'Fine,' I say. 'As you can see the place is improved no end.'

Marcia is watching Martin in habitual pose up a ladder. 'He's not bad,' she comments, her eyes surveying the sweep of his back and down to his perfectly balancing ankles. 'Fit, or what!' She probably would like to borrow *him*, too.

I scarcely acknowledge her observation, hand her the necessary packet of Daz, only it's not called that now but something like Bold or Penetrator or…

Penetrator!

I notice Edmund comes home from university more frequently now. I thought it's perhaps to keep an eye on me but I find him gazing out of the windows watching Martin at work. And Marcia's visits are more regular too, and I also see, rather like Edmund, that she makes brave attempts at conversation.

Suddenly the house is busier, more purposeful, on the mend. And one evening I too am looking at Martin, gazing at his swarthy back bronzed by the warm rays of the sun. And I realise perhaps that we don't *need* many words and that maybe its sheer economy expresses something else; something more elemental.

His hair catches the evening light and I mean to tell him, to say to him…

The next morning I'm up early as I have to go to a conference. It's an annual thing and I don't want to go but non-attendance means no subsequent work, albeit of a spasmodic and part-time nature.

In the vast rambling hotel that has been selected, I find the company more irritating than usual and the constant reference to work is grating. Are there no other things to talk about, I wonder? And then it dawns on me that Martin is alone, rattling around the empty farmhouse, or maybe not because predatory Marcia has popped in, or even Edmund.

One time Martin had no idea what Edmund was talking about and he ran a hand of incomprehension through Edmund's hair. Unusually, I caught sight of my son blushing from the top of his temples down to his pointy chin.

And I realise too that I'm in a place without Martin, away for two nights in the dreary conference world for what they call 'standardisation.'

Standardisation. And I feel oddly uncomfortable.

I arrive back late on Sunday evening. I drive from the neglected railway station, where I left the car, to home, the vehicle unvandalised.

And immediately the place seems different, bearing the weight of absence, mine and...

Something is in the middle of the kitchen table. A piece of paper. A note. I fail to recognise the writing. It says simply 'Mum ill. I go. Tanks.' I notice painfully the lack of 'h'.

And I'm suddenly aware that this is the first, last and probably only time I shall see his writing, sculpted by the large hand into which Edmund's so comfortably slid.

Silence. The clock is ticking. I am aware of the difference now to the house. The change.

And suddenly the stillness becomes unbearable.

Signs of the Times

We usually work under cover of darkness. It's much better that way. Not that we would have to entirely as our operations are short and sweet; executed in a matter of seconds. But perhaps it's better not to draw attention to ourselves, to our activities, what with auntie being a respected member of the community and all that. You only have to look at her. Still slender, hair tied back in a graceful bun, and with a youthful, engaging kind of expression. She has attended several horticultural events; sometimes been asked to open them if a particular celebrity has got on the wrong train. Having given herself over to many years of gardening, this has naturally resulted in her acquiring authoritatively green fingers. And being out regularly in the cold air and the black soil has invariably sharpened her wits, her perception of things – not that they were ever wanting.

I was talking about our evening excursions. Our equipment for these trips is quite simple. Two or three stiff brushes just in case one of them should fail. One of them lost all its bristles last week, quite inexplicably, which made me think of Mr Adams of Albemarle Road and his tragic hair loss. The brush may have been left out on the garden table overnight and succumbed to the harshness of frost that coated everything in its wake. It is, if you like, a kind of artistry that auntie has *always* encouraged and, I suppose, in her invisible raids of necessary attentiveness, she has become a sort of minor Banksy. I said this to her one day but she replied 'Don't be so absurd!' I think deep down she may have been flattered by the comparison. Yet unlike the great Banksy, auntie's works or 'miniatures', as she likes to call them, will not sell and in some cases will hardly be noticed, for all she is doing is restoring the status quo, returning the language, in her words, to a 'more neutral and less excitable perspective, diluting it from its vulgar flamboyance'. Auntie has a way with words so it is inevitable in offering my account that I will pick up some of them, acquire such turns of phrases myself.

I remember the day when she first decided on guerrilla tactics. I had had a friend over from school and, as was our inclination, we would often depart from the confines of the stuffy, airless house to step out into the garden. It was more problematic in winter when the cold air and muddy or icy ground presented obstacles to our improvised games of cricket. Nevertheless, we would take a stroll around the garden towards the autumn raspberry patch, at the last minute diving quickly into the shed.

I don't think anyone would blame me for this. Marcus, my fellow student, possessed many engaging features. This, of course, included his rear end, which was of a neat and pert variety. In fact, my compulsive gazing at Marcus's prime asset was no more than anybody else would do. When we walked down to the shops I often noticed several people turn and stare. Bored travellers became suddenly distracted at bus stops when we would make our journey home from school. Marcus's attractive rear seemed to appeal to a wide selection of people and I was only one of them.

The darkened shed with its half-blocked window looking back onto the raspberries was an ideal place where we could show our mutual appreciation for each other. When Marcus obligingly lowered his school trousers he would let my hands slide over his tight yet soft skin. He had been doing a number of exercises to perfect the muscles on his lower abdomen and I suppose our shed sessions were a way in which I could monitor his ongoing and encouraging progress.

It was fortunate also that our shed was at the bottom of the garden, behind the raspberries and the apple trees so that sighs and yelps of appreciation at Marcus's treasured asset could not be heard from within any of the neighbouring houses. Nor was Marcus of the silent disposition. When he was about to reach his zenith, grabbing frantically and erratically at my reddish-brown hair, he would release a litany of vowels, some of which I had never heard before.

It was after one such session when I was surprised there was any hair still left on my head that we returned, via the house, for Marcus to say his goodbyes. It was a tactic of necessary politeness to ensure his ongoing visits could continue to our small terraced house.

Aunt Bea, for her name is Beatrice, which incidentally she doesn't like, was incandescent.

"I've had enough! It's got to stop! Absolutely!"

I felt a quick twinge of alarm. We had been rumbled! Our chorus of ecstasies must have been discovered as it wafted its way back towards the house.

"It really must!" she repeated. "Definitely!"

Instinctively, I pulled my sweater down, as in Marcus's presence I can only show continuous appreciation of his glorious being, his soft sandy hair, his pale brown eyes, his ready sense of humour, his firm but beautiful fingers, his…

"I'm so sorry, auntie…" I began.

"And in our very street!" she added. "What is the world coming to? Such an insertion is the height of vulgarity!"

I gulped in astonishment. How could auntie be so concise, so blunt? I felt myself blushing furiously, though Marcus remained unusually restrained throughout and calm.

Normally I would be scanning the options for alternative meeting places but being confronted with such sudden and unexpected exposure of our shed trips my mind went completely blank.

"I've a good mind to take it down!"

This seemed a bit extreme. If the shed were to be demolished where would we put our spades, forks, hoes and all the other garden implements? There was, I suppose, the redundant garage which could accommodate the evacuated tools.

Marcus was staring at the ground as auntie was sallying forth. I noticed a cobweb which had entangled itself on the top of his sandy hair.

"I wonder what Mrs Marjoram would think, being so closely involved."

I was puzzled for Mrs Marjoram lived at the bottom end of the road and we hardly ever saw her. How did...?

"Personally, I would *never* have a sign outside my house! It only compounds the misery, the inevitable trauma!"

I felt auntie was getting carried away.

"But this is what estate agents are like! As well as being invariably loathsome, smarmy and repugnantly self-satisfied, they do very little to earn the substantial amounts of money that come their way! If anything, the new breeds are even worse than the established rogues, and of course the Pendleburys, poor Mrs Marjoram's ex-neighbours, did not possess the wherewithal to resist them!"

"I don't see what estate agents have to do with all this, auntie!" I replied crossly. "This is between me and Marcus."

She would probably pick me up on my grammar, hopefully, and be temporarily distracted from the passions that had been discovered in the aptly named tool-shed.

"Don't have anything to do with it!" she quoted crossly. "Don't have anything to do with it! You silly boy! Have you not seen the signs?"

She sounded momentarily biblical. I could see Marcus bridling at the word 'silly' and I was proud of him. In those light grey trousers, which he so willingly relinquished, he appeared infinitely seductive.

"What signs?"

"I think you are a little obtuse at times, dear."

I was not familiar with the word but reckoned it had something to do with dim. Marcus appeared to register it and continued to gently seethe. It was almost worth the insults!

"The sign next to Mrs Marjoram's at the Pendleburys! The Pendleburys as were! Not content with putting up the word 'Sold' and exulting in their own sycophantic smugness, they have added an entirely redundant and completely unnecessary personal pronoun!"

It took both of us a moment or two to work out what this might be. Given the feeble aptitude of our educational institution, where few insights were given into the mysterious workings of our own language, this was proving difficult.

"They have added '*It*' next to 'Sold' along with an extremely gratuitous if not offensive exclamation mark!"

"Oh, I see." I tried not to make this an exclamation too and took a deep breath as the situation finally began to dawn on me. At times auntie's wordiness, not to mention erudition, tends to obscure eventual meaning. As I inhaled, relief descended upon myself and Marcus. Our secret was apparently still safe. We had not been unmasked. We could carry on with our garden visits. I glanced over at Marcus and he threw me a smile, which I reciprocated.

"You may think it's nothing but I tell you we are embarking on a slippery slope!"

Shortly afterwards I said goodbye to him at the garden gate. I strained my eyes towards the lower end of the street to see if I could spot the offending house sign but the fading light prevented me. As I leaned forward, he nibbled my ear, stuck his tongue briefly in it and went off.

"I'm not prepared to put up with such vulgar advertising!" Aunt Bea announced when I went back into the house. "In fact, there is a need for immediate action. Listen. This is what I propose."

"Really, auntie!" So thankful and relieved was I that Marcus and I had not fallen under the unfortunate spotlight of scrutiny that I readily agreed to all of auntie's plans and what appeared to be the simplest and most effective course of action.

Two days later, once the necessary items had been bought, we ventured out at dusk towards the empty Pendleburys' house. In its sorry transitional state it seemed more like a husk than a home. The wide expanse of lawn and garden was now unkempt so that thistles and nettles were everywhere and there was a general melancholy at the lack of activity outside or within. Swiftly auntie took a medium-sized paintbrush to the sign.

"Paint, auntie!" I said, reminding her of the essential ingredient.

"Oh yes, of course, dear."

I unscrewed the lid of the tin. She dipped her brush in and applied it to the sign's offending 'It!' that had been added to the word 'Sold'.

A couple of brushstrokes and 'It!' was soon gone. A rapid and successful application! But instead of turning round and making for home, auntie was heading off now in the direction of town.

"I've spotted a few more on my travels so I've taken down the details and the locations. Come along!"

We traipsed up and down suburban avenues awash with lobelia, salvia and alyssum. Then we trundled along the more solid terraces of town. I would hastily unscrew the lid while auntie applied her brush and aimed. In all, six more trophies were added to the collection.

"I keep an eye out. Whenever I see one, I take note and write it down."

Her excitement was making her repeat herself. She pulled out a notebook as if to prove the point. It was a different one from the smaller pad she used for poetry. For auntie was of this disposition too. She loved language, the skilful use of words, and it may well be that some of this had been indirectly passed on to me. I remembered that on one or two occasions Marcus berated me for wordiness in a prelude to our evening preoccupation. He was a succinct man of action, bold and direct, not unlike auntie, but in an entirely different way.

Whenever the signs reappeared and auntie's daubings were scraped away, we would pay a return visit to the property in question. For these we always favoured darkness in case anyone was keeping watch. There was even an article in the evening paper about the 'Local sign tamperings' so that auntie's night-time activities were achieving a certain notoriety. Letters of support for the 'anonymous erasers' began to appear in the 'Your Comments' column of the local Advertiser. A number of grammarians entered the fray. Auntie had kindled a new linguistic awareness it seemed.

About eight months later, the said estate agent responsible for 'It' and its accompanying ejaculation, exasperated perhaps at the frequency and persistence of the nocturnal raids, allowed itself to be subsumed in an unexpected takeover bid from Anatole and Blake. The new proprietors did not continue the odious policy and strategies of the former company so that the 'Sold' signs returned to more modest proportions. The 'It!' seemed to have been banished forever.

The evenings now became a little subdued without our routine sign alterations. The evenings, that is, when Marcus was unable to visit. Auntie wrote more poetry in the other notebook resting in her desk but I could see that it wasn't the same. Not the same zest and spirit of adventure, the feeling of confounding and improving on the abysmal norm. The tins of black paint and brushes remained unused within the confines of the shed only to be disturbed occasionally by Marcus and myself and our enthusiastic actions.

The winter months arrived with their long evenings. The Solstice came; there was heavy snow in February.

I remember coming home early one afternoon in March. It was a Saint's Day and we had been excused the last two classes. I arrived back to find auntie in a state of high excitement. She had her familiar crusading expression on as I wheeled my bicycle into the garage.

"I've just been listening to the radio, Anton! You know, the local one."

I leaned the bike against the wall and shut the garage door.

"There has been an alarming development! It would seem that the City of Cambridge Council has decided that they are going to do away with apostrophes on *all* their notices and signs!"

"Apostrophes?"

It was something she held dear. Their frequent misuse was deeply painful to her.

"On what grounds?"

"It makes it simpler apparently! Clearer! Well that's what *they* say, the fools!"

I saw beneath the agitated gestures a rekindling of the determination, the spirit that had brought about our first excursion and necessary readjustment to the estate agent signs. I could tell what she was thinking.

"Only this time we would be adding, restoring, embellishing rather than taking away or obliterating! If we are to lose the apostrophes in Cambridge, the seat of such mighty and noble learning, then nowhere else is safe!"

In the garage where the bicycle lives, we have plenty of tins of black paint and brushes. The evenings are still relatively dark and auntie has made a note of all the signs and places that will need our attention. We are out on the road again.

In a wave of excitement I picked up the phone to ring Marcus.

The Smell of Apricots

They only told her at the last minute that he was coming. Almost with irony they said, "It'll be quite low key. Just one or two photographers."

"And what if I *don't* want to be photographed?" she asked them. "If this is a family visit, a social opportunity, what right has anyone to…?"

"It would be churlish not to," they said. "A moment of *real* history in the making and instead you'd rather turn your back on…"

"History's got nothing to do with it," she replied. "He's *my* brother. If I want to see him, then surely…?"

"We're talking about a brother, though, who is Head of State. He runs a country of his own now. Or rather, he *attempts* to."

"I'm not concerned about what he does. I'm just looking forward to seeing him again. It's been quite a while."

A long time, in fact. A very long time. She put the kettle on the stove and opened a tin of biscuits. There would be enough for when he came. Or maybe some cake? She could make a cake. The one he liked especially when…

She sighed. Absences had followed a familiar pattern before the last self-enforced one. As a young man he had been imprisoned as early as nineteen thirty five, the charge being anti-State activities. Only when the war had ended, was he released, finally being able to bid farewell to his damp seclusion in Cottbus.

He had no regrets, he said. He *had* to do it. And then, afterwards, at least, given the various provocations, to put some *bit* of the country on the right track, on the path to proper Socialism. She could come too, he'd said, but she'd declined. The mining world of the Saarland exerted a pull on her just as Socialism had spirited him away to Berlin, the proper capital, and beyond.

When she saw him, she decided, she would tell him off for that unwholesome addiction of his. With some it was women or fast cars – very often both – but for him it was the perverse fascination for the shotgun. Perhaps he saw himself as a latter day Franz Josef, an Emperor parading trophies before visiting State Leaders. And so for the allocated weekends, the carnage would begin. Rabbits, pigeons, wild boar, deer! Once they'd shot an owl and she'd been incensed. The local Saarland papers had got pictures of it and there with foot placed imperiously and disdainfully on a bison's head was brother Erich, scarcely taller than the fallen beast.

It was distasteful, she thought. Harked backwards instead of forwards. An Achilles Heel; a chink in Socialism's otherwise meticulous armour. Were there bison in the East, she wondered? Or had they been shipped in from the Polish forests, sedated in their clumsy waggons only to totter briefly into daylight and be fired at? No, it was *more* than distasteful! Its cruelty harked back to previous excesses when instead of animals in railway carriages there had been…

Her thoughts were interrupted by a knock at the door. Beyond the panels of crinkled glass, she could see a tall figure. Definitely not Erich, then. The door yielded to a damp afternoon. She sniffed the air.

"Sorry to bother you," said the caller, "but could we go over a few details for the visit?"

"Details?"

"Yes. We have possible arrival and departure times."

"You make him sound like an aeroplane," she said.

The visitor did not react. "We have a second set of times in case there's an extra stop-off on the way. Now could I take a look at your roof?"

"I beg your pardon! My *roof*?"

"Yes, we'll need to have someone up there in case."

"In case of what?"

"Security. There'll be three officers in the garden, one each in the neighbour's, and an additional armed officer on the roof."

For some reason, she had a sudden vision of one of Erich's hunting sprees.

"It's quite normal for Heads of State. Nothing out of the ordinary. Also for government ministers, too."

"Oh," she said. 'Heads of State.' That's what he was, she supposed. She had remained largely oblivious to it; sometimes, when he appeared on TV, she'd turn it off. It was a little too raw occasionally. And some of the neighbours had long memories. Some of the newer ones, too, were abusive. One had even told her, the man who had just set up a letting agency that she belonged 'drueben,' over there!

"I was born here," she replied coldly. "Grew up here. Why should *I* move? I'm not accountable for history nor for what was perhaps a logical consequence." The words rested uneasily with her. "I'm not responsible for someone else's decisions...*or* mistakes," she added.

There! He had succeeded in making her pass judgement and that was something she had always wanted to avoid. Erich belonged *there* just as she belonged *here*. Ganz einfach! Simple!

"But to authorise the shooting of your *own* citizens!"

She turned tail out of the office. She had only gone in to make an enquiry for a friend who was thinking of moving here, wanted a ground floor flat, no stairs.

"Can I see access to the roof?" the visitor was asking.

"Oh, yes. Yes, of course." She took him to the room with the balcony, which provided the easiest way to clamber over the tiles. "Bitte sehr!"

"Thank you," he said, closing the glass door behind her.

He was an unconscionable time, probably counting and checking each slate. Every so often, she would hear a thud from above and she had a vision of him landing in the living room.

She remembered being in England once and watching her friend Sophie's TV. There was an advertisement for tea where a man in a parachute lands in an opulent lady's living room. The lady was quite unperturbed. "People are always dropping in," confided the hostess, "for Horniman's Dividend Tea." They went to a supermarket round the corner to purchase the tea but she'd been disappointed as there was no reference nor picture of the parachutist on the packet. "And what means 'dividend'?" she asked Sophie.

The man was shaking her hand. "Alles in Ordnung," he said and left.

On the appointed day she awoke early and for the first time felt strangely nervous. On the way over to the local grocery store to buy the ingredients for the afternoon cake, she was sure some bushes were quivering rather too readily. At the large house on the corner, she peered over the wall to take a look but there was no shape crouching behind nor could she see any tell-tale feet.

In the shop they were behaving differently, it seemed. Did they perhaps know about the unofficial stop-off? Had it become common knowledge? Were they aware she was making a cake?

Back in the kitchen she basked in the companionship of her ingredients. There was something wholesome about mixing flour, of watching the wayward trails of icing sugar. The cakes baked themselves to perfection – fit even for a king, or an emperor, let alone a Head of State. She thought the man in the shrubbery might like the apricot slice so she rolled the oats with a heavy pin. The kitchen smelled like childhood when she, too, had been the recipient of industrious baking.

A shape appeared, silhouetted against the glass. She let in the man who was going to perch on the roof. From outside there were voices in the garden.

"Oughtn't to be allowed."

"Bloody cheek!"

"Taking things too far!"

"They'll want the shirts of our backs next!"

"Don't we give them enough money?"

"Buy their old people."

"Détente was a joke!"

"Tear down that bloody wall! If the Americans had any bottle…"

They were not happy, then, she gathered. And their polite yet studiously indifferent way suggested that they held *her* responsible too. The association perhaps of guilt and blood. For a moment she found herself sitting down with one or two of them saying, "Young man. Somebody has to do it. Would you prefer it if the Russians did?"

"It *is* the Russians," said one.

"Even the Russians are reforming themselves," said the other. "It's just those old hard-nosed Socialist dinosaurs!"

She had never heard her brother called a dinosaur before. She found it rather funny. But any hostility would melt when they saw the cake. The way to a man's heart was through…

She could hear the click of the gate. The tall shape from earlier was on the doorstep directing operations. A group of people were behind him. Two photographers at the ready. The man hiding in the bushes, the sentry on the roof…

He probably had been obscured by the group but, like the parting of the waves, they stepped aside and then she caught sight of…

Small, smaller still. Old, greyer, yet greeting her with a smile he ran forward to kiss her and they hugged each other in the garden. There were tears on his cheeks but she was thinking of all the concealed men, positioned like chess pieces around the place. The photographers flashed and there were TV cameras with attendant crew.

Such a long time. Imprisonment, war, no news, the end of the war, the new States, the two countries nestling together in distrustful co-existence. The exodus, the 'haemorrhaging of the German Democratic Republic' – his words – and then the Wall. The Wall *he* supervised. The Wall that *he* built. The Wall which sprang up overnight when all the Allied leaders were conveniently and perhaps suspiciously on holiday. The surrounding of Berlin with a virtually impregnable barrier.

But he was back home now. They talked together. She forgot about the hunting, handed round the cake. They walked out into the garden. He admired the house, the plants. It was homely, he said. 'Gemuetlich.'

I must be off now, he said at last.

The retinue followed. The TV cameras dismantled. In the ensuing silence she realised she had forgotten the apricot slices. She looked up but the man on the roof was no longer there; his colleagues in the garden had also departed.

She paused for a moment to take it all in. It had been like a dream – a fleeting sort of vision. But she *really* had seen him – and not 'over *there*' but *here* – in the comfort of her own house and garden. And they had clasped each other, touched…

And now the high wave of emotion had broken and subsided she sat down in the quiet of the kitchen where the smell of apricots still lingered.

Then she realised. Everything became clear. "Erich," she said, addressing the furniture in his absence, "they have lured you into an indiscretion." She thought of her own Leader, the bulky and unattractive Cabbage, who really was called Cabbage, rotund and heavy with all the seductive powers and charisma of an uprooted beetroot.

"The Cabbage has secured an important victory," she murmured. "And *you* have made a miscalculation. A great miscalculation. For in travelling here to the West your citizens will say, 'Why should *Our* Leader be the only one to do this, when we ourselves are denied, shut, locked up, stuck like bears in a cage?' She looked at the chair where he had briefly sat. "The trip to the West was perhaps one trophy too many in the hunting lodge. Of course we could meet but..."

There was a loud crash from outside, something falling from above. Those with powers to see into the future would have said it was perhaps the Wall collapsing, the demise of the sister State. But for Katrin it was a large tile that had slid from the roof, dislodged by the tall, silent man who had scrambled up there.

The Ambassador's Son

It may be of interest to you to know how the incident happened, how it all began. It was something that could not have been entirely foreseen. Planned a little maybe but all the same it was a rare opportunity.

I remember the day he came; the haze that surrounded his gentle appearance so that he looked like someone out of a dream or a film even. There was little natural light on that occasion and what there was came filtering softly through one of the far lancet windows. Yet it was the fusion of light both natural and from candles that made his entrance seem all the more memorable.

At the time my thoughts were somewhere else, as they often are, leading me out of the semi-darkness of the building and into the sunlight of the garden. I think I was making plans for the section beyond the shrubbery, pictured myself between the fruit trees amongst the radiant blossom of almond and peach. I used to think these trees grew everywhere but when I made my trip to England once I was disappointed by their absence.

Of course at the time my husband was unaware of the object of my attention. As usual he was too involved in his own devotions, his particular brand of piety, which, like certain church goers, he is apt to wearing in a prominent if not ostentatious position. There is an expression in English, which I studied for three or more years, and actually heard during my visit there, that says 'to wear your heart on your sleeve.' I liked it very much and immediately thought of Enrique, only in his case it is his religion he is happy to parade.

The day that Julio – for I may call him that – took up his position is recorded in my diary. There are many empty entries in keeping with the lack of incident, of eventfulness, but the twenty-third of March is pleasantly inscribed. A mild spring day, an auspicious day. Of course the diary is carefully tucked away and concealed in a locked drawer. It is better to play safe with these kinds of things.

Easter was late that year. Easter which follows the particular tendencies and inclinations of the Moon. There was talk in 1050, apparently, of getting it changed, of restricting it to a particular day but I doubt whether anything will happen. We must accord change with the reverence it deserves and therefore achieve it painstakingly. However, it does seem to call into doubt the veracity of a certain event, the accuracy of date, if we are given over to following the whims of nature. Navidad, or Christmas, is always the same, though for us more significance is ascribed, in material terms at least, to the day of the Kings or Los Zapatos.

I ended up seeing much of him over Easter; the various rituals and ceremonies. It was with eye contact that it all began and who could fail to notice the prominence and beauty of his eyes? It was through them, his and mine, that the pattern and process began of what some might call flirtation.

Because of this I chose the occasional moment to indulge in brief snippets of conversation, if only to experience the novelty of his voice and in that soft regional accent which he had, which most of us have, except of course Enrique. I enjoyed the gentle wisdom, the simple expression of the content. He did not speak like a book, as some do, nor did he indulge in platitudes or clichés but merely spoke naturally, spontaneously, honestly as I afforded myself the opportunity, as listener, to gaze into the realm of his eyes.

In the carrying out of the various ceremonies, and in daily life, too, an inordinate amount of robes and garments have to be worn. I felt for him in his black attire under a sweltering sun. There are obvious reasons for this in obliterating the physical contours of the body, yet the eyes cannot be covered and it was through them that I believe we first gained awareness and appreciation.

I felt too, when I closed my eyes at night, I could conjure up his image, his shape, and I pictured him staring back at me. When I yielded to the routine, mechanical intimacies of my husband, I discovered that there was often a third person in the undertaking.

I'm sure I don't need to let you know how I *first* became personally acquainted, with Julio, I mean. I'm certain you can imagine it for yourself; let it appeal to your romantic or innermost tendencies.

Suffice it to say that it was a day when a sudden downpour delayed my departure from the building. And when I eventually stepped out into the cooler air, took in the smell of the revived trees and plants, with which I could identify, I found myself formulating a plan. A plan which would combine innocence with deception. Innocence.

It was in early summer on a Day of Obligation that an extra party came to take part in the celebrations. There were quite a number of them and they passed us by in the aisle to take their allotted seats near the front. Naturally, the colour of his hair was sufficient to single him out. I made a point of gazing at him in an obvious way so that even my husband, wrapped up in his many devotions, took note. I sighed conspicuously at the abundance of auburn hair. It is a rarity for us in our geographical location. And I took to staring at him, seated as he was just a few rows in front. His skin was pale like the bud of a magnolia with the odd sweet freckle. Intermittent bursts of sun sent shafts of light through the windows to expressly illuminate his soft, gently reddish hair. Occasionally, he would glance around, perhaps taking in the novelty and splendour of the surroundings, and when I caught his eye, I would smile at him. The first time he failed to respond but on the second instance I must have beamed more obviously, like a crocodile anchored on a reed bank, and he reciprocated with a look of appreciation and natural radiance. Enrique was witness to this and his fingers executed a peremptory tap of admonition to my seated thighs. I gazed down at the floor in temporary contrition but it was not long before my eyes took up their nomadic quest again, were on the move and alighted on the tall shape of the boy.

"You seemed readily distracted!" complained Enrique when we returned home.

I pleaded ignorance; replied with a look of incomprehension.

"The visiting ambassador's son," he explained.

"Ah, so you know them?" I said.

He nodded.

"I would like to have been introduced."

"I'm sure you would," he replied in that pithy, pompous way which makes him seem so much older.

"I was struck by the colour of his hair, that's all."

"Yes."

"It was beautiful."

"Perhaps." There was a pause after his concession. "And so you were distracting him?"

"I merely smiled."

"And not just once?"

"No."

"Why?"

"He was a visitor. It was a gesture of welcome. Besides…"

He gazed at me intently.

"He was very handsome. Very!"

"He's a mere boy! No more than twenty!"

"And I am thirty one! Beauty is not restricted to any age."

"What's that got to do with it?"

"And he is twenty. Or so you say. What's *that* got to do with it?"

"It was improper. For you to look at him so ostentatiously! To smile! To give him encouragement!"

"Improper! Encouragement! To do what?"

You can see I was arguing convincingly. That evening after we had had supper, he asked me about it again.

"So when you saw your vision of beauty, did you have any other thoughts?"

"Other thoughts?" I laughed.

He became quite angry. "Yes. Intimate thoughts?"

The question was so ridiculous that I found myself blushing in annoyance, which in turn worked to great effect.

"So you *did*?"

"It was a *long* ceremony."

This was guaranteed to rile him, to spur him on to further vexation. I am frequently chided for my so-called lack of commitment, my disinterest in ritual...

"So you don't deny that your thoughts were improper?"

"I was simply responding..." And here it struck the right provocative note. "...To visual stimuli, to the agreeable nature of my surroundings."

"Then you have sinned in thought."

"If you say so."

"Your marriage, your bond is not enough for you?"

I laughed at his stupidity. "Don't tell me you don't think the same sometimes. I mean..."

He banged the book he was holding on the side of the table. He may have grazed a knuckle.

"We are not discussing myself! It is *you*!"

I stood up angrily, which I hope was convincing enough. "So what is it you want me to do? Go to confession or something? Expiate...?"

He was disarmed by my solution, my sudden apparent willingness.

"Indeed. Yes. It would be a start. And then..."

"I shall go this Saturday," I replied. "Yes."

He became quieter, placated by my readiness. And I, for my part, waited for Saturday.

When I entered the church it was dark as usual. There were two women seated on one of the benches and so I sat down a little way behind. As I waited there I hoped nobody would come after me. If they did, I would wave them on and continue to wait my turn. The first woman's visit to the large wooden box over in the south aisle was quite brief. Barely had the door closed than she seemed to be out again. And I wondered perhaps if these elderly women were such frequent visitors that there was very little to relate.

The second woman hobbled over whilst the previous penitent joined me on the bench. It rocked a little according to the nature of her supplication and I could hear the smacking of her lips in the darkness, rather like the sound of a fish in an ornamental pool when it swims to the surface in expectation of food. However, she quickly got up and left. A little while after, I saw the second woman re-emerge but unlike her neighbour she did not stop to recite a parting prayer.

I glanced around. The church was empty. I walked towards the confessional where Father Julio would be waiting. I knelt in the cosy darkness of the box, saw him outlined behind the grille.

After a few preliminaries I came to my tale. Of course, I added one or two bits for embellishment. I may even have produced intermittent sobs and sniffs.

"Did you feel anything towards this boy?" he asked, not without tenderness.

"He was worthy of attention but there is someone else for whom…"

I wondered if I had kindled a spark of jealousy just as I had done with Enrique. There was a long pause and then I saw him get up, leave his side of the confessional booth and open the door. He was standing next to me, drying my tears with a large white handkerchief, holding me. I could feel his warm breath upon my cheek.

"I shall go and lock the door," he said.

I heard him slide back the bolts of the heavy oak door that leads to the street. When he returned…

Again I shall condense the details for you. I'm sure you can imagine the tenderness that such close proximity begets. But in this we were both grateful recipients and there was enough room on the penitent's side to accommodate the two of us. I felt the warmth of his body contrast with the cool smoothness of the confessional wood.

"I should be going," I said to him at length.

He smiled, accompanied me to the door and unlocked it. As I stepped out into the street I heard the bolts grind back reluctantly on the other side.

"My confession was not good," I said to Enrique later. "I was distracted all the time."

It was true. I could still feel it.

He glanced up from his book. "Then you will have to go again," he said. Such words of encouragement even if they were spoken in his customary chilly style! "It's one of the first things they tell us. An imperfect confession. What were you thinking of?"

"I don't know." And yet I did. I floundered. "Various things. My mind was wandering."

"No doubt the image of the ambassador's son. It's truly disgraceful."

I could feel Julio pressing down on me, squeezing…

"Possibly."

"So go and make a proper act of confession."

"Oh yes," I said with a certain amount of eagerness. I would clearly follow that direction and for that I would need Father Julio and more of his time.

As before, I waited until the last moment and stepped inside the box. On hearing my voice, he immediately stood up and went to lock the door that leads into the street. As he drew back the bolts, I experienced a frisson, a wave of excitement.

"Come," he said, calling me out of the box. "Follow me."

Once inside the vestry, where there was far more room, we disrobed as fast as we could. His hands seemed much more eager than last time.

"How did you manage to come again so soon?" he asked.

I was not entirely sure what he was referring to. He has the hands of a seasoned lover.

"To confession."

"I told him that the last one was imperfect. That I became distracted." He ran his hand along my breasts, pressed his lips against my neck'

"As is this, of course."

"Of course."

I was able to relate to Enrique afterwards of my continuing distraction; that I couldn't get the ambassador's boy out of my head. He was disapproving as always. I also told him that I had admitted my imperfect confession to Father Julio.

"And what did he say? Angry no doubt that his time was being wasted."

"Not entirely. But he was quite strict with me. He told me I would have to keep doing it, atoning, until I got it right."

"I expect he will want to increase your penance."

"Without doubt," I replied as Enrique returned to the spiritual comfort of his book.

The Tale That Dare Not Speak Its Name

"I think," said Clarissa to Humphrey Everley, "that Lavinia, our new judge, may have gone a little overboard this year."

"Overboard?" replied Humphrey only partly hearing. "Overboard? She hasn't gone out on a punt or something? They all want to do that when they come to Cambridge." For a moment he had a painful image of Miss Lavinia Windburn being extricated from a sludgy River Cam.

"No, no. Nothing like that. No, it appears she's done four!"

"Done for!" gasped Humphrey. "Oh my word! How terrible! How are we going to find a replacement for our competition at this late hour?"

"No, no!" said Clarissa, slightly exasperated at Humphrey's last-word listening technique

He had once been a scholar of German where the verb, the all-important, invariably lurks at the end of a sentence. It was perhaps in part responsible for Hitler's rise to power. The element of suspense cloaking a content of banality.

"Not *done* for!" explained Clarissa. "She's done *four*! Chosen four! Adjudicated four!"

Like a new dawn on a misty horizon, the realisation gradually settled on Humphrey Everley's face. However, any subsequent joy was to be short-lived.

"Four? But we can't possibly have four! The Highly Commendeds and their feedback comments take us easily up to the break. We can't have things running late for the interval! The fellow members will get most agitated! Fidgety!"

Clarissa gazed at Humphrey for a moment or two and then realised. Break was an immovable feast, a sacrosanct shuffling of cups behind a mysterious wooden partition. It was perhaps what most people came for. The tea and coffee interlude heralded by the whistling urn and sandwiched on either side by a little literary icing.

"Didn't she read the rules? They're very explicit."

"Lavinia's quite insistent."

"Well it's most irregular!"

"I thought perhaps," volunteered Clarissa, "that one of the other stories, the Commendeds was a little too long. You know, in its variety of locations. Bermondsey, Upton Park, East Berlin. And then there's the incident where the heroine gets assaulted on the platform of some station called Shippea Hill…"

"Weltläufigkeit!" affirmed Humphrey, seeking comfort in a spot of abstract philosophical German. They always managed it so well. Angst! Schadenfreude! Zeitgeist! The language was just made for it! "Er, I think you'll find the story you're thinking of doesn't feature a railway station. The tale in question is 'I Was Assaulted on my Boyfriend's Grave' by Sylvia Delawney."

"Well where is Shippea Hill anyway?" asked Clarissa, ignoring Humphrey's correction.

He waved his arms in a vague gesture. Hills were in short supply in this neck of the woods. It was probably some location nestling in the vertiginous heights of Essex or possibly even Huntingdon.

"We shall have to explain the situation to her when she arrives. But four! It's unheard of!"

There was a sound of windows rattling as a taxi driver pulled up outside. Such was the delicate arrangement of the structure in which the literary group met that the panes of glass invariably wobbled. When the Charrington's coal lorry used to deliver to the old people's home opposite, one pane of glass actually fell out.

Lavinia, safe from any unexpected immersions with the Cam, stepped out of the taxi. For a second her peroxide spray of hair reminded them both of Dame Barbara Cartland but without the poodle and the vitamin pills. Humphrey quivered briefly.

"Good evening!"

"Good evening, dears! I've brought the scripts along with me." There was a pause. She smiled. "Well, naturally, how could I not? It would be like a wedding without a ring. A dinner-party without a gong."

"Allow me to take your coat," Humphrey offered helpfully. Barbara Cartland or no, chivalry would not be laid to rest!

"Thank you, luvvie!" said Lavinia, betraying a hint of northern accent.

Clarissa, who had a cousin from Ramsbottom, ushered her into the meeting room.

"Clarissa says you've nominated four. Amongst the Commendeds."

"Yes, I have, dear," beamed Lavinia, looking as if she had just invented the steam engine. "Most commendable!" She laughed at her little play on words.

"Humphrey's a bit worried about the timings," Clarissa explained. "He gets jittery with these kinds of things."

"I understand," said Lavinia. "But it *had* to be four. I couldn't have chosen one without the other! It would not rest with my conscience!"

Clarissa saw the chosen scripts spill out of a folder as Lavinia deposited them on a desk. Aha, she thought. Berlin. She could spot that one. There was one of those long German words stacked together rather like a famous railway station in Wales. That was a giveaway. Then there was a tale about vegetable marrows, no doubt the work of Roy Harding, and a

story about a loft conversion – still quite topical – and then…
She froze. She caught sight of the opening line, which
normally would have been praised for refreshingly opening
with dialogue… Yet the juxtaposition! The expression! The
word 'Cat's' – or was it two nowadays, you could never be too
sure? – had sidled up to the following word 'bumhole.'
Clarissa gasped at the outrageous coupling.

"Everything all right?" enquired Lavinia on seeing her co-
host turn rather pale.

"Oh yes," lied Clarissa. "It's my knee. A touch of
sciatica." Could you get sciatica in knees, she wondered?

"Yes, very unpleasant," agreed Lavinia, unpacking her
briefcase.

She seems well organised, thought Clarissa, apart from
her deviation in selecting four manuscripts. Again her eyes
drifted to those two horrendous words in partnership as
Lavinia looked for a pencil. It couldn't happen, she reflected.
Mustn't be *allowed* to happen! Emilia Bottomley, a generous
patron of the group, was also Chairman of the Cats'
Protection League. Any outburst of coarseness, however brief,
could throw their sponsorship into jeopardy.

She found herself beginning to identify deeply with
Humphrey's anxiety. He had currently gone to check the
smooth workings of the tea-urn. Clarissa glanced around. The
room was slowly starting to fill, with the devotees of the
Writers' Group choosing their favourite places to sit. It was
strange how conservative people were, she thought. Even
from an early age we tend to look for our securities, the
positions in which we feel comfortable. There was Mr Tom
Wainwright, who favoured the back row. Often his neck and
shoulders could be seen resting against a pillar, a combination
perhaps of fatigue and despair. And then there was Henry
Woodgate whose large frame should really not be occupying
the front row. Clarissa had sometimes spotted demure and

diminutive members such as Hazel and Cynthia anxiously straining, inclining their heads to either side of his ample build.

Whilst Humphrey was filling Lavinia in about the finer details of the meeting, Clarissa quickly slipped the offending manuscript, poised in number two position, to the bottom of the pile. There, that would be the immediate insurance if Humphrey stuck out for three! However, there was something in his demeanour, his body language, his enthusiastic gazing into Lavinia's hypnotic eyes, which suggested his resolve was rapidly weakening and that Lavinia might well get her way. We are often defenceless against charm, she reflected. It is so easy to be killed by kindness.

She paused for a moment. Her last three words assumed a literary quality that seemed stunningly original. When she had an opportunity later, she would jot them down in her writer's notebook.

But then despite basking in literary originality, there came another hiccup, a qualm, a nagging doubt. Was she not embroiling herself in a despicable act of censorship by removing the 'bumhole' from its rightful place? Was this not against the very essence of artistic expression, of creative freedom?

A lump gathered in her throat and failed to adhere to the principle of gravity. Furthermore, she had also contemplated a more radical removal by inserting the offending manuscript into the 'Also Ran' pile. No, that would not do! Besides, her deed might eventually be discovered as Lavinia did not appear to be of the 'scatty speaker' variety.

But as Humphrey and Lavinia continued their discussion in which the former seemed to have already consumed his weekly smile ration, Clarissa glanced across at the upright figure of Emilia Bottomley, who also caught her eye. Emilia waved a few enthusiastic gloved fingers and beamed.

Cat's bumhole! Bumhole! It could not be. Absolutely not! For the greater good then, for the continuation of seventy-three Hawkesley Lane, sacrifices had to be made!

Deftly lifting up one of the stories from the reject pile, Clarissa inserted three of its pages into the Berlin tale. Its writer, she noticed, was an Ernest Cottesley, a retired upholsterer who commanded an almost universal respect amongst the group with his varied combination of European travelling and stately home furniture. However, he was not in attendance at present to witness the unsolicited adjustment to his script. In the case of a writer's absence, the task of reading would most likely fall to Judge Lavinia.

"I think we should begin," announced Humphrey.

After a brief introduction, the adjudicator picked up the script and read.

"Well that was a mammoth one!" she commented afterwards whilst simultaneously observing a partly snoozing front row. Henry Woodgate's head was almost horizontal, thereby affording a view of Cynthia behind. "I'm not entirely sure whether the guided tour of the Tyrolean castle fitted into the story of the Berlin underground but it made for an intriguing contrast."

"Yes, yes," waggled a few front row heads, temporarily reviving.

Lavinia reached for the next tale. She was sure she hadn't read about the vandalising of the Alpine chaise-lounge when she had originally selected the piece! From the front row too, Humphrey grinned in tacit approval. He was always very partial to furniture. A good choice, his smiling encouragement seemed to say.

Now came the tale of the vegetable marrow with its lengthy build-up to the horticultural show and the glittering prizes on offer. This was a nice parallel with this evening's proceedings, both he and Clarissa reflected.

The clock was ticking swiftly to within ten minutes before the break. The marrow was duly applauded off, triumphant in its pale pink runners'-up rosette. Next came the story of the loft conversion. On its conclusion it was already twenty-five to nine.

"And now," revealed Lavinia, "a tale that made me laugh and is perhaps rather like a soufflé after a prat principal, a hog roast. The fourth commendation…'A Windswept'…"

But by now the front row was in agitation. The tea-urn was singing impatiently behind the partition while Stanley and Hilda were poised to fling back the screen.

"I think…" Humphrey began, struggling with the ocular temptation that came from an over-enthusiastic Lavinia, "we perhaps…er…"

There was a sudden clatter and a scream. The heavily dormant Henry Woodgate had fallen off his chair and onto nearby Dorothy Sedgwick.

"I think that settles it!" announced Clarissa boldly. "I feel we must adjourn for a break."

"No more Highly Commendeds, then?" asked Lavinia. "Just the winners after?"

The partition flew open. The participants were on their feet.

"Well that went very well," Humphrey congratulated Lavinia afterwards.

"Did it? I was a bit confused in the first tale. I'm not sure I read it with enough conviction. You know, I had the funny feeling I'd picked up the wrong script."

"You'll find we're quite an experimental group here," confirmed Clarissa. "Anything goes."

It was in the company of the last two words, the malaise of a fraudulent opinion, that Clarissa joined the eager tea queue. She was ushered in near the front by a deeply contrite Henry Woodgate, himself only a few positions behind Emilia Bottomley whose blushes had been so judiciously spared.

"Thank you, Henry," Clarissa acknowledged yet politely declined his offer.

In the aftermath of her successful strategy, she felt now was perhaps the time for penance. Humbly and thoughtfully she walked over to the periodicals table and joined the back of the lengthy queue.

The Meta Effect

"A Miss Dubrovnik is coming at two."

Walter looks surprised.

"For the meeting."

Meeting? Walter puts down the paper whose crossword he's trying to decipher and offloads his specs. The removal of the latter is a sure sign that he's listening.

"The theatre group," Larry reminds him.

"Ah yes."

"It seems she has some bright new project that she wants to share with us."

Walter is trying to picture Miss Dubrovnik. The name seems vaguely exotic; he imagines her as tall, dark, mysterious, fashionably dressed with a fabulous wasp-like waist.

"Dubrovnik. I've heard the name somewhere."

"I think it's a port," suggests Larry. "Not far from Oslo, I believe."

"Oh. I thought it might have been somewhere off the Belgian coast."

The mention of Belgium seems to diminish the special qualities attached to Miss Dubrovnik.

"What's her first name?"

"I can't read the writing. It looks a bit like Marmite."

"Well we can't have that," declares Walter. "I shall call her Elena. Elena Dubrovnika. The 'a' will give her a suitable Slavic feminine ending."

"Just as you wish," replies Larry. "Even though she comes from Belgium?"

The meeting takes place as arranged in the dimly-lit Village Hall.

"It's better attended than usual," observes Larry.

Perhaps similar minds have also attributed the exotic factor to Elena Dubrovnika and have turned out in force. As the adjacent church clock slowly pings the hour a flurry of figures enter the hall.

"Good afternoon everyone!" It's Miss Pinkerton addressing the assembly. She beams. "And I should now like to introduce our honoured guest, our esteemed visitor, Miss Tracey Dubrovnik!"

A small woman, slightly chubby and with a smudge of close-cropped hair smiles to the group. Walter gazes over in disappointment. The sensuous concoction of his dreams seems to have abruptly vanished.

"Thank you," says Tracey. "And this is my co-ordinator, Albert."

Albert smiles in the manner of uneasy consort. Walter notices Larry casting a long look at Albert's enticingly lanky frame.

"The first thing we need to attend to is the little matter of rebranding."

A vague murmur materialises amongst the listeners.

"The South Hambleton Actors' Group is perhaps an unfortunate acronym which may impede understanding and so we have decided to rename the company!"

There follows a slightly more anxious murmur.

"The South Hambleton *Amateur Theatre* is what we shall *now* be known as. It conveys more simply, more purely, I would say, if not quintessentially, the love of theatre. Love! Amateur!"

She purrs.

"And now our next task is to produce a people's play. A play that comes from *you*! The hearts and minds of the people!"

A few oohs and ahs follow.

"So first of all I'd like everybody to stand up and hold hands!"

Walter takes hold of Miss Pinkerton's pale paper-white palm.

"And close your eyes!" encourages Tracey.

He imagines for a moment that it's Elena Dubrovnika dressed in a Marlene Dietrich-style costume with a long cigarette-holder and a…

"And open them! There in those seconds what did you see? What did you experience? What thoughts or exciting ideas came into your head?"

Walter reflects for a moment. The lack of any warmth in Elaine Pinkerton's icy hand makes him wonder whether she is entirely in the world of the living.

"Did anything fire your imagination?" asks Tracey.

There's a sheepish silence. She glances around hopefully.

"I see. And now I should like you to be an animal. Yes, we shall go round where you will act out your animal and introduce yourself."

Seeing as most of the troupe know each other already it seems mildly pointless and a little embarrassing. Walter is somewhat alarmed at how vehemently some of the performing artists are throwing themselves into the part; from cockerels to spaniels to donkeys and a pugnacious boxing hare. He has never acted; merely alternated between composing occasional monologues and being front of house. When the unfortunate spotlight falls on him, he finds himself reciting the 'ribbit' mantra to suggest a frog.

"That's fantastic!" throbs Tracey. "What a shame you didn't do the movements to go with it!"

If he had, thinks Walter, he may have done himself a severe injury and found himself being towed away to the nearby Princess of Wales hospital. He smiles weakly.

Once everyone's settled down and recovered from their brief metamorphosis, Tracey unveils her next plan. "In a few minutes I shall invite a group of actors, *my* actors, to come and perform for you."

This brings about a few more moos of contentment. "This scene is what I call my Trigger Scene, though nothing to do with guns, I assure you." She permits herself a brief laugh, which is strangely unreciprocated. "From witnessing this scene I would then ask you to go away and write your *own* scene which can be attached to the Trigger appetiser."

There is a short puzzled silence.

"Before we proceed, though, I'd like to go through the various stages of playwriting to cement in your mind the possible methods and approaches that can be applied."

Enthusiastically Tracey throws large oblong sheets of blank paper across the floor.

"First," she explains, "we have the Background which in turn leads to the Exposition." She daubs the paper with her eager black ink marker. "Now comes the Development. This can often be accompanied by a series of Parallels."

"Parallel what?" enquires Miss Pinkerton.

Tracey stolidly ignores her. "Then we have the Transposition which often leads to the Meta Theme."

There's another pause but Miss Pinkerton wisely chooses not to interrupt it.

"This is followed by the Climax, the Denouement and what we might perhaps call Legal Consequences." She's scribbling feverishly.

How does that fit in, Walter wants to ask? But then he remembers that in the current litigious society in which they live everything has a possible legal consequence. While he's puzzling the various categories out, the actors assemble to form a circle. They hold hands and perform a brief scene in which something appears to be rescued from a tree.

"I found it very powerful," remarks Imelda Wincott afterwards. "Totally convincing and empowering!"

"But what was it?" enquires Miss Pinkerton. "The thing that they rescued?"

"I thought it was a cat," volunteers Walter. "It was not unlike Eunice Thompson's."

"But they were using a fleece," Larry points out. "Wasn't it meant to represent a sheep?"

"Ah, the sacrificial lamb perhaps," suggests Imelda.

"What on earth is a sheep doing up a tree?" Miss Pinkerton asks anxiously.

Walter grins in approval whereupon Imelda hits him on the forearm. It is the tap of silence and she smiles mysteriously. "We must apply and adopt our own powers of disbelief, of poetic licence."

"I thought it might have been a takeaway," observes Miss Pinkerton. "They come in those great big boxes nowadays. Usually for pizzas."

"And now," announces Tracey, "I want you all to disperse, once you have discussed the scene, and to take pen and paper…"

Albert distributes stationery to each member of the group.

"…And after a period of contemplation, of quiet reflection," Tracey continues, "to write a scene over a nice cup of tea."

As if on cue, the urn at the back of the hall starts singing.

"We shall then regroup at six to discuss further ideas and interpretations."

Walter glances over at the stumpy figure of Tracey a little wistfully. He and Larry usually walk over to the Goose and Bucket for a five thirty pint. It's blissfully quiet there for an hour or so before the kitchen flings open its doors and the smell of vinegar wafts over the Bucket Bar to accompany the flowing ale and cider.

"We could have a quick one before we return," he suggests hopefully to Larry.

But Larry is already immersed in the task of his commission and wonders whether it's a good idea. For Walter a pint of frothy ale is the ideal panacea for his failed frog interlude. He seeks refuge in a bench on the green rather than inhale the melancholy atmosphere that now envelops the village hall. Several people seem to be successfully invoking the Muse to embrace the Trigger Scene.

He clicks open the latch of his garden gate, floats along the path flanked by hollyhocks and seeks the sanctuary and serenity of his own sitting room. It has been an unpalatable experience he thinks. His own imagination has conjured up an exotic now Balkan beauty, not from the streets of Oslo but from the muddle of republics that emanate from the former Yugoslavia, and has been replaced by a tufted hair apparition in a boiler suit with boundless and unflagging enthusiasm.

The kettle sings his grief; its eventual subsidence his deflation. He could choose not to go back but then his absence would be noted and frowned upon. It would become a talking point. He could even lose some of the privileges he enjoys as an associate member of the Hall Committee, which offers fifty pee reductions for a variety of engaging events.

He extricates the forlorn tea-bag from his cup, scorched and crumpled now and lets his mind drift back to the mysterious object rescued from the tree in the Trigger Scene. What on earth was it? Could it have been a white egret that may have had a mishap, collided with the branches of a tree perhaps? How would other people approach this memorable scene, forever etched into the memory?

Torn between the desire to flee, to souse himself in ale at the Goose and Bucket, he finds himself grudgingly retracing his steps to the Village Hall. Perhaps inspiration will take hold once again when he's back in Tracey's magic circle.

She gazes at him for a moment as he re-treads the boards. He's the last to return to the group and he has the impression that he's been holding them up.

"Now," says Tracey, regaining control and smiling to her consort. "Let's go round the hall and share the ideas that you've come up with. It's all about sharing, you see. Winifred, you go first."

"Well," mutters Winnie, slightly taken on the hop, "I was a little puzzled about the white object that appears at the top of the tree…"

Tracey is staring back, beaming encouragement.

"I took it to be a cloud, perhaps of Wordsworthian dimension."

"Fascinating!" exclaims Tracey.

"I wandered lonely as a cloud," rhapsodises Winnie. "So therefore I took it to be the spirit or even the embodiment of the poet impaled on a plum tree."

"We *have* got a wealth of ideas here!" explodes Tracey. "What a collection of interesting minds!"

"Thank you," mutters Winnie and sits down.

"Now, Henry." She motions to the man with a large name badge attached to his polo-necked jumper.

"I wondered," he begins, "whether we could call this White Alert."

"Hmm," ponders Tracey. "That's certainly very interesting."

"There was this series, you see, called The Prisoner and to stop anyone escaping a balloon came out of the sea called Orange Alert. It was quite scary."

"Interesting use of Parallels," muses Tracey. "I think you could really work on it. Fantastic!"

She marks the white cards accordingly, following Winnie and Henry's comments. "Now, Hermione."

The leader of the local Weight Watchers' Group stands up. "The…um…object in the tree, we thought might have been a sheep."

"A sheep! How exciting!" Tracey exclaims. "But how did it arrive there, Hermione?"

"Well, that's just the point. We thought it was tied inadvertently to a hot air balloon, only when the balloon drifted over the trees, the branches somehow punctured the skin or the membrane, and the sheep unfortunately got stuck.

"Hmm," reflects Tracey. "Intriguing. But I'm not quite getting the Meta Theme here." She glances despairingly at her oblong cards, uncertain as to where to put Hermione's idea.

"Perhaps Legal Consequences?" suggests Larry whose turn it is next. "Improper use of a sheep?"

"Oh, thank you," gasps Tracey, quickly reaching for her marker.

Larry turns over to Walter with a smile but he's no longer there. He has surreptitiously tiptoed out and sought refuge from the side door that leads out of the kitchen.

Out in the fresh air awash now with pig manure and silage, he contemplates a tall and enigmatic Elena Dubrovnika as he heads quietly towards the welcome bar glow of the Goose and Bucket.

Our Trespasses

What did he think he was doing? What was he playing at? To make such an offer after *all* that happened? For forty years! More than forty years!

Many of the neighbours had been up in arms, not least on account of the barrage of photographers camped outside their houses. Some had taken the opportunity to make their feelings known. If there was a spare reporter they would hold forth. And their views were invariably the same. 'Haven't we suffered enough? What good will it do to have *them* here? The two of them! It only perpetuates the memory, compounds the misery! And the Reverend Pastor, of *all* people! Look what they did to him! His family! Blocked all avenues of progress! He would have had more than enough reason to say no!'

But he didn't.

It was perhaps taking the Christian message too far. After all, it was more than a secular society they found themselves in.

It was not necessarily religious nor Christian, he said. More an act of kindness, the right thing to do. And, on reflection, how could they continue to recite the Lord's Prayer, the Vater Unser, if they were to turn their backs on them? 'Forgive us our trespasses…' No they wouldn't be here for ever. There would be somewhere, a refuge for them, in the end.

But who on earth would want them? No one! Their time had passed. Finished. Not even the Russians, whose puppet he was for so long, offered the arms of welcome. When it came to it, the man with the port wine mark on his scalp and his Glasnost followers were only too keen to dump him!

At the village shop the Pastor had been sworn at, spat at, a large globule of phlegm trickling down his cheek. He wiped it away with a tissue and carried on walking. Back at the house he saw the camped out flotilla of Press.

They had arrived late one February afternoon. They looked tired, especially him. His wife was possessed of more energy, tended to look after him.

The Reverend Pastor could see the illness in the General Secretary's eyes, and something else, although he wasn't quite sure what. The two of them were courteous and polite. Hard to believe he had held office so long, had masterminded the creation of the sister State and now here he was!

"They are quite ordinary people," he'd said to one of his church assistants.

"Normal people?" The lady doing the flowers was surprised. "Is it normal to build a Wall across one's own country? Separate brother and sister, as witnessed in his own individual case? Divide friends and family? Shoot at people who were following their natural instincts to flee?"

"It's history now," he said. "And fortunately behind us."

"It is very *much* the present. It *is* the present as long as *he* is here!" the assistant argued.

"It is the legacy of what occurred. What *we* did. How could people have believed in something that was to last a thousand years? Such madness! Lunacy!"

The assistant picked up a vase of flowers and walked away down the aisle. It was better not to continue such conversations, not to let emotions get the better of one. They were united now. Together. The Pastor was only doing what he thought was right, even though no one could understand him.

After they had their first meal together, he was surprised how the former First Lady took the plates from the table and into the kitchen. She had insisted that they eat together. No separate arrangements. No further divisions, perhaps. She turned on the kitchen taps and began the washing up. She was not here to be waited on, she said. They were no longer in the situation they were before. As guests for an indeterminate time in the Pastor's house, she was more than happy to pull her weight.

He smiled. The requisites of Socialism, perhaps. He saw her arms working vigorously away, dishes despatched to the draining board.

The former Secretary of the S.E.D, the Social Unity Party of Germany, would retire to his room and switch the television on. Sometimes he would read but most of the time he was glued to events unfolding on the screen.

One evening when the Pastor was at a public event, someone he knew came up to him. From the very first moment, he knew what was going to be said, the diatribe lurking within.

"What right have you to forgive that man on my behalf? To forgive him? What right? You are getting above yourself!"

"I'm not forgiving him on *your* behalf. I'm doing so for myself."

The accuser was aghast. "Didn't you suffer enough? Your family? Your children? Thwarted, blocked, denied at every opportunity!"

"Yes, they did. We *all* did. But now we find ourselves in happier times."

"I hear you had an unfortunate encounter," the former Secretary said. "I'm sorry for that."

"There's nothing to be sorry for. It was none of your doing. Not your fault for the way he spoke to me."

"Even so."

The Secretary turned back to the TV screen. It showed scenes from Parliament.

In the evening the Reverend Pastor saw him take a turn round the garden. The doctors had advised a daily walk to help with his condition. He did it late in the day to escape attention, to avoid the camera lights, the flashes of fewer photographers. Next day, they would be back again, sometimes in greater numbers; a flock of scavenging crows.

He watched him walk around the garden, stroll slowly beneath the trees. He had not spoken of politics since he came. Not a word. It was as if a separation, a divorce had taken place within. And it had all happened so quickly; a snowballing, domino effect. Perhaps he should have seen it coming, seen the inevitable rise of the flood waters.

As he came back in, shaking off the damp spring air of the garden, he gave that brief peremptory nod of recognition. It was perhaps the nearest he came to a smile.

"We've been here for over four weeks," he said one morning. It was in response to the news that they might finally, eventually, be on their way. "We should say our thank yous to you."

"There's nothing to say thank you for. You have been our guest."

"Oh but it is," the former Secretary maintained. "Your kindness."

They were sitting round the large table, books piled on nearby chairs. There was a short silence.

"I would put it to you," said the Reverend Pastor, "that recent events are of no coincidence. In 1949 we were split into two states and in 1989 reunited. That's exactly forty years. In the bible God's period for retribution, for penitential reflection and humility, was also forty years. God has levied this on us for the sins of the Reich. And now we can be a country again."

The former Secretary thought for a moment, a frown drifting over his face. "Well if you look at it like that, I can't really put up an argument against it."

There was that near nod of agreement. From the kitchen they could hear a clatter. Margot Honecker was putting away the breakfast dishes.

Cognitive Recipiency

"I don't know what I'm going to do about all these results," said Hamish McLaren to Miss Beazley one morning.

"Are they not good, then?" she asked anxiously.

"Take a look for yourself."

Emily stared at a maze of intoxicating graphs and hieroglyphs. "Oh dear," she said, comprehending nothing. "I see." Men with graphs were like boys with train sets. "Shall I make a cup of tea, then?" she suggested.

McLaren gazed at the obliging Emily. It was her solution to everything. Dry rot in a basement, roof in danger of imminent collapse, an impending invasion somewhere in Eastern Europe. A cup of tea. And yet her choice of liquid pragmatism often seemed to work. She was at it now, standing by the tea-urn with its urgent arpeggios and eventual apocalyptic whoosh as it sent the water bubbling on its way.

They never stayed long in the job Emily thought. It was a stepping stone to some other position, usually in a pharmaceutical factory. McLaren was only one in a long line of failing trouble-shooters. Yet with his light gingery hair and shy Glaswegian smile he was a little more appealing than the polished oaf straight out of Public School. They were generally even more brainless – said all the right things, of course – but when it came down to it, they invariably had the intelligence and imagination of a doughnut.

"Is the exam still the same?" she asked.

"I'm not quite sure," he replied. He held up some papers and endeavoured to sift quickly through them.

"Mr Weelkes said there's something about a recipe in one of them."

"Bear with me," answered Hamish scanning the various sheets. "Bear with me."

He would be more attractive, she thought, if he refrained from using a wide range of clichéd expressions. But then it seemed to be greatly favoured at present within the Board. The fashionable word of the day was 'challenging' as 'difficult' seemed to have vanished out the window. Yet pleasant though 'challenging' was, it gave little indication as to the nature of the problem or any clue to its resolution.

"Mr Weelkes rang up to complain about onion bhajis," she continued.

"Oh." Hamish wasn't aware that the Exam Board had a culinary helpline. "Would that be the process question, by any chance?" he asked.

"It seems he went to somewhere near Brick Lane where all the candidates chose onion bhajis as their 'process.' He also complained that they used identical connectors."

"Was that in the *making* of the bhajis?" suggested Hamish helpfully. "I wouldn't have thought kitchen implements would have been a problem."

Miss Beazley sighed. He still had a lot to learn. "Things like 'the magic ingredient is…' or 'more importantly' and 'the last but not the least.'

He stared at his skilful tea maker and then realised. "Oh, language connectors, you mean!"

"They had been primed, apparently. However, after twenty four successive onion bhajis, although there may have been a vegetable samosa in there somewhere, Mr Weelkes admitted defeat. He was on the verge of despair. In fact he said 'I never want to hear another fucking recipe again!' And that was on the phone!"

Hamish was momentarily shocked. "Perhaps we should send him a letter for inappropriate interaction. I think it's a P85. Abuse to a member of staff."

Miss Beazley looked up from the now tranquil tea-urn. "I don't think it would serve any purpose really," she explained. "Mr Perkins, one of our other examiners, said a week of recipes is really an insidious form of torture and wondered whether interlocutors should be compensated in some way."

Hamish became silent. The fear of litigation was enough to stifle any form of literary reprimand. "They're not very good for the other levels either," he added, pondering a second tier of results. "It makes us look like the exam board that likes to say no instead of…"

"I thought that was the university one," suggested Miss Beazley, raising the unwholesome spectre of their main competitor. She struggled to remember the name of it but for some reason – and she wasn't sure why – it called to mind the Archers on Radio Four.

"I'm just wondering what we can do to…"

"Massage the figures?"

"Surely you're not suggesting?"

For a moment she had a pleasing image of a stressed-out Hamish extended on a massage table. He was naked down to the waist whilst a slim Mediterranean woman was squeezing his freckled Celtic back. It was not unromantic, she thought, particularly as she saw herself as a lady with the Latin touch looking not unlike Sophia Loren or the more flamboyant Gina Lollo…whatever her name was.

"Back to the drawing board, then," sighed Hamish.

She handed him a cup of tea, deep chestnut brown swimming in orange porcelain. Emily steadfastly refused to use plastic or even cardboard cups.

For the rest of the week Hamish was in deep gloom about the figures. "I'm sure we shall lose customers when they receive their results."

Emily quivered at the word 'customers.' She did not like it. They used it on the railway instead of the more optimistic and less static word 'passengers'.

"They may even seek alternative awarding bodies," he fretted.

She glanced up at the mention of the last two words. He appeared to be losing weight and, whilst agreeably slim, she wondered whether he was eating properly.

"Would you be amenable to going to Ciano's after work tomorrow?" she suddenly suggested. "You see I've become an auntie again and I'd like to celebrate."

It was a small white lie as Emily had in fact attained auntie status some three months ago, a week before Hamish arrived. He seemed to hesitate for a short while as if pondering whether it was wise to combine work colleagues with pleasure.

"Well, if it's to celebrate a new arrival," he said.

Miss Beazley went home in a state of high excitement.

"I've booked the table," she announced when Hamish arrived the next morning. For a moment he appeared nonplussed and then he remembered the celebration.

"Seven o'clock?"

They invariably finished at six. What would they do in between?

"There's a pub opposite," she informed him, as if reading his thoughts. "We could have a drink there before."

It felt like going on a date. She made him an extra cup of tea.

In the Frog and Nightie Miss Beazley shocked Hamish by ordering a pint. She seemed to drink it rather quickly and then appeared ready for another.

"Same again?" asked Hamish.

"It's my shout," she insisted. "What would you like?"

"Oh well, just a half," he said modestly.

Her bemused expression had immediate effect.

"A pint then, perhaps."

"Halves seem to disappear more quickly," she replied. "They're no good from that point of view."

Shortly afterwards they walked across the road to Ciano's.

"It's a strange name," said Hamish. "Ciano. Do you think they meant 'Ciao' and spelt it wrong?'"

Emily looked at him for a moment. His own name suggested a wild chieftain from some obscure Highland tribe. "It's short for Luciano, I believe. Personally, I think it's a lovely name. *And* he's got the most beautiful eyes."

Hamish gazed at her briefly. Emily seemed strangely effusive. Perhaps it was the release from the office of annoying statistics. He noticed that she also dabbled in a little Italian and was mildly flirtatious with some of the waiters.

"I had a great-uncle called Luigi," she explained, "but everyone called him Joe. He used to teach me to swear in the Neapolitan dialect. Red or white?" She passed him the wine list.

"Erm, I'm not quite sure."

There was an instrument tinkling somewhere through a speaker. It was possibly a mandolin.

"The Cavalcante Apollinario," she informed the waiter.

"Very good, my lady."

It sounded vaguely medieval thought Hamish as he noticed Miss Beazley's eye trained on the movements of the waiter's energetic back.

"To success!" she cried when their glasses were filled.

Hamish lifted his tentatively. "To success."

"You're not still worried, are you?" she asked him. "You must *try* and switch off, Hamish. Relax."

"It's easy for you to say but I find it quite difficult."

A dish of olives was put in front of them. They were dark and enticingly wrinkly.

"Have you ever thought," asked Emily, "of perhaps reversing the process?"

"Reversing?"

"Well, yes. Instead of getting the student to describe whatever's involved, why don't you switch it over to the examiner? You know, those awful processes and the recipe. Mr Weelkes still says…"

"But…"

She was replenishing their near empty glasses. "I heard a fascinating programme on the radio the other day. She was pleased not to have said 'wireless,' which occasionally dated her.

"Oh yes…"

"Yes. It was all about cognitive non-verbal recipiency."

It sounded oddly like the language they spoke in those meetings, thought Hamish. "And what would that be?"

"Oh," she said, slightly surprised. "Are you not familiar with it?"

He shook his head.

"There's this American, a Mr Flywheel, H. J. and *he* came up with the term. It consists of wagging your head at appropriate times to show that you're following an argument or type of discussion."

"I see."

"So if you reverse the process where the examiner does all the talking, then all the student needs to do is to behave appropriately and wag."

"You mean nod their head?"

"Precisely. Consequently, the success rate would be enhanced significantly. Your abandoned 'customers' – she again shuddered slightly at her own use of the repulsive word – "would come flooding back. Everyone would want to do the new syllabus!"

Hamish took a large gulp of wine. It was chalky and rough on his tongue. "That's really not a bad idea! Yes!"

"Of course the candidates with St Vitus dance might be unfairly advantaged but I'm afraid it can't be helped. There could perhaps be a note made in the marking system."

Hamish looked momentarily blank in response. But as he raised his glass again, the idea seemed to have considerable merit.

"You're an angel, Miss Beazley!" he said.

"Come, Hamish," she replied. "You can call me Milly."

Milly? He thought she was Emily but perhaps this was a coquettish truncation.

"I shall put it to the Board tomorrow," he promised. "There's an extra-ordinary meeting."

"Well there you are," she said. "Everything's sorted."

"I'm so grateful! Really I am! It's brilliant!"

"Not at all," beamed Milly.

His hair caught the subtle lighting and reflected an amber glow. Hamish glanced across at Miss Beazley, whose features in the subdued yet cosy ambiance suddenly seemed Mediterranean. For a moment she reminded him of an actress he'd once seen. They called her 'La Lollo' or something.

She smiled and raised a glass.

Ars Gratia Artis

"**M**ummy is so looking forward to meeting you," said Katya at the breakfast table.

Alex's spoon engaged in the act of lifting a clump of Shredded Wheat ever upwards dipped slightly.

"Really she is," affirmed Katya, noticing the temporary slump in Alex's cutlery.

"Yes, well it'll be nice," breezed Alex without conviction, simultaneously avoiding eye contact.

From their upstairs window they could see Mrs Hilderson walking between the gnomes of her back garden. There was a small arch at the end of the gnome cavalcade over which a rose by the name of Rambling Rector slumped.

"What shall I take her, *we* take her?" Alex asked. He felt that Katya's mum's affections needed buying. "I don't even know her name!"

"Dried fruit," replied Katya in answer to the first question. And then, "Nastasia Filipovna. But you can call her Nastya."

Alex thought for a moment. The name sounded oddly familiar. He felt he had met it somewhere. In an epic Russian novel perhaps. "Has she got a nice house?" he asked.

"It's smaller now. After the separation. But she likes her garden."

Garden, thought Alex. A world denied them from their second floor flat, whilst Mrs Hilderson in her own one person abode had the freedom to walk uninhibitedly through her corridor of gnomes.

"I'm late for work," he said glancing at the clock, which unhelpfully corresponded with the right time. He stood up quickly, knocking over his plate and knife, sending them clattering to the floor. He was always extra-clumsy when he was nervous. "Nastasia Filipovna," he muttered, as he kissed Katya's cool cheek.

"Pardon?" she murmured.

"Nothing," he said. "Just thinking aloud."

On the bus he had to stand, a further ignominy on the way to work. The driver took corners quickly, braked suddenly, causing his passengers to crumple together and fold like a pack of cards. At work, the coffee machine was out of order so at eleven o'clock he had to make his way over to the overpriced snack café across the road, where the staff wore blue and white uniforms and oversized hats. It felt like some kind of parody of the NHS. The hissing of the various coffee appliances obliged him to visit the unisex loo and donate a urine sample.

"I've got to meet the mother-in-law," he informed Vince after work one evening.

"Sounds like a drink is called for," suggested Vince. "Build up your Dutch courage."

Alex did not dispute the wisdom of Vince's recommendation. But why was it Dutch, he thought? Why should they come off so badly in this comparison? And then there was 'Going Dutch' when the spirit of socialism and magnanimity was cast to the wind. What had they done to offend the compilers of the English language?

"So it's Sarah's mum, is it?" asked Vince.

"Katya," Alex corrected him.

"Pardon?"

"Katya. Sarah was the last but one."

"Shows how much I know," smiled Vince.

Shows how much you listen, thought Alex.

"And she's not the real mother-in-law? Prospective?"

"Prospective," echoed Alex.

Vince was passing him a beer, its flat head in contrast to the blousy pints up north. His cousin Rachel, who worked in a pub in Huddersfield, would have been shocked.

"Thanks, mate."

"When are you seeing her?" Vince asked.

"Saturday. Katya can't wait. She starts going all American when she's excited."

"It should be a piece of cake. Just employ your innate acting skills."

Alex's work tapered into two parts. The first half of the week saw him at Hellmann's Photographics while Thursday and Friday involved an evening stint at the Very Small Theatre Company.

"Such as…?"

"I don't know. Your natural gift for insincerity."

"Thank you, Vince."

"Anyway, where's this Katya from? It sounds a bit Eastern European to me."

"Spot on, mate. Her mum's Russian."

"Throw in the odd word, then. It all helps the charm offensive."

Alex gazed at Vince's rapidly diminishing pint. An odd combination of words. Charm coupled with offensive. It sounded as incongruous as military intelligence."

"I don't know any," said Alex. "Apart from 'Nyet.'"

"Yes, I don't think that would help very much. Not in the general flow of things. Though I gather in the course of history it was a word they tended to favour."

"I go all clumsy when I have to meet people," Alex confessed. "My coordination seems to disappear out the window."

"Seduce her with the occasional word, then," persisted Vince. "It invariably works. It shows a willingness to connect with their level. Respectful, sort of. You'd be an idiot not to!"

That was it! Idiot! Alex coughed into his beer, partly choked and slathered on the table. Of course! Nastasia Filipovna!

"Nastasia Filipovna!"

"And good health to you, mate!"

"No, no! Nastasia Filipovna! The name!"

"Yes, I know it's a name. I'm not entirely daft."

"No, no!" insisted Alex. "The Idiot."

"Well there's no need to be rude either! I'm only…"

"Yes, I know you are. Dostoyevsky."

"Sorry, mate. You're falling apart here."

"Nastasia Filipovna. A femme fatale. In Dostoyevsky's The Idiot."

Vince's face showed partial enlightenment. "Oh I see. This is some kind of literary game."

"I was trying to remember where I'd heard the word before." He took a large swig of beer and drained the glass.

"Well just 'cos she's got the same name as…"

"It's an omen," whispered Alex anxiously. "Perhaps I can get Katya to postpone it. The meeting. Recurrence of back trouble, perhaps."

"You're only putting off the inevitable. You'll have to do it sometime."

Alex saw Katya's face, eager, expectant, wreathed in smiles, then pucker into a welter of disappointment.

"Let me get a few Russian words for you. Meet you here for a drink tomorrow. My brother Andre's got loads of language books. I'm sure he's dabbled in Russian in his time."

When Alex returned home he was slightly the worse for wear.

"You've been to the pub!" snapped Katya crossly.

"Only a couple of pints, dear," lied Alex. "I said I was meeting Nastasia at the weekend and Vince said it was a cause for celebration. A milestone!"

"Really?" replied Katya, partly charmed. "Oh, Alex!"

She bestowed an enthusiastic kiss over his designer stubble.

"Andre's got a few words for you," announced Vince when they met up in the pub the following evening. "He says you can get them online, too."

"No matter," said Alex. "It's easier via Andre."

"Well," began Vince adopting his confidential tone. "You can start with 'Privyet.' That means hello."

"Privyet," repeated Alex. "Sounds easy enough."

"The only problem," confided Vince, "is that it's a little informal. Perhaps not so appropriate for the first meeting."

"Privyet," said Alex again. "Hello, you say? But informal. What kind of hello would that be?"

"Perhaps a 'wotcher,' or something like that," suggested Vince.

Alex winced slightly. The combination of wotcher with the regal grace of Nastasia Filipovna did not rest easily. "How about another hello?"

"I was coming to that. It's more usual, so Andre says, to use Zdrastvootyer."

"Oh dear," replied Alex. "That's tricky."

"Yeah but it's a lot easier if you say 'Does yer arse fit yer?'"

"You're putting me on! This is a wind-up!"

"Straight up, mate. My brother never lies. He's too much of a geek to do that."

Alex felt momentarily sorry for the fraternally abused Andre.

"You can't seriously suggest…"

"If you don't believe me, we can try it out on Dasha."

"Dasha?"

"Yeah. She works at the station coffee bar."

"I appear to be in the middle of a Slavic enclave."

"If you don't believe me…"

They left after three pints with Alex wondering how he was going to explain this one to Katya. He looked at his watch. It was already ten to eight.

"Come on! We should just catch her."

A slightly plump and despondent Dasha was marooned in her narrow shell of a coffee booth. On seeing Vincent her expression changed.

"Hello, Vincente!"

"Vincente?"

"I told her I had Latin forebears. She says she's always wanted to go to South America." Then pointing to Alex. "This is Alex." Then to Dasha. "Zdrastvootyer!"

"Zdrastvootyer!" replied Dasha.

"See it works," said Vincent smugly. "Now you try it."

Alex regurgitated the catchphrase question.

"Oh very good," enthused Dasha, offering a rotund paw. "Such lovely pronunci…whatever it is."

"His better half has a Russian mum," Vince informed her.

"Better half," mused Dasha. "What is that?" She was handing them a couple of coffees in woefully thin paper cups.

"I'm fine," protested Alex.

"So am I," replied Dasha. "On the home!"

"She means on the house," explained Vince. "Cheers!"

"Cheers!" yelled Dasha.

"Cheers!" yelped Alex, squeezing the cup awkwardly.

"Another celebration?" queried Katya when Alex stumbled over the hall mat. It had a habit of tripping people up sometimes, highlighting their ignominious downfall.

"Vince had some good news," lied Alex.

"Good news?"

"Yes. He's won a poetry competition."

"Really?" queried Katya. She had met Vincent once. "I wouldn't have thought he was the poetic type."

"Well there you are," reasoned Alex. "It just goes to show. There's a hidden poet in all of us."

"Very hidden," said Katya. "And the dinner's cold." She pointed to a forlorn plate sitting in the middle of the table. It had been ostracised from the oven some while ago.

Alex wanted to reassure her, to tell her that everything was going to be all right. That he was investing in courage of the Dutch variety and was acquiring words of a welcoming nature to break the ice with Nastasia. He could greet her in a questioning catchphrase, although it seemed he had already forgotten the 'Nice to meet you' and 'Thank you' offerings.

The Saturday for the meeting arrived, the weather being amiably warm and sunny. They took the train to Sittingbourne and then a bus as the car was still unobligingly in a garage. In the circumstances it was probably better not to be driving, thought Alex. Katya had a tendency to backseat drive from the comfort of her own front pew.

"Welcome!" cried Nastasia Filipovna flinging open the door. "Please come in, Andrew!"

"It's Alex, mum."

"What I said," insisted Nastasia crossly. Her outstretched hand pointed towards the sitting room, where there was an uncomfortably low-lying sofa. At Alex's heels a mouse-like object yapped.

"Be quiet, Looshka!" yelled Nastasia.

Looshka scrabbled her claws on Alex's trousers. Then there was another bellow and Looshka plummeted into a sulk.

"She is always curious," explained Nastasia. "Katya, did you come by train?"

"Yes," admitted Katya meekly.

"But why?" demanded Nastasia. "It is easy for me to collect you. Both of you. Why?"

The insistence of the questioning in part contained the answer, Alex thought. He gazed at the bewildered Nastasia and smiled. "We didn't want to trouble you," he began.

"No trouble," insisted Nastasia. "No trouble at all. I can easily…"

"We're here now," confirmed Katya.

"Yes!" replied Nastasia. "But why so long? I am waiting."

Alex was wondering whether Nastasia's immaculately and formidably kept house might contain any beer. It would be of some assistance on this occasion. Perhaps she had a dazzling array of flavoured vodkas in a dark cupboard waiting to be unleashed.

The leather settee squelched uncomfortably to Alex's gyrating buttocks. It sounded unpleasant.

"Alex works in a theatre," said Katya helpfully.

"It is good!" responded Nastasia. "You are actor?"

It was too difficult to combine the variety of his two menial jobs under one satisfactory title. Instead he just nodded.

"I love the stage!" enthused Nastasia. "Do you like Pinter? His plays have many beautiful pauses."

Alex wasn't too sure. He knew that the last theatrical offering was a musical version of The Waltons whose main attraction in the second half was a whistling cow.

"How often do you perform?" she asked.

"Most nights," replied Alex truthfully. Furniture required moving on several occasions and in numerous productions, apart from the minimalist Hubert van Glimp, who dispensed with both props and actors.

"But that is wonderful!" continued Nastasia. "I am sure you have lovely voice."

And now the combination of Katya's eager smile and Vince's, via Andre's linguistic accomplishments, persuaded Alex to intone with full aspirated inflexion and a minimum of elision.

"Madam, does your arse fit you?"

He smiled in triumph at the success of his ice-breaker, his dipping of hitherto timid toes into the uncharted regions of a mysterious foreign language.

But the smile was not reciprocated. Firstly, Katya was gazing in horror at her unpredictable partner. "Alex…!"

Her voice faded into the background as Madame Filipovna Jones sailed upwards from her seat like an indignant hot air balloon. "I leave you to see yourselves out!" she muttered darkly.

As she paused at the foot of the stairs Alex thought he could detect a further 'How rude!'

He was out in the street now, the front garden full of mocking sunshine. He had heard Katya's footsteps behind him but when he turned round there was no one there. Instead there was a crescendo sallying forth from the hall and stairwell of the house.

He reached the gate, heard it click in a decisive sort of way. And there was one of those things that Nastasia had mentioned. One of those long meaningful Pinteresque pauses.

In Aqua

I married far too young. It was the thing to do, of course; the best form of escape from an overcrowded council house. And it was good for my parents, too, the rest of my siblings, to see the added bonus of a vacated bed.

I first met Sergio – Serge as he sometimes liked to be called. I think it was that record which was banned by the BBC with lots of grunting and very little music that might have been the inspiration. Anyway, I met him shortly after I was 'volunteered' as a girl guide. I realised afterwards that those two words in their alliterative glibness were perhaps some kind of metaphor for life. It was women who constantly had to fix and stabilise the unreliable paths of men. It was they who had to improve their faulty and frequently faltering attempts at communication. When they were together I noticed how far apart they often sat. It was a wonder in those brief moments of listening, of pricking up those inattentive ears, that they could ever hear each other. Given that the subject matter was seldom interesting, an unflagging diet of football, cars and football again, they were unlikely to be missing much anyway.

Weekends meant that I was usually lolling around the house with a range of younger siblings, which resulted in the place becoming even more untidy than it was; more clutter within a severely cramped space. It was Uncle Edgar, a short, glib man who had never sired children, who came up with the novel idea. He knew someone over at the Pigden Branch, a name that invariably became transmuted, who informed him that they were in need of recruits. It was therefore suggested, and I was 'recommended', driven over one wet Saturday afternoon while boys in shorts, many of whom were my brothers, screamed themselves hoarse over muddy football pitches.

I was soon presented with a drab, starchy uniform of unappealing sludge-like colour, which made me feel like a district nurse or an escaped nun.

"How was it, Gemma?" they asked when I returned home after the first meeting.

I cannot hide my feelings. My nostrils involuntarily flared, opening and closing like an extractor fan.

"You'll soon get to like it," they cajoled, exuding false and misguided optimism.

I was unconvinced.

And then one Saturday, the world turned itself on its head. I was completely derailed!

At the other end of the busy hall, responsible for some dismal gathering or event, I could see an unruly flotilla of boy scouts. Their deep-green uniform combined with our pale brown mud attire meant that from the balcony we must have looked like some kind of mobile forest; maroon dwarves overshadowed by gangling teenage boys in ill-fitting shorts.

It was because of this unexpected addition to the assembly that I became partly hypnotised, sucked in by the beam of a pair of dark brown eyes. I gravitated ever closer to them until I was within speaking distance. I remember he had a roguish smile, not unlike some of the street traders on the Wednesday market. Before I knew it I was volunteering my name.

"Gemma," I said. It seemed to come out very strangely. I sounded particularly hoarse.

"Sergio," he said and he squeezed my hand quite brutally.

I felt myself becoming hoarser and was sure that I was colouring furiously.

I read somewhere that in the mists of time we had once been possessed of a tail, along with a great variety of other animals. If we were to behave in the way, say of a golden retriever or labrador, then my tail would have been thumping furiously upon the floor or against the rickety furniture in sheer uncontrolled appreciation. How transparent then our feelings would be! How difficult to stay 'cool' and conceal our innermost emotions!

Sergio smiled knowingly, confident from a mighty victor's perch, beaming as one who has suddenly made a conquest. And within the smile he revealed a row of radiant white teeth, whereupon I felt myself melting further and for some reason experienced a tinge of moisture in a more intimate region.

From that time on we met up regularly. If we travelled anywhere we would plump for the lovers' seat on the top of those bright double-decker buses. As we journeyed I would thrill to the throbbing of the engine as my leg drifted against his boy scout shorts. I would wait for him after meetings, where they were no doubt acquainted with every type of knot imaginable. I stood outside like a proud parent, waved at his emerging smile and mop of hair. But it was in the cinema that I experienced the deepest intimacy, languishing in the back row of the balcony seats, away from the usherette's twirling beam. Sergio seemed to like foreign films. I suppose French or Italian was no problem to him. And in those moments when the sometimes minuscule subtitles were drowned by dazzling sunlight or decided to slip off the screen altogether, I would alleviate my boredom and uncertainty by nudging closer to him, feel the sharp shock of the hairs on his legs prick against my soft skin.

And then one afternoon, in the library car park, after it had got dark around four thirty, Sergio procured the keys of his brother's Ford Cortina and I did a deed that auntie had once told me to beware of. In the cramped quarters of Giuseppe's smelly petrol wagon, Sergio's scout shorts somehow became disentangled from the rest of his body and flew over towards the vacant driver's seat...

He did, we did, the honourable thing. I found myself treading the uneven flagstones of a church floor, bedecked in fluttering wisps of white, walking slowly up the aisle where Sergio and a stooped priest stood patiently waiting. The ring placed on my finger secured me, captured me as his bride. It was a shock to see him out of uniform and in long trousers.

For our honeymoon we went to the Channel Island of Sark. It was a haven for bicycles, no cars or Ford Cortinas to remind us what had brought us here. Our daily routine over the five or six days was to get up late, have lunch, then go for a stroll and find some romantic place overlooking the sea. There I would get to know Sergio's varied litany of passionate vowel sounds after which he would promptly fall asleep.

Back in the hotel I would sit with the window open, listening to the soft sound of the nearby sea. I pictured myself on exotic beaches with palm trees and glasses of Tia Maria. I saw waiters in penguin-like uniforms quietly approach with silver trays...

Not long after, we moved into a little house in Rathbone Terrace, which Sergio said he would do up. Our belongings were placed in the spare bedroom while the decorations were to take place. It would have been far better if we had paid someone to do the job as Sergio was a dilatory worker. When I suggested it, he pleaded poverty, which was true, of course. But this was hardly helped by the frequent interruptions of nuptials, sometimes three or four times a day, and something we were powerless to do anything about. I was naturally more than compliant as that shiny hair, glossy almost under the electric light, and those appealing dark eyes sucked me in, assisted in the shedding of my clothing...

As I lay on my back listening to Sergio's impression of a steam train, I thought to myself 'Bang go the living room windows,' or 'the painting needed to protect those flaking sills' and even 'the curtain rail in the spare room on which to hang the neglected curtains.'

But I was without the willpower to stop it and found myself in the middle of an irresistibly wholesome addiction. And when I managed to thwart the temptation of those seductive eyes, then some other part of his body, those trim legs or firm thighs, the neat cheeks of his highly pert buttocks, conspired against my wavering resolve. From the first floor perch of our curtainless bedroom window, I became adept at recognising certain clouds that drifted nonchalantly by before and after our interludes. And afterwards, when I went downstairs to make a cup of tea, I felt a tinge of regret, of guilt almost, that we were forever postponing the embellishments to our nest.

During those following months I arrived at work frequently late and in a kind of breathless soreness, but by lunchtime, which at weekends was the time for one of our many upstairs interludes, I began to feel quite hungry for it. Was this because of the aforementioned addiction or was it simply my body clock sending out a reminder for some exercise?

I found myself frequently gazing at Hugh the delivery boy when he came in with the post from head office, observing his long legs, his slim stretch of back as he bent down in front of the water dispenser partaking of its cold, tasteless, slightly fragrant liquid like some animal grazing at a water trough. I began to look forward to his visits, to welcome his late afternoon arrivals, to float on the dissonance of his strange Midland vowels.

My vigilant appraisals of Hugh did not go unnoticed by Sonia, whose lunchtime trips to the pub served as a prelude to her habitual afternoon fatigue and indolence. We discussed the merits and failings of our respective partners, commented on Hugh's external features, talked of holidays, escape.

"How long is it you've been married?" she asked me one day.

I had to think. I always confuse May with March. "Five years," I replied. I mentioned the combination of boy-scout, girl-guide, the Cortina and the library car park.

Five years.

"You should go somewhere special," suggested Sonia.

She was right. Ever since our trip to Sark it had been summer holidays up in Yorkshire, lying close-up to purple heather on the vast expanse of moors. The next day we went to the travel agent's in an extended lunch hour, followed by a swift drink at the nearby pub.

"We always go to Yorkshire," I said.

Sonia turned up her nose.

"Not that it really matters." I explained that much of the holiday was spent in the horizontal position.

"Lucky you," said Sonia. "It only seems to be Wimbledon that makes Gary randy. And that's just for two weeks a year!"

I judged it unwise to volunteer that I would willingly forgo some of my 'surfeit' if only for the poor neglected rooms of the house.

"How about Italy?" said Sonia when we had returned to the gloomy confines of the office.

I handed her the coffee that would disguise the smell of beer. It wasn't a bad idea. Besides, I loved ravioli. "Sergio's part Italian," I explained to her.

"Well, there you are, then," she said. "Take him back to his roots."

I wondered about Venice; I pictured Sergio on a gondola.

I booked it later that afternoon, came back home flapping the plane tickets in triumph and a reservation for a cheap hotel.

At first he was slightly nervous, taken aback; seemed to be missing the Lincolnshire Wolds and the North York Moors. "Come here," he said in eventual celebration. We christened the kitchen table.

The weather when we got there was almost autumnal; a mist clung in the air. Venice reminded me of Sark with its absence of cars. I gazed across the shallow lagoon as we waited for the vaporetto to take us across to Giudecca. Immediately after we'd checked in and opened the tiny attic window we were in the Cortina position. Our birdsong floated through the aperture, drifted towards the bobbing pontoon and across the murky waters to the Zatterre.

That evening we ate in a small fish restaurant tucked away behind one of the churches. But when we returned to our small hotel, Sergio was strangely tired and promptly fell asleep. I'd never known anything like it. Not once in all our time of conjugal involvement had there been an evening…

The next day we explored the labyrinth of narrow streets around the Rialto; discovered how the city lay, according to one of the guides, on a bed of sinking mud. How robust the local inhabitants must be, I thought! The nonnas, who had to climb so many steps, scale numerous bridges and keep their balance on the wildly waving pontoons.

I mentioned it to Sergio but he merely stroked my hand. I expected him to make some comment about toning up your muscles but he remained oddly quiet. And then again, when we got back to the hotel, he fell almost instantly asleep.

During our time there we saw much of the city and the islands; we explored most of the boat routes, visited monasteries. There was, however, a mid-week interruption to our unusual spell of abstinence, so there was nothing amiss in that direction. Sergio held me tenderly as his scale of sounds drowned out the siren of a passing vaporetto.

And then it somehow became apparent. A revelation, if you like, as I gazed at the sparkling water with its shoals of tiny fish. Venice had somehow calmed Sergio's rampant libido; had offered an interlude to sex. It was as if all the surrounding water had mesmerised or tranquilised his powers of application. The Chinese say it does you good to look on water once a day. Was this perhaps a remedy to a domestic problem and one of overpopulation?

As the plane took off into the clouds, speeding us on our homeward journey, I closed my eyes and had a momentary vision. I saw a home with one or two decorated rooms. I saw the embellishment of curtains, of boxes cleared away! And I saw Sergio up a ladder, paintbrush in hand, adding his Italianate frescoes, with me clinging onto him, holding his legs, propping up my ever-resourceful and now obliging boy scout...

Hard Cheese

I remember the day I was chosen, although it was touch and go initially. It was just after eleven as I'd caught some of the wafts of Saint Angela's less than enthusiastic chimes. I don't know if you've ever listened, you probably haven't, but there's a strange pause halfway through, as if the whole process has ground to a halt and given up in a sudden bout of world weariness.

That was it. I too was weary. Had virtually given up hope. Hope of ever being adopted, taken in, acquired, whatever you want to call it. And on a more ambitious level, appreciated! That odd but necessary transaction where coins or notes are placed into the stallholder's soil-blackened hands and the fortunate, selected individual is tenderly placed into floral wrapping paper or sometimes a plastic bag…

They've got these new bio-degradable ones now. The twenty-first century has finally hit the marketplace. I heard Ernie talking about them the other day, only he was grumbling about the price. Council's orders apparently.

I could hear some voices nearby and I could see them fingering and touching my neighbour with interest. I've seen a fair few of that type in my time; have seldom been able to strike up a relationship with them. They're often only here for a day or so, waving their ferny fronds, leaving me on the shelf, quite literally!

I sometimes wondered if it was the position I was in; the actual placement of pot plants on display. You see, Ernie has a certain routine, a ritual which he always sticks to, with me on the end as a kind of afterthought. I think he has a structural picture in his head, a system all worked out. And because I'm slightly taller than the novices now, I generally feature top left.

It's not an enviable position, I can tell you. There are constant draughts and violent squalls that blow across the marketplace, flapping against the canvas awnings and sending things flying. And I've had my share of accidents, too. I was rescued once by the fish lady into whose stall I blew one Wednesday afternoon. My landing spot was amongst the fillets of plaice and dyed haddock, the smoked variety.

Doreen, I think that's her name, was rather annoyed at the amount of soil and flecks of Vermiculite that had found their way over to the King Prawns. Ugly looking creatures if you ask me. I had quite a fright. Those dark brown eyes! Weird! I heard her remonstrating with Ernie, who was largely unapologetic, and kept saying 'That wornt 'appen agin, dallin!' But it did.

And this is where I'm deeply indebted to Gareth, Ernie's teenage son. Ernie had gone away on holiday to some place in Spain, the Costa del...The name escapes me. It does after endless months of icy and fruitless vigils. 'The Costa Lotta,' Margarita, the cheese plant, wittily said one sunny afternoon. I greatly enjoyed the company of Margarita. She was a happy plant, never bemoaning her fate, unlike those perennial Weeping Figs. It was she who first drew my attention to Gareth's underpants, tapping her large glossy leaves against my rather frazzled stamens. In the current trend, Gareth wore his boxer shorts halfway down his abdomen so that those pale pink cheeks with their endearing cleft were exhibited to all the specimens on display. He seemed quite unconcerned, unaware of the draughts that whistled round his back and below. I could sense Margarita quivering; you know, in the way that plants do when they conduct the mysteries of semaphore to one another.

Gareth was picking up a petunia pot that had tumbled off the shelves, reaching deep into the dark recess that lurked beneath one of the wooden tables. I could tell we were not alone in our vigil because Mr Protheroe, who works in the solicitor's office on the corner, was also watching, eyes partly obscured by one of those blousy and, to my mind, overdone mimosa plants. I've noticed also that Mr Protheroe makes more visits to the stall and actually *purchases* a number of plants when Gareth is on!

I wondered if perhaps my luck might be in, but in truth Mr Protheroe does not strike me as a plant lover – not of house plants, anyway. By now he must have a border stacked full of pansies and primroses. You see I've been here that long. Nearly a year now of constant toing and froing, from nursery glass house to windy ledge on the market stall.

But while Ernie was basking in the beauty of Benidorm, a place no doubt dedicated to the advantage of sleep, Gareth was revolutionising the order of the usual suspects. On that Wednesday I was removed from my lofty location over on the left and stationed one layer down in a more central position. Initially I regretted the loss of the observations of the sapient Margarita, but to be placed further down and being able to luxuriate in the sporadic bursts of sunshine was altogether a more pleasant experience. I know it goes against that human logic which would have viewed my 'rearrangement' as a kind of demotion from the ladder of opportunity, but all I can say is 'You try it, dear, suspended on the top shelf in full range of a biting north-easterly!'

It was when I was partly dozing off, succumbing to tenderising torpor, that I heard her voice.

"Julian!" she announced. "What about the space over by the stereo?"

I thought I was dreaming, that this was some kind of surreal concoction and we had entered one of those human dwellings. But when I became a little more attentive I could see she was sketching out a plan of the living room.

"What about it?" said Julian. I assume it was him although I think there may have been three of them.

"Well, what do you think?" she asked.

"I don't mind," he said in a tone which I considered rather rude and truculent.

I could see her pale hands deliberating under those long fronds of golden hair and I quite understood why that plant I have referred to a tad sourly on occasions, might be called a Maidenhair.

"I think that one, Sally," said a third voice cautiously, one whom I later came to realise was Hamish, Julian's younger brother.

Sally's hands were fingering his suggestion, a short and unattractive specimen to my left. It's clear that men have very little taste. "No," said Sally. "I want something more structural, more iconic."

Iconic? Did she say iconic? For a plant? Perhaps I misheard. It may have been 'ironic'. I felt momentarily rebuffed. But to my great surprise I was being lifted off the shelf by two hands, carefully – a great contrast from that clumsy oaf Ernie, who often carried several plants between his fingers, like pint pots being collected from a pub. There's one opposite the market, in fact.

The next thing I knew was that Gareth was wrapping me in a gentle bridal veil.

"I think I'll take a Maidenhair, too," she said. "A small one. It'll look good by the bathroom window."

Sweet and sensitive was the floral paper that enveloped me, and the little patch of sellotape that bonded the crack, the overlap of wrapping paper, somehow felt like an accolade, a final seal of approval. I was held up, momentarily, as a valiant trophy by liberator Gareth and passed over to Sally. I was a bit embarrassed, however, when I heard the asking price and felt that I could have warranted more. I was also slightly aggrieved at being bundled off with the Maidenhair but I gloated at her prospective period of exile in a cold and very likely draughty bathroom, subject to its enormous variety of odours.

As I took in a last glimpse of the market stall before being carted off by Sally, I tried to catch the cheese plant's attention but it seemed that she was in serious contemplation of Gareth's posterior as he was looking on the ground for a wayward coin. I was now firmly in Sally's basket, travelling off to a different land. I was brimful of expectation!

I fervently hoped that they wouldn't make the mistake that so many humans do of plonking me in a window only to be frazzled by the morning sun. But no, Sally was looking me up in a plant encyclopaedia for I had no label attached to me. It had been lost in that long passage of time and only added to the complexities of my adoption.

I was in a book! A fleeting burst of fame! She was speaking to someone, reading out loud.

"Away from direct sunlight and draughts. Mist occasionally."

Mist. Ah yes, we love it! The total indulgence of spray; a veil of fecund opportunity!

In fact, I was not far from the aforementioned place by the stereo, although I was slightly anxious by the proximity of the hi-fi speakers. But all in all, I settled down quite compatibly. I never saw the Maidenhair who had been banished to the bathroom.

Sally worked from home while Julian was away in some kind of office. She strolled about the house in a loose-fitting top and a pair of pink panties. I enjoyed her comings and goings from my strategic vantage point; relished it when the days were warm and she sighed her sultry sighs before coming to land with a deep squish on the sofa. There she would flip through catalogues, some of them to do with seeds, and get up and put the coffee machine on, which made a frantic, whooshing sound rather like a steam engine. As the open-plan kitchen/living room frothed and bubbled to impending coffee, I would gaze out into the garden beyond, squint through the open blinds and contemplate my comrades basking in al fresco liberty.

I liked it particularly when the doors were open after the smell of rain. If only the gentle drops from heaven could be placed in Sally's mister, or even the slightly less glamorous boiled water, then I would be in a kind of sixth heaven. Or is it eighth? I've never been that good with numbers.

Julian would come home from work about seven and then they would eat, somewhat belatedly, I thought, around nine, and sometimes out on the patio where the sliding doors would admit to a pleasant draught. Julian would eat quickly, burp, watch telly, drink a glass of wine and go to bed. There were seldom conversations in the living room, more a punctuated silence, although they seemed more animated out on the patio. In the early morning, he would get up and leave; Sally would surface a couple of hours later.

At this point I should tell you I was not the only plant in the room. Over by the bookcase and partly concealed in a corner was a Dieffenbachia, which someone impolitely, and possibly incorrectly, referred to as Mother-in-Law's Tongue. It was a somewhat introverted plant, and no doubt due to its German background, given over to lengthy philosophical contemplations. Much more exuberant, though mocked by some, were a pair of spider plants sitting opposite. Over a period of time, they would send out offshoots or 'babies' as Sally liked to call them. Occasionally, she would pot them up and give them away to friends. I liked their cascading vigorousness, their kinetic tendencies, although Julian dismissed them as 'hardly subtle.' Subtle!

After a few weeks in my new home I came to realise how the second man figured in the scheme of things. I'm talking about Hamish, Sally's brother-in-law, of course.

He would usually come round in the afternoon after Sally had nibbled at her vegetarian quiche and rocket salad. Personally, vegetarians make me uneasy. I much prefer carnivores. You never know if in a fit of intoxication, they might turn their attentions to the houseplants.

Sally and Hamish would skim through a variety of documents and he would give his opinions on the designs. After which they would often have a coffee and sometimes a piece of carrot cake. I later learned that there was a deli across the road called Ricardo's or something.

And then, usually on a Wednesday, they would both drift over to the adjacent sofa and indulge in a spot of petting and leather couch lovemaking. As Sally was seldom on top, I was more often than not treated to Hamish's pale oval-shaped buttocks contrasting with the smooth, darker colours of the settee. They were infinitely superior to Gareth's, who seemed unable to wear his trousers properly. In the late afternoon they gently reflected the living room side-light. The noise that came with this was quite extraordinary, not unlike a bird I had seen on a wildlife programme. Of course, it wasn't helped by the sliding sounds that came from their various positions on the sofa. I couldn't bear it! Some weeks the breathless ritual would be acted out more than once and when Julian went off to Torremolinos it seemed to happen every day. I have to say, on reflection, that Hamish's bottom was not in the same league as Gareth's, and that as plants we had been vastly spoilt.

Then one day disaster struck. During one of the settee springboard sessions – they never appeared to favour the bedroom for some reason – the heavy sofa experienced a puncture. Sally got up slowly, ashen-faced. Hamish with his outstretched arm was trying to placate her, reassure her, but the suggestions were met with scorn.

"How could it have happened?" she yelled. "How could you have been so careless?"

I gathered that the clumsy oaf Hamish had skewered the settee with his big toe. They didn't speak very much for over a week, merely confined themselves to attending to the various bits of daytime office work.

One evening, during a sudden flare-up, no doubt caused by contemplation of the visual crack – I'm not referring to Hamish but to the lengthy scar on the sofa – Julian hurled one of the spider plants when he returned from work. The poor innocent went whizzing through the open doors towards the patio and was never seen again.

I subsequently began to worry about my own safety as the other spider plant had also disappeared. I knew that Julian, like his brother, never appreciated them and wondered whether he was prone to commiting further horticultural homicide.

Imagine my surprise when I awoke from a brief mid-afternoon slumber to see the familiar fan-shaped fronds of an ample cheese plant. Furthermore, it was no ordinary cheese plant, for as I gazed more closely, I could see that it was none other than my old friend Margarita. I was overjoyed and deeply indebted to the generous nature of Sally, who had oddly abandoned her various vegetable quiches and taken up a new passion for fresh mangoes. It had to be mangoes and the kitchen cupboard was full of them. If I wasn't mistaken, her shape gave the impression of being slightly altered and that she too was looking like a mango or an avocado. Oddly enough Hamish's visits were now extremely peremptory and to the point. The sofa was left to convalesce but I thought the solution would have been to clip his toenails.

Margarita laughed when I communicated to her what had been going on; a kind of shimmering of her shiny, glossy leaves. She seemed quite disappointed that the afternoon sports were not resuming and then I related the incident of the spider plants and how I began to fear for my own safety. Margarita looked concerned and her protective instinct came to the fore. "No te preocupes," she said. Or something like that. "I will look after you, carino."

I was still wary of the unpredictable Julian; apprehensive of further flare-ups.

"It's okay," Margarita said one afternoon. "I have a plan."

On Thursday mornings, when Sally retreated to the shade of a subtly floral garden, the interior was left to the attentions of Agnieszka, a cleaner from Gdansk. It was Margarita's firm view that Polish girls were all called either Agnieszka or Malgorzata, leading no doubt to the diminutive nickname of Gosher or possibly Gusher. I said I had met a Staniswava once – probably spelt with an 'L' – to disprove her theory, to which she just replied 'Oh, Stasher.'

I'm sorry, I'm digressing. Anyway, Aggi had a routine whereby she would move all the plants, a little too enthusiastically, I thought, whenever she was vacuuming the living room. Margarita was put over by the front door and had to shiver in the most terrible draught.

Bang, clunk, bonk, went Aggi, who clearly would have been a disastrous candidate for the settee were Julian perhaps to offer a reciprocal arrangement. Mercifully, he didn't. I was lifted back onto my customary podium as was, eventually, Margarita. But when I gazed more closely at her, something seemed different, although I couldn't work out what it was.

Later that afternoon, there was a message from Sally on the answering machine to say that she was going to be late. Julian played it back on his return, replying acidly with the one word 'Typical!'

It was as he was going out of the door, presumably to have one of those dodgy takeaways from the end of the road, which invariably stink out both the kitchen and the sitting room that it happened.

There was a quick swishing sound and a sudden wail. It reminded me of Hamish and Sally's sessions. This was followed by a low groan and then silence. The front door lay open for quite some while and I could see Margarita flinching, fluttering away in the draught.

Round about eleven, when pinky darkness lurked beyond the windows, I could hear Sally's voice suddenly shrieking. "Oh my!" Then, "Oh my! Oh my!" She was quickly dialling something on her mobile. "Yes, yes!" she yelled. "Ambulance!"

Two green paramedics arrived. They came to remove Julian, who had apparently tumbled down the stairs. They comforted and consoled Sally.

"How could it have happened?" she wailed, blowing her nose several times.

I would have liked to console her too. Place a shiny leaf around those neat, freckled arms.

"Tripped probably," suggested a man's voice. He had large feet and a shabby raincoat. "Not drunk?" he added, glancing round the room at the unopened wine bottle that lay on the table.

The paramedic was picking up something from the carpet, placing it on the table, asking Sally if she was all right. Sally sobbed continuously into her handkerchief.

"Tripped on something," the big feet man repeated. "Just went headlong."

I listened to Sally as she phoned Hamish when the police and ambulance had left. In the silence of the empty room I looked at what had been deposited on the table.

It was a large, rubbery, glossy leaf. It looked like it had come from a cheese plant.

People Like Us

All around her was noise. A relentless slow clapping of hands. Once she'd got off, the driver wrenched the wheel and with one sharp movement she saw the bus blow up a cloud of dust and disappear into the heat.

"It's the other side of town, my dear," Mrs Montgomery-Smith had said. "Take a taxi."

Caitlin had looked at the map. It *was* perhaps too far to walk.

"Out of the question," continued Mrs Montgomery-Smith. "Besides you'll be walking through certain areas."

It was the curl of Ernestine Montgomery-Smith's lip that seemed to say it all. A gesture that was half snarl, half sneer. Caitlin had a list of taxi firms and numbers at home. She would look them up later.

"Another drink?" suggested Ernestine.

Caitlin shook her head. The list beckoned. She took a last glimpse from Mrs Montgomery-Smith's veranda, a sort of terrace to survey all beneath. It was the best thing about her squat and ugly house. She got up to go.

"Thank you," she smiled. Mrs Montgomery-Smith extended a regal hand. It was soft and sweaty like putty or kneaded dough.

Caitlin wondered how Robert would be feeling. Would he be awake now that he'd had the op? He had collapsed just outside the library and when they took him to hospital they said it was very likely his heart. She had thought about staying somewhere near the clinic but they had advised against leaving an empty house. Besides, it was only a taxi ride away. But then Caitlin remembered that taxi rides contained hazards of their own. A number of people had been abducted from them in recent months. It was perhaps too risky to undertake. She would take the bus.

The path through her neighbour Connie's garden was lined with bright orange flowers. She could never remember their names whereas Robert, a dedicated botanist and plant enthusiast, knew both their Latin and their everyday names. Large bees with amber bottoms buzzed around them, their backs and legs liberally dusted with pollen.

"Come in," said Connie. "Would you like a coffee?"

"I can't stay," said Caitlin. For a moment it sounded rather blike a snub. "I just wondered if you knew the times of the buses. When I ring up, no one answers."

"Buses!" exclaimed Connie, making it sound like an expletive. "For your servants, I take it!"

"I don't have servants," replied Caitlin. Why have people for the jobs you can do yourself?

"No, of course," said Connie remembering. "No, of course you don't. But why would you need to know the times of buses?"

"Robert's in hospital," she said, faltering for a moment.

"Oh, my dear!"

"I'm sure he's being well looked after."

Connie looked doubtful. "But why would you go by bus? It's for the…" She stopped short of saying the word. "Everybody takes taxis!"

But there's the risk, thought Caitlin. The risk of being spirited away. And that would hardly help Robert's predicament, would it? It would impede his recovery.

"Are you sure?" asked Connie. "I mean it won't be very pleasant. All those…"

No worse than buses anywhere. A bit cramped perhaps; crowded definitely. It would be the same as in any large city. Reluctantly Connie gave her the times she needed. "They're not very frequent, my dear. There's one at ten, one just after mid-day. Every couple of hours, it would seem."

Immediately after lunch Caitlin made her way to the pick-up spot two blocks away. She would try and buy Robert some fruit, choose a variety of the things he liked. The heat was shimmering off the road as she walked to the makeshift stop. There was a small shelter from the sun but it smelled heavily of urine. Passing cars slowed down to gaze at her, an exhibit in the heat waiting at a bus stop. The slowing cars didn't offer any prospect of a lift but then again to enter one, a stranger's domain, might be imprudent.

Eventually, she caught sight of something like a moving flag of faded grey and blue. For a moment she thought it was going to go past her so she waved her arms vigorously. The driver seemed surprised that she wanted to make a journey. When she stepped inside it was full of boisterous townspeople, a wash of animated voices that wafted over to the driver's seat.

"The hospital, please," she said.

The driver looked at her strangely. She really *was* making this trip. "I go near," he said. "Then five minutes' walk."

"That's fine." She gave him the fare, coins tumbling onto his mini-counter. The voices in the bus began to quieten a little as she walked down the cluttered aisle. When she reached the only vacant seat there was almost total silence. They appeared stunned by her unexpected entry; the pale colour of her skin amongst a sea of darker ones. She had surprised them. White folk didn't do things like this. The man on the seat next to her was sound asleep. His large head lolloped around his shoulders, at times touching hers. Gradually the voices accelerated in volume though never back to their previous exuberance.

Caitlin peered out of the dust-covered windows. There were bits of town she knew and parts that were unfamiliar. She was trying to recognise particular streets or landmarks that might herald the arrival of the hospital area. She had forgotten to ask the driver to tell her when it was her stop. Would he remember? She would ask the woman behind her who was engaged in animated conversation as her companion still slept.

White folk did not take the bus. It wasn't done. They had other better means of transport. Otherwise there was no problem in doing so, although she did regret the lull of voices. It was something that happened when you visited isolated pubs in England. Voices dipped so they could take in the stranger but sometimes it was painfully, uncomfortably quiet. It was done perhaps to emphasise outsider status, to underline divisions.

But now as she glanced out of the window she could see a familiar building at the end of a long avenue. The bus headed towards it and she saw the ugly glass front catch the sun. Faces turned to stare at the unexpected detour. 'Driver!' one voice called. The vehicle had driven in to the hospital entrance.

"Hospital, lady!" the driver called out to her. "Hospital!"

He had not forgotten. The voices dimmed as she retraced the aisle. As she waited for the driver to pull over, it suddenly started up. A sharp twanging of hands being put together, slowly and deliberately. She had experienced it once at a cricket ground when the crowd had become impatient, irritated at what they saw as painful scoring by the batsmen. The military barracking of a slow handclap.

And they were doing the same thing now but this time smiles replaced impatience. The grins confused her. It felt like some kind of dream. She thanked the driver and he smiled back. The barracking became louder and then the bus pulled away.

Robert was sitting up in bed when she arrived, his face ghostly against a fluffy blue dressing gown. He grinned sheepishly. As she went to kiss him Caitlin realised her hands were empty of gifts, of coloured fruits.

"A few days," he said. "Maybe a week. I'll have to take it easy."

She reached out and stroked his arm. It was reassuringly warm.

"Have you booked a taxi back?" he asked when it was nearly time for her to go.

"I came on the bus," she said.

He seemed taken aback. The nurse who had come in to the room stopped fidgeting with a vase of dead flowers.

"I think I was booed or something. Given the slow handclap. Although they seemed quite nice about it. Smiling even."

"People like us don't get buses," said Robert. "Apparently."

"Is that so?"

"And it wouldn't have been a slow handclap. Not in the sense *you* took it to be. It's an accolade, a sign of approval."

She could hear the noise still reverberating in her eardrums.

"Really? You're sure?"

"Completely. Given that people such as us don't take buses it would have been approval."

She kissed him on the cheek. "I'll see you tomorrow."

She was walking down an empty disinfected corridor. The driver said he would pick her up again at four. That was when he made his return journey.

Caitlin braced herself again for the lull in voices, the barracking hands of approval.

The Call of the Hoopoe

It's early morning. The blackbird's singing, noisily as it happens, outside my window. And from my brother's room next door there comes a strange sound; a humming or a singing maybe.

We used to share a room the two of us but now that Sam, the eldest, has gone away to college, Danny has taken Sam's room. It's emptier now in my bedroom but it's probably for the best.

Danny often complained that I used to snore. A noise like a drainage pump, he said. I didn't believe him. Not at first. And when he used to come to bed later, he'd put on the light and that would wake me up sometimes. I'd stare at him as he took off his socks, balancing on one leg like a stork or a pink flamingo. And I'd notice the hairs on his legs tapering down towards his ankles as he'd swap over, balance on the other leg; fling off the remaining sock.

It was odd at first with both of us in separate rooms. It felt like some kind of divorce or marriage split but that'd already been done and dusted by our parents. The old man, as Sam always calls him, was living now in the south of France. I tried to picture him. Walking down an avenue of palm trees; white shirt, dark mysterious sunglasses. And I wondered perhaps if he was some kind of spy.

"Don't be stupid," said Yvette. (She's my sister. Sounds French too, maybe) "He went off with Miss Watkins, didn't he? His secretary! Dad's always cheated! Cheated on everyone!"

I was a bit disappointed. I hoped that he'd keep in touch somehow. Invite me down for a holiday. Take me out and pay for everything because he was the one with the guilty conscience. And *I* was the favourite. Or so I thought.

When we later compared notes, Sam, Danny, Yvette and myself, we found out that we were *all* the favourites.

"Don't tell the others, son," he'd confided to Sam one day. "It'd only upset them. But I have to be honest. *You* are my favourite. I know I shouldn't have them but I just can't help it." And he'd clasp each of us by the hand to emphasise the fact that we truly *were* the favourite. All four of us!

"He's a toe-rag!" grumbled Yvette one evening. "A bloody big toe-rag!"

I didn't say anything but I felt uncomfortable all the same. I mean, he hadn't exactly done right by us, by mum particularly, but even so, to call him that amongst other things seemed a bit disloyal.

I couldn't get used to the space; the extra space! I was able to use Danny's old bed to put things on and remove most of the chaos from the floor. And there was more room in the cupboards, too, the chest of drawers. It felt like a room of luxury.

So it's early morning. The blackbird's making a racket and Danny's doing this strange singing sound next door. Later, at breakfast, he's in a white T-shirt for college, hair sticking up and with a large smudge of raspberry jam on his chin.

"What were you doing?" I ask him. "That noise. It sounded like you were singing."

At first he looks nonplussed, as if he doesn't know what I'm talking about.

"Singing?"

"Yeah, singing. Early morning."

"Oh yeah, that."

"Hmm."

"Hoopoe," he says.

"What?"

"Hoopoe. I'm trying to imitate one."

"Imitate what?"

"A hoopoe. That's the noise you heard."

Of course. He's into birds. Or at least I think he is. Looking at him now, his hair is like ruffled bird feathers. And when he changed, when we shared a room together, he balanced on one leg...

"Why do you want to imitate it?" I ask.

"Why not?" he says.

And he presses his thumbs together and blows through them. He makes a very good owl sound. Only that wasn't what I heard.

"Hoopoe?"

"Yes."

I ask him to spell it for me and he smiles. I like it when he laughs. His face changes and his white T-shirt throws light onto those dark eyebrows. He runs a hand through my hair, which he only very occasionally does. He's acknowledging my presence, I suppose, and I like it.

"Father Flanagan needs a helper."

This is mum interrupting the ornithological breakfast.

"A what?"

"Someone to serve."

"Don't look at me," says Danny. "I've done my time."

"Exactly," says mum. "So Billy, it's your turn!"

A cloud passes over the breakfast table. A cloud of messed-up Sundays, of duties and...

"But it's Sunday, mum!" I protest.

"Yes," she says. "It's Sunday. It often is. And then, of course, there's the holy days, too."

She gets me off early the following week. I walk sulkily down to church on my own.

Father Flanagan is a large man with peppermint breath.

"He had a skinful last night," Brian the other altar server tells me confidentially. "Always makes him a bit grumpy. It's a good idea to be quiet. Gets better, though, after the communion wine."

"What's your name, lad?" asks Father Flanagan returning to the vestry.

"Billy," I say.

"Well, Billy, you'd better jut watch today. Observe carefully. See what needs doing. And remember!"

I sit in the front row with Cathy Casey. She keeps looking at me and giggling. And then I think that I'll be on the other side of the rail next week, the communion rail, and she'll be there watching me. Grinning at me with that stupid mug of hers.

I glance round uncomfortably and I meet Danny's eye a few rows behind. He has a smirk which is slightly sneaky and smug.

I've got a book out of the library. It's called 'Collected Birds of the British Isles'. I want to see what a hoopoe looks like. I thumb through the pages but it's not there. I thumb through the back and eventually I find it under a section which is called 'migratory birds'. It's a funny looking thing, rather like a cross between a jay and a magpie. It's got a sandy brown tummy and a long pointy bill. It's a bit like a curlew only the bill doesn't bend at the end. And the hoopoe's got an odd sort of crest on the top of its head, a bit like a lapwing's only messier. I wonder why Danny should be so interested in this bird and why he wants to imitate it. The book tells me that hoopoes are summer visitors to the southern counties of England. They're quite common in France and most other European countries, in fact.

I see dad walking along a boulevard of palm trees with Miss Watkins on his arm; pale cheeks and red lips, and hoopoes watching disapprovingly from the branches of trees. I expect their crest goes up in the air in indignation. But dad won't see them. Instead he's gone all doey-eyed and he's gazing at Miss Watkins.

It's Sunday again and I'm getting a pep talk from Father Flanagan.

"Like this," he demonstrates. "And then you go backwards, Billy, to genuflect. No, no! That's too much!"

I remember going to an Anglican church once at Rothwell. They didn't do anything with their knees but that's maybe because the people there were so old. They just bowed stiffly. I can't remember what the occasion was and why I was there but it went on for a very long time and the sermon was nearly half an hour! It was to make up for their lack of attendance, Danny said, seeing as that lot didn't go every week. A sort of revenge, perhaps.

The bell goes and we're walking out, Father Flanagan, Brian and me. Brian's swinging the incense and a bit of singing breaks out. Everything's bathed in a grey, smoky cloud; the sun's coming in through the windows. I must be dreaming.

And then I sneeze. Not just once but several times. After the fourth one, Father Flanagan gives me a dirty look. I turn the other way and see Cathy Casey smiling in the front row. Perhaps I can tell mum later I'm allergic to it and that it might bring on an asthma attack but I think she may be wise to it; all the excuses that may have come from Danny and Sam. Suddenly there's a loud thud and the heavy book I've been carrying falls to the floor. Eyes are staring at me and from where Cathy Casey's sitting I can hear a loud snigger.

"Not too bad," says Father Flanagan afterwards, ignoring the sneezing and the book. "But you must learn to go a bit slower, Billy. It's not a skating rink."

"No," I agree sheepishly. But for a moment I picture it and smile.

"Oh, by the way, boys, there'll be a new lad joining us next week. You're away then, Brian, aren't you?"

"Yes, Father."

I wonder where he's going.

"So, Billy, you'll need to help Kevin out."

Me? But I've only done it once! I won't remember anything! I feel a sense of dread and panic.

"And how's butterfingers?" Danny asks when I get home.

He's referring to the large book I dropped. And then suddenly I realise I'll have to wave that incense swinger. Next Sunday. The one that Brian was holding. The very thought of it makes my nose itch and start to run.

"I think I've got an allergy," I say to them over the dinner table.

"Is that why you keep dropping things?" asks Sam. He's home for the weekend from college.

I begin to think college is an excellent idea. It gets you away from the all the nuisances and inconveniences of family; the slavery of being an altar boy. It must be bliss. Sam shows me some photos but it's mainly pictures of people on bikes. Perhaps that's what goes on. Just having fun, hanging out with friends, drinking, the odd bit of study.

"I expect they'll have to up the insurance with you there now."

I ignore Danny and pretend to gaze more interestedly at Sam's collection of photos.

Next Sunday sees my unwelcome promotion of duties. I realise now I miss Brian, his calm awareness of where everything is.

"Am I late?" asks a voice.

I turn round and find myself staring at a giant.

"Kevin. The new altar boy." He smiles.

I wonder if he's been pressed into it, is carrying out the orders of unreasonable parents, but he looks oddly keen, enthusiastic even.

"Have you done this long?" he asks me.

I find I'm unable to say 'Just a week.' The truth escapes me and I'm unable to spit it out. It might spook him and then he'd be less willing to undertake those duties. Besides, I don't want to show my inexperience. It's a pride thing.

"Not long," I reply.

He's shaking hands now as an afterthought and my palm quickly disappears into his. I wonder how tall he might be. Six foot seven? And then I wonder how old he is.

"Well done, Kevin," says Father Flanagan. "You've met our Billy. He's also a new kid on the block."

Any attempt of experience I had has vanished; blown away by Father Flanagan's bluster. I can see him responding to Kevin's eagerness, his sense of purpose. And then there's his height too, which gives him a kind of natural authority.

I tell Kevin a few things from the little I can remember but he seems to know them all already. He gives a great big grin and runs a hand through his long hair.

"Oh, before we start," says Father Flanagan. "I need you two boys to help me move a cupboard."

We follow his eyes in the vestry and they land on a great squat, vault-like object.

"No problem," says Kevin.

Father Flanagan is quickly directing operations as to how to attack the beast. I wonder if the cupboard'll floor me and I can have a few weeks off. But Kevin, with his soft Irish accent, his steady hand, has everything under control. It sails across the room, gently lands in a new corner, large and oversize like some kind of police phone box.

"Great," says Father Flanagan. "Well done, Kevin." He rubs his hands.

Kevin and I put on our surplices. Father Flanagan has found one to fit him so obviously there have been giants here before. I glimpse at the size of Kevin's feet and can only guess. Thirteen maybe.

During the mass I'm supposed to go off and fill the censer and put the incense in. I'm not sure if I've done it correctly as it only gives out a solitary puff of smoke. Father Flanagan attends to it quickly and I feel myself reddening. I can sense Cathy Casey staring at me so I glance away and catch Kevin's eye. He smiles good-naturedly.

And now I have to swing the censer so that it makes clouds of smoke. I want it to make a screen so that I don't have to see Cathy Casey any more or her silly, goofy face. The smoke's going well. Ting, ting! I swing it before me, let it bounce against the chain. I swing it again and...

Something's flying through the air; flies through the wisps of smoke and out into the audience. Only I shouldn't say 'audience'. It's comm...con...or something.

Somebody gives a sharp yelp and I look back at the censer. The top bit's come away somewhere and the contents are spilling out onto the floor. Father Flanagan looks furious; he snatches the thing off me. A man in the audience is being attended to. He seems to have a large bump on his forehead. He touches it gently and gives an un-Christian-like glower towards the altar in my direction. I'm only new, I want to say. A novice. Yes, that's it. I'm still at the learning stage.

"Yer clumsy great pudding!" snaps Father Flanagan afterwards. "Yer didn't screw the top on properly!" The three of us gaze at the hazardous censer. "I've got a bloody homicidal maniac here!"

I'm hoping for the sack, a swift dismissal, but it's not being offered to me. This is my penance, then. To stay.

"Be more careful next week, Billy," he advises. Then he remembers. "At least Brian'll be back."

I have it in my head that Brian's gone fishing somewhere. He's sitting by a little stream or a gurgling river with hoopoes in the background, and he's reading a book.

"I expect they'll issue the congregation with helmets and armour-plating next week," says Danny. "In the light of unidentified flying objects." He giggles.

Congregation. That's the word. Its sudden rediscovery helps to temper Danny's insult.

"You must be more careful, Billy!" mum pleads.

"It wasn't my fault! It's because Brian was away."

"You can't go blaming others!"

During the week of early summer mornings I hear the hoopoe again. It must start softly because I notice the sudden rise, the increase in volume. And it's all the louder as Danny has his window open.

"There was a green woodpecker in the garden yesterday."

"Oh." He seems uninterested.

It's a funny bird. It has this mortar board thing on its head, a little crest and it laughs away to itself. Apparently it's picking up ants as they emerge from the cracks in the path.

"Gotta go," says Danny. "Bye, butterfingers!"

He taps me on the head. The reminder makes me cross.

Then he's back again, having forgotten something and he hits me on the nut a second time. The people you have to live with!

The following Sunday we're all there, the three of us.

"I heard about your mishap," says Brian, scarcely disguising his glee.

I wonder if it was Kevin who told him but as I glance across he looks like an innocent party. It's probably common knowledge now; a talking point amongst the audience. Or it could be grumpy Father Flanagan. At least we don't have to move a cupboard today.

"Ah, Brian you're back!" exclaims Father Flanagan. There's relief, I'm sure, in his voice.

"We had to move *that* last week!" says Kevin to Brian, pointing at the cupboard.

"Bet it was heavy," replies Brian.

"No sweat. I could have done it on my own," boasts Kevin.

Brian looks doubtful. I think otherwise.

Kevin walks over towards it. "Just bulky, really." He catches my eye. "In fact, I could lift this one up with one hand."

Brian doesn't react. Perhaps he thinks, as senior altar boy, that Kevin, the novice, is overreaching himself.

"Really?"

A little later the censer is back in Brian's safe hands.

"Now just watch Brian," suggests Father Flanagan to Kevin on his return to the vestry.

I'm clearly out of the running now and, after last week, strategically demoted. But I don't mind too much. I'd feel nervous about doing it again. With my luck, I'd probably set fire to the building.

Brian shoots off straight afterwards. I imagine him returning to his fishing spot, where he continues a conversation with a trout.

"Better today, boys," says Father Flanagan to Kevin and myself. "Yes." He has a flicker of a smile.

"No flying objects," says Kevin to me when he's gone. I allow myself a reluctant grin.

He's tying up his boots, enormous platforms for those sizeable feet.

And suddenly, from nowhere, I say, "Could you *really* lift me up with one hand?"

He pauses over a shoe-lace.

"No sweat," he says again and looks up.

"So?"

"Okay, then."

He's coming towards me now, blotting out the sun drifting through the vestry window, and he tells me to open my legs. I stand like a pair of scissors. Then he places a huge hand, clutching onto my behind. In a second I'm sailing up towards the shifted cupboard, gazing momentarily at the dust that's lying on top there. I like this unexpected view of the world. I slide back down.

"I'll do it properly this time," says Kevin.

And I'm floating back up beyond the cupboard, into a sunbeam and towards the ceiling.

And then something happens, takes hold of me. There's this feeling; this sudden hot rush. And something seems to have happened to my pants. And in all of this, there's this noise, a kind of gasp that I've never heard before. And it comes out of my chest, my throat, from deep within, and it makes a racket!

I slide upside down, along Kevin's back and onto the floor. And as I slide I realise that I've heard this sound before. I recognise it from Danny's room.

The singing. The sound. The call of the hoopoe!

The Glass Cabinet

As he turned to the left the house immediately came into view. There it was; the long haul up the steps to the entrance above. Suitcase gripped tightly in one hand, he reached out to grab the rail beside him, smooth and cool beneath his dry fingers. For the last few steps there was no rail and this was where he turned, as he invariably did, to look at the view.

Maybe it was this that kept him calm; a period of contemplation after a long tiring journey. He could see the river gleaming in the distance; playing fields beyond. The willows and Lombardy poplars gathered round its banks made him think of warmer times and happier places. And he'd been back again, hadn't he? It seemed to have done the trick. Well, perhaps...

The key slid into the lock and he stepped into the darkened hall. On the polished table there was nothing except a card for taxis and one for window-cleaning.

Squirt! Squirt! The sound came from behind him and Mrs Connelly's active aerosol cut into the silence.

"You're back early!" she called out cheerily. "How was it?"

Michael Hannigan grunted. Far too early, he thought. Too premature! "Fine, fine!" he answered.

"We got your postcard. The one from the Christine Chapel."

The aerosol went on squirting.

"Sistine."

She stopped briefly. "How many?"

"No, no," he answered, and irritably picked up the suitcase.

"I'll bring you a tea, presently," she offered. "A nice cup of tea."

Father Hannigan shuddered. Mrs Connelly's teas did not require cups. Their sheer strength enabled them to stand up of their own accord.

He walked across to the study with its long shelves of books. They too hinted back at happier moments – before it had all started. Some of the volumes there spoke for periods, places and contentment. The window was open a little and he averted his gaze from the shiny cabinet, illuminated by the sun, and out into the garden. Delphiniums waving in the breeze discreetly screened off the vegetable patch, although his keen sense of smell detected something from the onion family.

At one end of the garden was Father Broughton kneeling in front of a large mop-head hydrangea. One way or another he spent most of his time on his knees. Father Hannigan wasn't sure which had the greater effect, but the garden, in spite of its muddle, its casual chaos, seemed to console him, take him away from the dark interiors of halls, church pews and porches.

Father Hannigan picked up his case and went upstairs. From his window he could still see the curate kneeling, planting, praying.

"Was it a good trip?" Seamus asked him later that evening.

"Superb!" he replied, with an enthusiasm that startled even himself. "Every day there was just the right amount of travelling and I..." He was going to say something else in his thankfulness, his gratitude, but checked himself in time. Why dwell on things, after all?

"It's not been too bad here either," said Seamus, "except Wednesday was a bit wet..."

And Father Hannigan drifted off to the olive groves while Seamus gave him a weather report.

"They say it'll rain again later tonight."

"Really?"

"Save me watering, I suppose."

Father Hannigan ran a finger round his neck and studied his colleague. Always philosophical, always accepting. Perhaps it came from spending so much time outdoors.

"Where else did you go?" Eager eyes were on him once again.

"I took some photos. Would you like to see them?"

"Indeed I would."

"Mrs Connelly was pleased with the Christine Chapel," Father Hannigan smiled, but his curate simply nodded and gazed on uncomprehendingly.

The night was rough, inhospitable. Whatever he'd had to eat caused recurrent dreams, snaking back and forth in a circle. In one he was haunted by a gleaming golden glass. It stared back at him in its three-dimensional boldness and brilliance as if it had been taken from a jeweller's shop window. The glass itself was empty. It seemed to wait and in the dream so did he. It lingered this vessel, then became a wine glass, sparkling at him from the base of its elaborate stem. There was a raucous squawking sound from somewhere. As he reached out to touch the glass, it smashed into a thousand pieces and his outstretched hand turned from pink to deep magenta scarlet.

Wiping away the sweat on his forehead he glanced at the luminous dial on his alarm clock which ticked away at twenty past three.

The bird which had woken him was tapping near the window. He lay awake for some while then eventually went down into the hall. What day was it now? Friday? Holidays erased any sequence of time, befuddled, addled routine. And the house itself was so quiet; a kind of sleeping vault. Through the sitting room windows trickled the first rays of a sickly sun, but he didn't welcome it, not at this hour.

His feet were padding across the cold stone floor of the kitchen then stuck for a moment on an odd sheet of lino. A tap dripped softly. In the refrigerator there was a carton of bright orange juice. On its packaging two children were depicted dancing under a heavily laden fruit tree. No doubt some kind of allegory. They seemed very similar to the pair that danced around carousels licking the pale whipped-up cones of ice cream adverts.

Father Hannigan poured the liquid into a clean, clear glass imagining... He closed his eyes and ran his fingers round the rim. For the briefest of moments the word 'escape' drifted into his mind. Escape to warmer climes, to peach trees and orchards! To live somewhere where nobody knew your name! He peered again to examine the glass but this was not the one which had woken him. He put the dancing children back into the fridge.

"Sleep well, did you?" Seamus Broughton asked.

"Excellent. Like a log," he lied.

"It wasn't a bit cold after your holiday?"

"Oh, no."

He looked blankly out of the window. He could hear Mrs Connelly's vacuum cleaner humming a dirge in a distant part of the house.

"I've got some calls to make," said Seamus Broughton, his chair scraping noisily as he got up. "I'll see you later."

Father Hannigan nodded. He watched him stride eagerly down the steps, rushing out to meet the day. His head was throbbing now and the phone was ringing; insistent ringing. It was usually left to Mrs Connelly to answer it, but remembering who it might be, he stepped out into the chilly hall.

"Father Hannigan?"

A voice was introducing itself – a soft, soothing, gentle voice. He knew what it was going to say.

"Good holiday? Good... Fine weather too? Great."

A hesitation.

"You must be feeling better already."

"I am."

Another short silence.

"Now about your particular problem..."

It was 'little' the last time it was mentioned so it was no longer a belittling voice.

The speaker cleared his throat, making way for some kind of announcement. "I'm afraid it can't be changed. It has to be. We've looked at various options and I know you've suggested alternatives but blackcurrant juice is for the chapel folk up the road. Wine, it has to be. I mean, it's hardly the same!"

"The same," echoed Father Hannigan.

"Pardon?"

"I said, I see."

The same as he put down the phone. The same. Sunday. The same. The same Sunday...

He suddenly felt weary, debilitated by the telephone voice. He went upstairs to bed but no dreams came. He slept for an hour. No glass, no waving lombardies.

A little later, he got up, went mechanically through the day, tidying things, doing little. The sermon lay unwritten but instead a decision was shaping itself.

When Seamus Broughton went off later to chair a youth meeting, Father Hannigan piled some things into a shabby suitcase. It was lighter than the one he returned with, contained a minimum of clothes.

Clutching it tightly, he descended the steps and into a light haze that seemed to spring up from nowhere. Plants and trees lost their shape and form as they so often did when he woke up in the morning with a splitting head. But this time nothing had passed his lips. His mouth was dry. Keeping his eye on the uneven paving stones, he fervently hoped he wouldn't meet anyone on the way.

The road began to lose its houses. He walked on further between open fields. The river snaked lazily in the distance but he failed to notice it. Suddenly he felt tired again and sat down on a large expanse of rock not far from the lane. The wind was getting up, dispersing the haze, setting about whistling through telegraph wires. For a long time he sat there, coat wrapped round him, collar flapping in the breeze.

As he viewed the landscape around him, pockmarked with years of quarrying, he suddenly realised there was literally nowhere to go. He didn't even have enough money for a hotel or a taxi. Nowhere. Nowhere to go.

The steps back to the house seemed steeper. Damp moss made the last few steps treacherous and slippery. The key slipped into the lock and the door gaped eagerly open. He walked quickly through the hall and into the study.

There it was in front of him. The bright cabinet, the assorted collection of bottles, the glinting glass decanter. Quickly he opened the cabinet door, listening to its scraping sound fill the room.

As he poured the clear amber liquid his hand began to shake. He glanced at the clock. It was still quite early. Several hours to go. And in that time many happy moments…

Worm

I haven't been here for a while. No. Quite some time really. I used to come here regular. Like a dose of prunes…That was before…Well, you know, what happened. Danny said I should come back. Try and…

It's changed a bit…I'd wheel me kids here after school. Weekends, too. We'd spend longer then.

It was a nicer park before. Not so many notices. Less grubby.

Eventually I moved away. Further up the line. Between Shippea Hill and Brandon Creek. I couldn't afford to live here. No. Them rents! It's because of all the students, you see. Places became so short, even out here, and so they stuck the rents up.

Then when Frank buggered off there was no way I could stay on here. Not long term. Went off with his P.A. Personal Assistant, they call them. I should say it was 'personal'. Till the extent they were sharing a hotel bed together! Him and Miss Doubleday. Did it to save on expenses, he said. Simple economics. Did I know how much those single rooms *cost*?

Well, of course I didn't. It wasn't me going off and shagging me secretary, was it? Naturally, I didn't believe the silly tosser and so in a matter of weeks he was off. Permanently anchored and having it away with Miss Doubleday and probably one or two others. His prick was never in his trousers for long. Said it was a clinical condition. CSS or something. Compulsive Sex Syndrome.

Well, I'm all for that, too, but perhaps with just the one person.

So that left me and the kids. I had to get an evening job. Emmie left pretty soon after college. Got married, moved somewhere on the South Coast. Managing some B&B they were. I waited for an invite. A holiday there with Danny would have been lovely. He was still young. Ideal, really, but the invite never came…

So that just left the two of us. We came here quite often. He'd stick his boat in the lake. Hours I sat here.

They called me up from school one day. I went with me heart in me mouth. Well you do, don't you? Thought he'd done something, you see.

'We think he's Uni material, Mrs Claypole,' they said. Little ginger man with specs.

Uni? United Dairies? United Biscuits?

'No, University,' they said. 'Oxbridge.'

Uxbridge, I replied. It was a station on the Piccadilly Line. I didn't even know there was a university there. There wasn't then. There probably is now. Universities all over the place these days. More common than phone boxes.

'Oxbridge. Oxford or Cambridge.'

Cambridge? Well, he could travel there from home, couldn't he?

The time went pretty quick. I didn't come here as much – to this place. Had to get a weekend job, too. Help with the costs. And of course Frank wouldn't cough up any. All his cash being spent on Miss Moneypenny or whoever it was.

I went to the service, the Gradualation.

'It'll be in Latin, mum,' Danny said.

'What will?'

'The ceremony. The passing out parade.'

'Why's that, dear?'

'Because things change *very* slowly in this country. Especially in Cambridge.'

I wish we could say the same for the rent 'cos in Danny's last year it rocketed.

'It's a bit of a con all that Latin,' Danny said. 'Mutton dressed as lamb. Making the ordinary seem exotic.'

I didn't mind it. It reminded me of when we used to go to church. My brother Sam used to be an altar boy but then he stopped going all of a sudden…

I found it quite touching. Danny kneeling in front of an old boy with a pink robe and a red nose, hands clasped together. The old boy called Danny something like 'Me Commissar' and it made me think of Russia.

In the thirties, this place was full of communists so I suppose it was quite appropriate really. I wondered if it had gone like that again. I looked around for a minute and thought no, probably not.

I was proud of him. He looked so handsome, kneeling down. No wonder the old boy wanted to clasp him.

He got a job soon after. Snapped him up. Down in London. Got a flat. The day he left, the house seemed so empty.

So I came here, to the park. Just to think. Think about everything. Everyone. All the different things. Emmie, Danny, all around me.

And I sat on this bench and looked out. It was peaceful and quiet, sunny even. A lovely day.

And as I looked ahead, something slipped into my eye. Creeping into the bottom of my eye.

I saw it, that thing and them. Saw them just ahead on the other side.

Like a worm creeping into the bottom of my eye…

There was the sound of voices, laughter. Up and down they went. Ducking, divi…

And then it happened. A sudden gust of wind. And I saw it from there. From that bloody bench!

Those voices turned to cries, shouts, screams… Screaming!

And I sat here rooted. My feet were like stones.

I wanted to get up, do something.

But they wouldn't move... Wouldn't...

They said it was the shock. Sitting there watching it. Slowly. Like in slow motion.

They found the knife. Found who did it.

They took me off to Addenbrookes...It's more like a factory there than a hospital. Sent me home two days later...Took me half a day to find me way out.

And then I moved. Because of the park. The money. The place was no longer the same because I couldn't bear to look. Couldn't look to where it had happened.

Those kids.

Danny said I should go back. One more time, he said. Exorcise a ghost. Yes.

So here I am.

There are plenty of memories. Plenty.

But even so, I can't really look ahead. Not over to that place. You know, where it happened... I'm trying but...

So it's good to come back. Yes...He might be right.

But even so, I still can't...

Chapter and Verse

"New in the parish?" she asks. "Just arrived?"
There's a slight sneer as she says the last word and, if I'm not mistaken, a vague whiff of disapproval.

"Well, yes. A few weeks now."

Beyond her blustery almost matronly frame I am watching a line of birds waddle past the pond. They approach and shuffle by with a stiff military air as if this is some kind of bird manoeuvre which will form part of their training later in life. I can see that the participants are a species of duck but I'm not quite sure which variety. They all possess ample if not rotund bodies, rather like the speaker before me.

"I think you'll find this is a *very* welcoming church," she assures me.

I consider this for a moment. Yes, perhaps it is. I nod in agreement. "In fact I've just been inside." I sound like a released convict in a moment of candour.

"Marvellous!" she exclaims as if I've just notched up a notable achievement; an exam, a sports award, a runner-up in Master Chef…

"Yes. Very light."

"Light. Yes," she echoes.

I prefer churches when no one's in them. When you can see your breath, mixed with the hang-over of incense, waft down the aisle, or, if the weather's warmer, the snap of wood in summer heat. When I walked round the nave of this one, I noticed somebody had left a beer bottle over by one of the family tombs. It said Mac's No.1 and with its red and white label it seemed to be a variety of pale ale. I wondered if this was some type of sacrificial offering to the occupants of the tomb; a covert ritual perhaps.

"What did you do?" she asks. "Before you came here."

I was a bingo caller in Streatham, I want to say; a plumber in Basingstoke; a vet with a PHD in fleas. But my admission, when it comes, is a humble and truthful offering. "I was a lecturer," I say. A word that is sometimes difficult to pronounce.

She issues a smile which banishes all remnants of a sneer. "How fascinating!" she exclaims. "A lecturer in what?"

"In Literature," I apologise.

"How interesting!"

I've had enough of these ejaculations.

"You'll be pleased to know there's a U3A group in the village given over to just that!"

"Aha." I'm unable to offer more. Discussing literature now that I've hung up my laurel garland would be nothing short of a busman's holiday.

She's waiting for more response and so the smile becomes more impatient. For some reason I find myself thinking of Hattie Jacques and Charles Hawtree. The latter is pushing a trolley round a hospital ward. I wonder if I'm correct in thinking they were both in the same film.

"The vicar's very keen on guest speakers. Absolutely loves it. We have a series of talks in the Parish Hall."

"I see."

"I must have you over for coffee!"

"That would be nice," I lie.

And so we turn to part. She's following the ducks that are frisking in the shallows of the pond. Their raucous quacking sounds like the response to an earthy joke. Either that or they're laughing at themselves, or even us.

"I didn't catch your name," I call as she's rounding on an eider.

"Imelda!" she wafts. It catches on the breeze and blows up into one of the poplars.

Imelda. I'm thinking of apricots or peaches with a soft layer of vanilla ice cream.

Peach Melba. As I close my gate, which gives out onto the village green, I have a vision of the participants of the University of the Third Age Literary Group stepping gingerly out towards their class. And I briefly shudder.

Two weeks later, the phone goes. I can never quite get used to it. Its shrill and raucous wail takes a delight in shattering pastoral peace. I pick up the receiver slowly, uncertain as to what it contains.

"Hugo!" The voice sounds familiar.

"Ye-es." I'm turning it into two syllables as I'm still unsure.

"Imelda here!"

Imelda? I have to think for a moment but I am aided by Charles Hawtree and an imperious matron. "Ah, yes."

"Not an awkward time, is it?"

Yes, well we *are* having a bit of an orgy here at my place, I want to say. Few Romans just popped in. But I'm a slave to convention and say "No, no!" The thought of an orgy with some of my former more inventive university students is not unappealing.

"I've spoken to the vicar," she announces.

"The Reverend Catchpole."

"Clatworthy."

"Ah yes."

"And we wondered awfully if you'd be kind enough to cement your arrival here in the village by giving a little talk."

"A talk?"

"Yes."

"A talk on what?"

I say the words very quickly so they become a compound. Atawkonwat?

"Anything you like, my dear." She oozes generosity, a free rein...

"Well, I don't really..."

"Good!" she shrills. "That's settled then. We look forward so much..."

We. The vicar's mouthpiece. The oddly absent vicar. 'A talk to cement my arrival.' Still, once I've carried out my duty, a debt of honour, my 'cementing'. Perhaps they will let me go, leave me alone.

Atawkonwat? The words follow me round over the evening, a mantra of doubt. I gaze at Bob's picture staring at me from across the piano, the first friend to deflower me at university, and I seem to see a grin of encouragement.

But several days on and various glances over at the conspiratorial piano and I'm still no nearer my eventual subject matter. I suppose I could talk about students, about their decreasing powers of imagination, of resourcefulness, neutered as they are by the demands of a technological age, but I think it may not be very kind; a touch disloyal and Bob's encouraging grin seems to agree. If he were here now, putting the final touches to the washing-up, whipping me with a wet tea towel as I straddle the hyacinths in the garden, attempting, unconvincingly, to escape his unerringly accurate flicks, it would all be so simple. And as I sit myself, cumbersome and self-conscious upon the podium, his ready smile from among the audience would make it all so easy and relaxed. Ah well!

"Tolerance," I say to the darkness beyond the telephone.

"Pardon?" queries Imelda.

"I thought I'd give a talk on tolerance." There's a brief pause.

"I see. Yes." Another pause. The idea is being digested like lumpy custard, like a lead balloon sprayed with molasses. "We shall look forward."

We shall indeed. I glance over at my assembled photographs. They exude smiles of radiance in their various states of undress.

The subject has been decided, seized upon; the nettle grasped. I feel a sense of relief now.

"So can I pencil you in for the fifth of May?"

I think for a moment, consult a non-existent diary devoid of entries. "Yes, that's fine," I say.

Tolerance begins in my ready acceptance of the date. It's only a few days after the first of the month when brightly coloured dancers will be jigging around the maypole, rejoicing and honouring an ancient phallic ritual.

The days start to get warmer. I sit outside on the lawn where surreptitious insects take a liking to my ankles.

The phone rings again. "We're greatly looking forward to your talk next Tuesday," says the voice. And from my contemplation of a pale striped potter wasp I am plunged back into the land of commitment and timetables.

"I wondered whether we could meet up the week before, just to go through the themes of your talk."

There is only one theme.

"And then you could have that coffee we talked about."

A dual purpose visit. Did we discuss coffee? I can't remember. It seems like I've made a commitment.

"Shall we say the Wednesday before?"

The non-existent diary agrees. I wonder whether to go through the motions of shuffling pages within earshot of the phone.

"You'll find me on the second lane after the church, just past the old brewery."

I put the phone down, feel a tinge of regret for the redundant beer dispensary. I wonder if Imelda makes good cakes – the kind that have little almond flakes sticking to them. I glance outside. The light is going. I draw the curtains on the fading evening and for the first time I feel a flutter of apprehension. It starts from somewhere within my stomach, churns round a little then gently accelerates.

I'm walking across the green now in the direction of Imelda's. The grass is soft and comforting, dips occasionally under my steps and from the previous night's heavy rain. It's relatively early but the curtains are being drawn in the windows of nearby houses. I think of some TV programme, a murder mystery, where the inhabitants of rural villages are systematically bumped off. From canons to bell ringers to inflated gentry and oversexed postmen. Perhaps it's on the TV now and the drapes are being closed to make way for the reality everyone craves for.

Suddenly I regret my acceptance of coffee in the evening, wonder if I'll be expected to stay for longer or whether along with the coffee there'll be a bottle of something stronger.

I ring the doorbell and it clatters from within. Behind the lattice window and the adroitly carved wood I see a shape billowing like a cloud to answer the summons. The door opens.

"Hugo!" she exclaims.

"Imelda."

The names seem to go quite well together, like a couple from the upper strata.

I'm beckoned into a room with floral patterned furniture, soft settees and a fireplace with an inglenook. I quite like this room. It makes me think of an inn.

"Coffee?" she asks.

"Yes, please."

From somewhere I can hear the opening of a tin; some kind of biscuit accompaniment. She's back with a tray which is floral too; it could lie in subtle camouflage across the sofa.

"It's so lovely to have you in the village. A real professor!"

I lift up a biscuit from the plate, a kind of macaroon and it disintegrates onto the carpet. We both pretend not to notice and I crouch slightly to scoop it up, but I only make matters worse. There's a clock ticking in the background; a precise, heavy and measured tick. I glance behind me and see the deliberate swing of a pendulum. She follows my eyes, humours my distraction.

"Now your talk…"

"Ah yes."

"Tolerance, you said?"

"I did."

"A good choice. Thought-provoking, too."

I'm being gently patronised on a bluebell and tulip sofa.

"I just wondered. *We* just wondered…"

"Yes."

"Whether you would supply some biblical references. To go with your talk."

"Biblical references?"

"Yes."

There's a pause and the only sound is the tock-twack of the clock punctuating the living room silence.

"We find it's generally helpful. Reassuring. It also gives a relevance. A context."

"A kind of validation, then?"

"Yes."

It's dark outside. There was nothing stronger on offer within. No concealed ten year-old malt to honour the occasion and mellow, befuddle the senses. I close the gate and walk back across the green, wondering where the brewery might have been. The acrid taste of coffee sticks to my mouth, dries it out with the powdered macaroon in the cooler night air.

A talk on tolerance. With references. Little hooks to cling on. References. A precedent in print. A validation.

I see an owl swoop from a tree, its outline catching the remains of the evening light. As it gives its obligatory hoot I look back at the house I have just come from and I think about the futility of words.

The Aftermath of Bingo

After Madge left me for a bingo caller in Dulwich I found myself thinking about the meaningful things in life. Firstly, why a bingo caller? Secondly, I wasn't aware that there were any such operators in Dulwich. It was much too genteel. There was even a number twelve bus that had Dulwich Library as its destination. Not many boroughs can boast transport to an outpost of learning. And then I wondered how Madge would adjust to this change in lifestyle, to live in a house peppered with numbers perhaps, something she had always been hopeless at.

I confided my various misgivings to Charlie down the Pig and Whistle one evening. Rumour has it that this strange animal combination is in fact a corruption of Peg and Wassail.

"What am I going to do?" I sighed as he downed his now rare if not almost obsolete combination of brown and mild.

"Take up bingo, mate! Get yerself a new interest! You might even win her back." It made her sound like one of the prizes.

"I'm not bothered about that," I replied indignantly. The very idea was repugnant, obscene. How could bingo break up a marriage? No, I found the quietness of the house deprived of its soft susurrations of sex daunting and depressing. We were usually at it most evenings just after the Nine O'Clock News. Madge would never agree to it before, just in case we overran.

"You mean find someone else?" Charlie asked.

"Yes, precisely." I was no longer bothered about Madge and her new enthusiasm for numeracy.

"Well," sighed Charlie, taking a deep sip of the liquid before him. "There is Tinkerbell's."

"Tinkerbell's?"

"Yes. That dating agency on the corner."

I nearly spat my bitter into his pint. "I couldn't possibly go to a place called Tinkerbell's!" I yelled. One or two heads turned round.

"Well, you won't go dancing!" Charlie was becoming defensive, accusatory. "I can't see any other options!"

I have to come clean at this point. I am the owner of a pair of flat feet, size twelve. It's probably even more in metric. The few occasions when I trod the dance floor – and I use the word advisedly – I squashed an impressive array of tender bunions and little-toe corns. I have a problem with co-ordination. When they say 'left', I go to the right and quite often vice-versa. When it comes to giving directions in the back of a car, I am also lethal.

"Suit yerself," said Charlie. I notice that dark beer makes him grumpy. Perhaps it's in the roasting of the malt.

I felt it was time to change the subject and leave Madge, no doubt subjected to a litany of bingo terms, 'legs eleven, clickety-click and two large ladies', to her own devices. I broached the subject of begonias and asked Charlie about his potting shed.

Nevertheless, a few days later I found myself in the vicinity of the newly resplendent offices of Tinkerbell's, radiant in its gentle colourings of pink and blue, no doubt delineating the allotted colours of the sexes. It was a cold and foggy afternoon, nearly five o'clock. I felt it better to visit the establishment under cover of darkness.

I was just about to go in, step over the threshold of the lioness's den, when I saw Mrs Jenner on the pavement opposite. I waved casually and walked purposefully by. She seemed to be there for some time, strategically positioned outside the entrance of Tinkerbell's. I wondered if this was a kind of blackmail ploy, a means to augment her income. It was rumoured that Father Donohue had been seen lurking not far from the premises. When I looked again I realised she was waiting for a bus, a number sixty-two, which would take her back to Shooters Hill.

As soon as the bus with its cheery singing conductor Desmond had taken off, I retraced my steps to Tinkerbell's doorway. I waited till the vehicle had turned the corner before entering, just in case Mrs Jenner was on the top deck and peering back with a telescope. I looked carefully in both directions and stepped inside.

A vision of loveliness sat within, glued to a desk and filing her nails. Her fluffy blonde hair obscured a pair of heavy specs. She looked like a naughty secretary. I sat enthralled as she took down my particulars.

"That's lovely," murmured the spectacles. I had to agree. She was. "Barbara likes to see *all* our clients. She'll be with you in a minute."

Barbara! It was a veritable seraglio. A lovely auburn-haired girl called Lindsey went by and deposited a cup of tea for the hidden spectacles.

"Mr Kitten!" Someone was calling me, drawing me away from the two counter graces. Would there be a third? A sculpture bearing the same name and boasting three well-proportioned and beautifully carved bottoms stands in the foyer of the London Tate Gallery, the older version. I'm sure it is positioned there to increase the number of visitors.

I stood up, beckoned by Barbara but there the vision ended. She was wearing a heavy tweed jacket and almost military footwear. As I accompanied her to her office, I found myself thinking of hockey pitches.

"Mr Kitten!"

"It's Kitson."

She peered again at something she had written on a folder. "Oh, so it is." There was no apology for my metamorphosis. "Nice to meet you!" she barked and held out a rather threatening palm.

I am not a lover of shaking hands. I visited Germany once and felt I had used up my annual allowance within a week.

She motioned me to a chair. "I get all my clients to fill in a form," she beamed. I was handed a couple of reams of paper. "The green one is more detailed and I would be grateful if you could undertake careful completion of this at home." I glanced despairingly at the green-tinted pages. What sort of questions lay within? "The smaller one is of course more concise. It appertains to age range, appearance…"

"Ah yes." I nodded.

I began to wonder if Barbara herself had a partner or whether she was removed from such mundane things, content simply to oversee the process of mixing and matching. Mixing and matching? Where had that come from? I found myself following the movements of Barbara's stonemason hands. The supermarket?

"We look forward to seeing you again, Mr Hudson," said Barbara, plucking the abbreviated form from me. I began to wonder whether she muddled clients just as she did names. It could cause some worrying permutations. I didn't feel I could correct her again – at least not so soon. She cast the briefest of glances at my signed confession of honesty and for a moment – was it my imagination but was there the very slightest curl of the lip?

Five days later, after I had returned the encyclopaedic tome with its oddly intrusive questions about footwear to Tinkerbell's, the phone rang.

"We have an exciting match, Mr Hudson," thrilled Barbara. "A Valerie Clenchwarton from Battersea. We suggest, however, you meet up in a mutually convenient public place."

A lavatory? "Thank you very much," I said.

"You're welcome," replied the thrilled Barbara.

I met Valerie two days later in the Cuthbertson Tea Rooms, which is a mile away from where I live and for Valerie four. She told me in great detail about her journey here and how it involved three buses. "Which ones?" I enquired politely.

"The one four seven, the nineteen and the sixty-two. I could have taken the seventy-eight…"

I could have asked her whether she had encountered Desmond, the singing bus conductor, in her travels but somehow I missed the opportunity. Valerie was not unattractive with a long mane of dark brown hair. She reminded me of a French film star now in her twilight years. I lifted up my 'croissant speciale', whereupon all the almonds fell off.

"Tell me," confided Valerie, lightly touching my finger. "Does the spirit ever move you?"

"Oh frequently!" I said. I may have blushed slightly because the way my trousers had risen against my newly purchased Petrobum underpants was having a similar effect.

"Oh." She sounded pleased and placed a card in front of me. I put on my glasses and saw the words in blue and grey ink with something about Healing Mission dance before me. "We meet every Sunday at six fifteen!"

She beamed and got up to go. It? Was that it? "It's been lovely." She was shaking hands. "See you soon. Well, Sunday, of course." She vanished into the crowded street.

I complained afterwards to Barbara about Tinkerbell's being penetrated by people assuming missionary positions. She merely gave me an Aberdeen Angus type look and offered me a biscuit. I shook my head. "It doesn't always work out," she sympathised. "We need to be patient."

It was several weeks before the phone rang again to offer hope. I felt that I was being chastised for my lack of malleability and that Tinkerbell's had gone into a reactive sulk after my conversation with Barbara.

"We're quite excited about this one," she said. "Jacintha. Seems a perfect match!"

I wondered what might constitute this but Barbara was reeling off the contact details and was unwilling to be distracted.

When I suggested the previously visited tearooms to Jacintha she was more forthcoming.

"What about that restaurant wine bar on Firth Street?" she suggested.

"Fine," I said. It was certainly better than a tearoom and had an added promise of alcohol.

I took the precaution of eating before I went as wine bar menus seemed to revolve around limp lettuce and warmed-up cheese.

Jacintha was slightly plump and cuddly. I liked the way she lifted her wine glass so that it caught the light. In her conversational enthusiasm she managed to send all her cutlery flying. This confirmed my wisdom in refraining from having something to eat. One is often too nervous to indulge in table manners. But being of inherently chivalrous nature and having an overwhelming desire to see Jacintha's ankles, I bent down to pick them up. As I did so, I felt a sudden sneeze coming on – it may have been dusty 'below stairs' – the violence of which caused me to drop the cutlery. Then Jacintha said something to which I banged my head on the table as I stood up. As the cutlery had travelled some distance around the wine bar restaurant, we tried unsuccessfully to catch the waiter's eye so I swiped a set from the adjacent table. Jacintha giggled enthusiastically.

We left the restaurant and were travelling back to Jacintha's on a number sixty-two bus. If I wasn't mistaken, this was one of the buses favoured by Valerie and I hoped there would be no awkward coincidences. Fortunately there was no sign of her. She was no doubt out somewhere on another mission terrorising other unsuspecting members of Tinkerbell's.

Jacintha inserted her key into her prettily patterned front door and we stood together in her dimly lit hallway. It seemed a romantic enough setting but as I stooped towards Jacintha's softly powdered cheek, the same seismic sneeze that had assailed me earlier in the wine bar returned again but this time with greater vehemence. It was followed by another and another...

As I reached for an obdurate hanky something was nudging me below the nether regions. I glanced down and saw the fluffy posterior of one of the country's many overweight felines. Jacintha followed my gaze and cooed what sounded like 'Piddy!'

"You keep cakes?" I wheezed. I meant cats.

"Oh yes," she said. "But only the six of them now." There was a flicker of sadness in her voice.

"I...I...I...I'm allergic to..."

"Cats? What a pity! Surely...?"

The only surely was I had to get out of there. My throat was on fire and my eyes were streaming a flood. I was safer lying beneath a car exhaust. "I'll ring you," I lied.

"Be sure to," she chided.

I didn't. And when I think of otherwise sweet Jacintha I see the bloated head of that overweight feline and my instinctive reaction is to...

I was beginning to think my second disastrous meeting had put me in bad stead with Tinkerbell's. The phone remained silent.

Shortly after the outing with Jacintha I had to visit Mr Cordle the dentist. The violent sneezing fit had unsettled one of my molars and I could no longer chomp with certainty.

"Four thirty," said an unsympathetic voice at the other end as I phoned to make an appointment. It was clearly thinking ahead to the screams and helpless protestations.

But as I stepped inside Cordle's I immediately noticed something was different. The Venus fly-trap, which always reminded me of Little Shop of Horrors, had been removed and a pale orchid had taken its place. Moreover the callous voice which had answered the phone was no longer in evidence. Instead there was a polite olive-skinned boy who took down my details.

"Mr Cordle?" I enquired.

"He is no longer here," the new receptionist informed me. "Some problem with Dental Estimates Board. Fraud maybe."

I felt my jaw involuntarily. Mr Cordle had always been a little over enthusiastic and zealous in his practices.

"Please take a seat," he said.

The leather seat gave me a sort of glutinous welcome and I slid along a little way. There were no other patients here to witness my anxiety and I breathed a sigh of relief. Fear can often be infectious. I glanced at the reading matter. Country Living had been replaced by Plumbing International, Readers' Digest had been ousted in favour of…

There was a squawking sound from beneath the receptionist's desk; a kind of intercom.

"Oh, auntie, I'm so sorry. I forgot." He looked over towards me. "The dentist will see you now."

I got up to go to the usual room and see Auntie. A lady with a heavily masked nurse was motioning me to a chair. I was wondering if the latter was preparing for some kind of heist.

"Mr Kitson," she smiled. She had deep dark eyes and I could see the family resemblance with the nephew on the desk. Hastily I explained the circumstances which had destabilised my molars and probably blown out half my gums.

"It's not a problem, Mr Kitson." I looked helplessly round the room as she and the masked nurse busied themselves with charts and my gaze alighted on a poster of familiar style and colours. An immaculately attired doctor was apologising to a lady patient, who was readjusting her underwear, saying 'I'm afraid we've been on a wild-goose chase, madam. It must be your tonsils!'

I felt a soft gulp within me then a snigger. The snigger transformed itself into something more vocal. I found myself chortling, guffawing in the almost horizontal dentist's chair. The dentist was momentarily alarmed then followed my eye line.

"You like Mr McGill, then?"

I gazed again at Donald McGill's banned seaside postcard now blown up in glory on the surgery wall. I could only nod. Liquid in the form of tears was pouring from my eyes. My sides were wobbling, aching.

"It's very popular with the patients."

Only when I had calmed down, and with the help of the nephew who managed to drape something over the distracting poster, was she able to stare inside my aperture.

"Which tooth?" she asked. She then went on a dental walkabout. "No, no. It's absolutely fine, Mr Kitson. Although I can recommend something for your gums."

"Really?" Nothing? I was all right? Mr Cordle would probably have taken out a whole row of teeth. I placed a tentative finger inside. The tooth no longer wobbled. "I'm so grateful," I murmured.

"Perhaps the laughter. The face muscles. Relaxed perhaps…"

"Put it back into…?"

"It's not impossible," she conceded.

The bandaged nurse muttered something about having to catch a bus and left. I was left alone with Marcella, my caring and solicitous dentist. With my facial confidence restored, we talked expansively about our various tastes and interests and we continued it down the Pig and Whistle. The nephew left us at the door of the hostelry and murmured a discreet goodnight. I looked around to see if Charlie was there supping his brown and mild but the world was our own.

When Tinkerbell's finally contacted me at the end of what was probably another punitive and petulant sulk I was able to tell them I no longer required their services. I could sense Barbara's disbelief at the other end of the phone.

"I'm fine," I said. "I now have…"

"I'm so glad," replied Barbara acidly.

"In fact, we're going away this weekend to the Isle of Wight. To the Donald McGill Museum."

"Donald who?" barked Barbara.

I repeated the name to her.

"Never heard of it," she said, a touch nastily.

It said it all really.

Swifts

Where did I first meet them? Now, you've got me. Good question that. Let me think. That's right. It was during the long hot summer. Quite ironic then that it should prove so productive, but yes it was during those endless weeks of drought.

I first saw them on the pier. I was walking round as you do and I saw her face under a ring of those coloured light bulbs. The sea roared and I could see the foam through the slats. It was slowly getting dark but there was still the last of the sunset which hadn't yet vanished behind the cliff.

They both looked very young, and so they were of course. Those eyes. Those pale blue eyes. They sparkled in the lights and I could hear laughter. In the distance the church tower loomed up, watching us, adding its blessing. Have you noticed how in that part of the country they go in for those tall church towers?

As they left the pier I followed, but whereas I walked along the esplanade, they abruptly turned right and up the steps. I remember the swifts screaming and flying low- the first real heralds of summer, as the swallows are apt not to bother with towns.

I sat and sipped my beer and said "you're beautiful", for beyond the amber glass and the sighing, shifting sea, those eyes imprinted themselves on me, and I heard her laugh once again.

The next day the rain came; a sullen drizzle and a sea mist. The town as empty and deserted as if an unexploded bomb had drifted up on the beach.

But on the Saturday in the Life Boat Café – I believe, I really believe- fate struck. At the next table there she was.

Quick, I thought, get a line, seize the moment, throw a line to a drowning man, but "could you pass the salt?" was all I could muster. It was in one of those big, heavy dispensers and wobbled manically across the table.

I passed the salt cellar back. I couldn't ask for it again. She got up...going...although she'd left her coat. But no. False alarm. She went to the counter and ordered another tea.

The seagulls were flying out after the fishing boats. Have you noticed that herring gulls have a nasty laugh? That is, when they're not screeching wildly across the harbours.

She came back and then suddenly lurched forward. The table leg had tripped her up and sent a shower of tea in my direction.

"Oh I'm so sorry," she said.

"No, no, it's okay, no damage done."

I hastily wiped the tea from my white flannels.

"It's these stupid legs."

"No problem."

She smiled in embarrassment. So tea had worked where salt had failed. We began to talk.

"We're going back on Friday. James works weekends."

"James?"

"My brother."

"Oh, what does he do?"

"In a hospital. Porter."

We talked and talked. The sea rattled the pebbles. Half an hour later James arrived.

"What kept you?"

"Left my sunglasses in the pub, didn't I?"

That evening we met for a drink. The weather had returned to normal and we sat outside, quaffing pints as the tide began to turn, dragging across stones on the beach and buffeting the frail looking supports of the pier.

I looked into those beautiful eyes and was hypnotised.

By the end of the week Anne's cheeks were glowing.

"The air's so fresh up here," she laughed.

"Nonsense, it's all that drinking. Honestly, she doesn't normally drink that much."

I smiled. We swapped addresses. Little bits of precious paper. And this time no idle holiday exchange. I would write. We would meet up. I'd make sure of it. Definitely.

I kissed her goodbye on both cheeks and James squeezed my arm. They stepped into the truncated train and were gone. A last wave from the window. A puff of blue between rolling hills. It's not as flat as you think...Silence. Solitude. I was back to being alone but it didn't bother me. I would definitely write.

Thereafter the post cemented our union. Hesitantly, at first. Little spidery writing. Amoebas crossing the page. Then more often. Come and see us. How about it? A train riding over the low marshes of the east, swaying in the breezy emptiness. I nearly missed the station. Small and unapologetic, only two carriages contriving a match with the platform. A wooden hut for shelter, a ticket office long abandoned, and James leaning against it, grinning at my brief panic.

"I'm afraid she's stood you up. She's playing tennis so she sent me to pick you up. Some knockout tournament."

We walked along a reedy lane flanked by dykes and drains.

"Fancy a drink?" said James. "Celebrate your arrival."

As we sat outside the weather-boarded pub I noticed how white his teeth were.

"This is why I didn't take the car. Excellent stuff."

The beer was heady and hoppy, and I felt uncoordinated as we approached the house. Trees waved around the low, stone building, offering scant protection from the wind. I stayed a long weekend. Played tennis every day. Balls lobbing in ballooning breeze. Canoed down the narrow river and was almost garrotted by overhanging branches.

They tenderly extricated me from the advances of willow, brushing off the leaves and stray bits of bark. I came back most weekends and was garrotted more. Anne came to London and so one day in late autumn, leaves still fluttering on trees, we tied the knot. Little café near Holborn Circus. Words nearly drowned by the Espresso machine.

Anne rang to tell them at home, then made another call to tell James. He was rambling in the Lake District. Buttermere. She had to tell him too. It was always like that. Instinctively thought about each other. Reflex action. Like mirror twins, except they weren't. She returned beaming after making the calls. We went to a restaurant to celebrate. Groomed spinach accompanied by paltry potatoes and lamb resting poignantly on three leaves of cress. We should have stayed in the café and blown up with lasagne.

After a while we moved. Anne didn't like big cities, so it was back to the countryside. It was all the same to me. More travelling but less hassle. We saw quite a bit of James.

At weekends when Anne was doing her stained glass stuff, we cycled off to obscure pubs with unknown beers. Roads that always went upwards whichever way you went, and a biting wind that blew into you. Many a time we saved each other from lurking ditches as we missed the zigzags of the road.

But Anne put down her stained glass and for our second anniversary we went back to the coast.

"I'm not camping!" she protested. "No way."

In fact the weather settled the argument. Grey skies and chilly winds buried the atmosphere of balmy evenings. The swifts had long gone, abandoning the summer, leaving the gulls to screech across the harbour. I wondered whether Anne would want James to come but she made no mention.

We walked along the beaches most days, taking in the crisp sea air. One afternoon we went on a longer walk and headed beyond the pier. Those beautiful eyes, I thought. Long stretches of sand tapering into nowhere. Constant ripples in slate-grey sandpools. Looking out to sea, a mist was beginning to form, and there was the distant sound of a foghorn.

The pier was what started it, I thought to myself, as we trod unexpected pebbles and skirted around rockpools. I looked behind us, but there was nothing but open beach and waves crashing against breakwaters.

We went up to the cliffs. A kestrel was drifting above. The ground was still moist after the morning drizzle.

We trod paths that wound through bracken and gorse. I had no idea of the time but Anne kept looking at her watch.

We turned back, Anne walking slightly ahead on the narrow path. Birds scuttled across, low-flying and scolding. The mist brooded on the horizon.

Even now I can't really recall it. You know, when your mind goes blank sometimes. But I do remember the foghorn. That bleak doleful sound.

Just at the bend in the cliff path Anne had slipped. It may have been the wet stones or sudden subsidence, although she was never that nimble on her feet.

Of course everyone was sympathetic...sometimes painfully so. But between those long staring silences I had James all to myself. He would be in need of comfort. Such beautiful eyes.

Hoodwinked

"**B**limey, she's barmy," muttered Ron as she staggered towards the taxi.

The hooded figure paused and gestured towards the suitcase.

"Lady, what you got in here? The kitchen sink?"

"No, the fridge," she replied tartly and gave her destination.

"I think it'll be shut, love."

"Don't you 'luv' me," she said by way of distraction, and got into the purring taxi.

It was getting dark, trees and shrubs paraded past the window.

"Are you sure you want to go there? He repeated. "It'll definitely be shut."

Hilda took no notice. The rhythmic passing shrubs made her think of heady days in the shop. The early mornings, oh so early, drawing back the curtains and treading on dew-drenched lawns. Just before she passed through the gate she loved to plunge her hands onto the cool grass and watch the droplets trickle up her arm. As she walked the mile and a half to work Hilda could see Trevor bending over the oven. She loved his arse. Simply loved it. There was nothing better than when she casually nudged past leaving floury handprints all over his neat blue- trousered bottom.

Time and again she did it, till he got narked.

"I kept getting funny stares all morning, Hilda, so cut it out."

She sniggered. He was so sweet and his eyes flashed when he got angry. Such lovely eyes.

"Excuse me for asking," inquired Ron, "but have you joined an order or do you normally dress up as a nun?"

Hilda started and looked at the broad neck in the front part of the cab. Not a patch on Trevor's bottom, she thought.

"Oh this? Well, we've been rehearsing and I simply didn't have time…."

Ron slowed down to approach a roundabout.

"And if you don't mind me asking, where do the roller skates come in?"

She clattered coyly.

"It's a variation of one of those Andrew Lloyd Rhubarb things. I have to circle round the stage singing 'the hills are alive…' I'm all equipped with flashing lights. It's going to be very visual."

"Must be," said Ron, who'd never quite made it further than the Cromer End of Pier show. And who was he to argue?

They passed down the long avenue which threaded through a housing estate. The battered bus shelters bore testimony to the fragile remains of the town bus service, the last of which was seldom seen after seven o'clock.

She remembered the queues sometimes outside the bread shop, and Charlie who worked in the cash cubicle of the butcher's. It was more hygienic then, when they didn't mix meat with money.

"Here's the church," she exclaimed," Wait here!"

She skated under the drooping oak and negotiated the two or three steps up to the porch. In a moment or so she was whispering through the grill of the confessional, her soft, sibilant sounds like the twittering of morning sparrows.

The clock ticked round. A candle flickered.

"Bless me father for what I am about to do…"

"I see." Fr. Joe listened. "Well, I concede you have a point, if a little drastic."

It was over. She left the confessional, shutting the wooden gate and was out on the porch.

A passing builder made her think of Trevor, and she was back again in the shop. It was Christmas and bonhomie was in the air. No tinsel as it tended to get tarnished with baking flour- but the heady smell of mulled wine….and after….

The toot of Ron's taxi disturbed her reverie. She scowled and skated towards the car.

"Some people don't know the meaning of patience," she grumbled. "It's me who's paying you!"

"I've got another job after this, lady," he remonstrated.

"Oh shut up!" she snapped. "And drive on!"

The spire of the church behind disappeared into darkness as they bobbed swiftly towards the ring road. Here was the smell of mustard factory mingled with the waft of beer from the remaining brewery. They climbed the narrow bridge over the river with the trees in the nearby park fading fast into twilight.

She sighed. Trevor and she had often lain under the bridge listening to the rain. Soggy crisps on wet afternoons. A pickled gherkin for Saturday night. A walnut whip on Wednesdays.

Life had been with its little pleasures, and she drifted back to the shop again. It was Easter; time for the occasional chocolate departure from a rigid Bakewell routine.

They were getting nearer now; in fact they were almost there.

Her sense of well- being gave way to nausea. There it was- awful in its enormity, like a kind of housing estate spread over the marshes. First of all came the lights of the petrol station, and then, in neo- lavatory style, the hybrid horror of the hypermarket.

She hated it. Hated it for everything. Not just for what it had done to high streets up and down the country, but she also hated it for the eventual closure of Trevor's shop.

Of course he no longer worked there, but it had been a baker's up till the last six months, and now it lay empty and forlorn, coated with green and yellow stickers for Billy Graham and Bhagwan.

This was double desecration of the shrine.

The cab circled a moment or two in the deserted car park.

"I told you, lady."

"Here," she said," help me with this case."

Hilda stumbled out of the cab and wobbled precariously with her suitcase. She staggered up to the huge glass doors of the hypermarket.

"'Ere lady." Shouted Ron. "What you gonna do with…?"

Ron felt uneasy as the veiled Hilda bent over and undid the flaps. Within moments she had produced something looking rather like…

"A ruddy bomb!" shrieked Ron. "Crikey, she's mad. 'Ere, give me that!"

It was too late, for Hilda had swiftly triggered a device and was skating like mad past Ron towards the exit of the car park. She cackled gleefully, invisible now in the darkness. For good measure she smashed a giant burger sign to the left of the automatic car-wash.

Ron seemed to freeze for a moment. Then a blaring car horn from somewhere jolted him into action. He jumped back into his cab and drove off.

The camouflaged Hilda was nowhere to be seen, as he drove frantically out of the car park, thanking him for his custom, and onto the main road.

Suddenly there was a loud rumble and the world was raining glass. The hypermarket was at least living up to its name, as parts of it orbited above the street lamps. Plastic seats from cash tills bounced furiously across the tarmac, while a thousand Angel Delights were now being reconstituted in the ornamental fishpond.

The following day, a taxi driver, answering to the name of Ron, had been apprehended. A write- up appeared that evening in the local paper. Ron's taxi had apparently been spotted by a distraught petrol pump attendant.

Apart from driving off at high speed, he appeared to have been badly concussed following the explosion.

Mr. Ron Bassetwood keeps referring to some story of a nun on roller skates singing 'The hills are alive...' and 'I did it for you, Trevor'.

Ever Decreasing Circles

The image of the rippling pool abated. Gradually with time and like the ripples themselves they burst and broke themselves upon the banks. Only grief hadn't quite receded. It was habitually present; a dull ache like a nagging tooth or a toe blister pressed against the shoe.

Leaves parted and he was hurtling through the undergrowth. Almost in slow motion, he could see the swaying branch. The pattern of shed leaves crunched on the floor under the urgent panic of his feet. Joe's cries for help had suddenly subsided. He was wading into the pond, dark, inky water that now bubbled evilly round his mouth. Then he was picking up that little shape, that sopping bundle and screaming wildly across the conspiratorial silence.

Caroline was next to him, hysterical. Then everything became confused, waterlogged, splashing. Breathing into that little mouth as he lay on the clay bank; futilely pumping that motionless chest-; that terrible stillness.

The family in room 3 let out a shriek. The word 'cheat' resounded in chorus.

He and Caroline had lasted nine months after that, but the drifting away from each other had begun before Christmas. They were each reminders to each other, and, in the ensuing numbness, somehow unable to console one another. They saved their tears for empty rooms as if the visible show of grief would infect each other.

They parted, wrote occasionally; postcard type letters, token platitudes. Everything was so safe.

Then he met Eileen, and shortly after, Caroline wrote to tell him about Ian.

The back street bed and breakfast was in a small seaside town. Eileen had inherited it from her aunt, and somehow the fresh, salty air, the compact garden, full of creeping nasturtiums, offered the change he needed. No nine to five. No spasmodic and overcrowded trains. Enough work with hotel and garden to keep him busy. And Eileen was so different. She was calm, methodical and seemed to understand him intuitively. When memory clouded his face, she pressed him against her shoulder and ran her long fingers softly against the back of his neck.

There was no pond in the garden, but stray frogs and toads hinted of a nearby presence. There was a greenhouse to which he retreated in the quieter winter months. In mid February or March, it housed a small paraffin heater, which glowed from the twilight hours to early morning.

As Easter beckoned, guests started to appear at the B&B. Streaky bacon smells wafted into the hall, and each morning he got up at six, leaving Eileen slumbering, to prepare the breakfasts.

There was one last shriek of 'cheat' and Miss Warburton was knocking at the door. It appeared her towel had gone missing again. "Can't have that now, can we?" he said and led her to the linen cupboard.

This was another tranquil place like the greenhouse. Various smells of comfort and pine combined with the smell of warm wood. A wholesome void, calm and still. No ripples.

When the Wilkinsons booked in on Friday evening, they were full, the first time that year.

"Looks like we're in for a busy summer," he said to Eileen that evening. "And the weather looks set to last." She looked up from her book. "I shan't complain." Then with a smile, "You never know, we might make enough to go on holiday."

"Maybe," said Michael, unconvinced.

"Either that or look for a bigger place."

"Hmm," he grunted. "Sounds like more hard work. And that way we'd never get to take a holiday."

"Pessimist."

"Let's see how the summer goes," he said as he went to put the kettle on. As the electric kettle chugged away, he wondered where they would go. Their first holiday.

"It' a bit early, I think," he said. "I don't know."

With the hotel full, he was getting up earlier to do the breakfasts. At half- past five he stepped onto the dew- soaked lawn, the grass soft and cool between his open sandals. Water…circles…He tried not to think. He went back to the kitchen and shut the door, quickly spearing a pack of bacon. The greenhouse glinted in early sun. The only sound in the kitchen was the sudden singing of the fridge, followed by the chinking sounds of milk bottles on the back doorstep.

Eileen had a headache that morning, so he told her to stay in bed. He'd be fine. Yes. He could do it all. He'd manage.

By eleven thirty, he was finished, washed up and all, and taking a mug of tea up to Eileen.

Suddenly his thoughts were interrupted by a soft tapping at the door. A girl and a boy stood in front of him.

"We can't get into the room. It's the door."

The girl had a wide spread of freckles emanating from the nose and with her red hair she looked like a spotty lion cub.

Michael accompanied them up the stairs.

"Everybody's out shopping," the girl said, "and we couldn't get in."

"Oh I see, yes. That door sometimes sticks. We'll get it fixed." He leant his shoulder hard against the door and it grudgingly gave.

"Try not to slam it too tight. We'll get it sorted later."

Two footsteps followed him, as he turned back downstairs.

"What's in the glass house in the garden?" the boy asked.

"That's my greenhouse where I grow the plants to put in the borders."

"Can I have a look?"

"Yes, of course. I'll just take this tea up and I'll see you down there in a moment. Don't go in, will you?"

"No."

The diminutive solitary figure had his back to him as he stepped out for the second time into the garden. The sun dazzled through the glass, glinting fiercely off the neat aluminium frame.

Michael slid back the door and they stepped into greenhouse heat. Spiders scuttled behind staging as they trod gingerly over the boards.

"There's sometimes a frog hidden under this plank of wood. Shall we see if he's still there?"

The boy nodded as Michael turned over the board. Squinting beneath the wood was a squat brown and yellow frog.

"Ohhh," said the boy and slipped his hand into his.

He put out the other hand to touch the tiny frog but Michael stopped him.

"We don't want to frighten him, do we?"

"No, we mustn't." The boy looked back at him and it was then, in the greenhouse of the sun, that Michael saw him clearly for the first time.

His mouth dropped open and he murmured the word "Joe,"

Joe's blue eyes looked back at him, that familiar studious and forlorn expression.

"Oh Joe," he whispered. "Joe."

He picked the boy up, that soft cheek caressing his line of stubble. Kissing him repeatedly, he held him tightly against his neck.

"At last," he said, "at last we've found you. Mummy will be pleased. She'll be so pleased."

He didn't hear the child's frantic screams. All he saw was the bright, radiant sun as he bundled him into the car and drove off at full speed to tell Caroline.

At Night

There was a monster in the back bedroom, Damian thought, as he looked at the rain pouring across the garden. He'd heard it hadn't he?

He snatched the battered Ford Capri and ran it along the window ledge, the neat suspension negotiating flaky paintwork. Inside, a diminutive driver sat motionless by a huge steering wheel. Footsteps in the hall. His mother going no doubt to the freezer to get some more beef burgers. Rain dripping outside the window. The lawn fluorescent green and looking like the bathroom sponge. Damian liked it whenever he trod the path, listening to the water hiss up from the grass and trickle down the cracked patches of concrete. But as for that monster, it definitely lived in the back room.

"You're going to the Garrick's after tea," said Marie, bumping a plate down in front of him.

Damian looked up at her with a disgusted stare.

"I don't want to."

"Tough," came the reply. Then to placate the inescapable stare, she added, "It's only for an hour," and ruffled his straw brown hair. "I can't really get someone to baby-sit for an hour, can I?"

He kept his eyes on her.

"Besides, Mrs. Garrick likes having you. She does. And I know Lucy isn't exactly your age, but she looks forward to seeing you too."

"It's boring," said Damian, chewing his beef burger in a deliberately ugly fashion. He reached mutinously for the tomato ketchup, smiting the bottom of the bottle a few extra times for luck.

A little while later, he was duly dropped outside the Garrick's. As he walked the few steps up the path he noticed the big Mercedes had disappeared from the drive. This was the one possible source of interest to him. It had buttons inside that made the mirrors go up and down. The aerial ascended and lowered like a periscope. He wasn't sure if it had a phone inside too but it could splosh water quite dramatically over its windscreen like a great whale. He looked sadly at the empty spot on the gravel path as the door swung open to meet him. Even worse, he was inside the house before he could press the bell that played a tune.

Damian looked around the hall. There seemed to be so many rooms leading off.

"Damian," cooed a voice. "Come on in."

He stood on springy carpets while Lucy was watching him on the stairs.

"Perhaps you'd like to go up to Lucy's room today. We've got some visitors coming."

Mrs. Garrick propelled him in the direction of Lucy. Lucy, tiny in her strawberry tights, was looking very smug for some reason. He followed the strawberry up the staircase. It was the first time he'd been in her room. As usual, toys formed an assault course on the floor over which Mrs. Garrick would gingerly tread.

As Damian looked at a row of glass tanks by the window, Lucy, lip quivering and face beaming, said, "I've got a parrot." And there, sure enough, immobile yet alive, a beautiful green and yellow parrot stared quizzically at the new entourage. It had a red spot on its bill and its red cheeks looked as if it were permanently embarrassed.

Damian stopped to look at it; at the same time his mouth dropped open.

"What's his name?" he asked.

"Well actually," said Lucy superciliously, "we don't know if it's a boy or a girl."

"Why not?"

"It's very difficult to tell when he's very young."

166

"So how do you know he's a he?" persisted Damian.

Lucy ignored him and stroked the yellow and green parrot.

"Buttons," said Lucy, "Mrs. Winch thought of Buttons."

Damian made a face.

"It's a stupid name," he said, but even so he moved a hand forward gingerly to stroke the becalmed parrot.

"Here's my doll's house," said Lucy after a while, seeing Damian might become too well acquainted with Buttons. "It was made for me specially."

Damian peered in through the various windows; the hall with its fitted radiators, the little study with its reading lamp. In the living room, figures sat in cosy armchairs round a log fire.

He watched mesmerised for a while. Everything was so calm and stable. The rooms with their leisurely figures seemed so permanent and still. Quite unlike...

Damian got up, rubbing a spot on his knee. Lucy's face required an answer.

"I like the parrot more," he said, determinedly. "You can stroke him."

Later, when Damian was brought home about eight, he noticed that uncle Larry had arrived. His black car was wet and gleaming in the drizzling rain he told them all about the parrot, that he'd stroked it five, six, seven times, even though it was only twice because in truth he was a little afraid of the bird with its sharp claws. They didn't seem very interested though.

"Time to go to bed." said his mother. "Say goodnight to Larry."

Damian went upstairs thinking of the parrot. He undressed and read his comic. Lying for a few minutes without any clothes on top of the bed, he could think of much better names than Buttons. Buttons. He said it out loud. Then he turned out the light and pulled the bedclothes round him.

The parrot nodded its head before his eyes, for Damian was now its proud owner. It had learnt to speak better than anybody else's. It was very tame and came onto his hand. It said lots of things and was particularly fond of sausages. At the school they were amazed. In the playground, a circle of admirers had gathered round, hands reaching out nervously and tentatively to touch it. Even better, the parrot pecked the hands of those it didn't like.

But at that moment Damian opened his eyes and the parrot disappeared. His bedroom stared back at him in darkness. It was raining again outside so that the water gurgled down the drainpipes and resounded off next door's dustbin lids.

The wind blew gently through the half open window; the window through which the parrot had escaped into the night air. The curtain fluttered and he shivered. He was now feeling a bit cold so he crept out of bed to close it. He tried not to bang the window or thump his feet on the floor. It was quite hard to shut as it had got stuck in the damp, but finally he managed to do it. The sound of muted rain could be heard outside.

Then, as he got back into bed, another sound. Damian stopped and listened. He listened carefully. The wind blew against the window, but he could still make the noise out.

There it was, without a doubt. The monster in the back room

Turning the door handle gently, he slipped out into the passageway. He stopped. Maybe he should go back in. Forget all about it. Maybe it would eat him though. But then, if he was in bed, it could come and eat him too. That would be worse. And the parrot that could protect him had gone.

No. He'd have to let everyone know. Raise the alarm. So he inched forward into the darkness, hearing the sound again. The floorboards creaked as he moved nearer to the door.

Then he heard a low gasp. He pressed his ear against the wood, but the noise wasn't coming from there.

Then suddenly another door opened. A man was in the passageway, his shadow coming towards him.

He heard his mother in the distance, shouting 'Don't, don't'! Then, anxious footsteps and Larry shouting "The little bastard! Spying on us!"

Larry's face was quite different. His arms were raining blows. From nearby and yet a long way off, his mother screeched. As Damian felt their full impact, he screamed and shut his eyes. The parrot had gone.

Not Drowning but....

"I'm sure," said Sheila, "…in time."

"No," Bridy said and shook her head.

Her eyes came to rest on the black and white swirls of the ball, taking pride of place, as Dave would have it, on the gloomy sideboard.

Sheila caught Bridy's line of vision. "Another cup of tea perhaps? Shall I make it?"

"No," answered Bridy.

The ball billowed like a giant squid on the lonely dresser. It was barely a year old, but now it festered like an unloving mushroom of remembrance.

Two days ago, they had done it. Decided. In an hour of incessant rain, scattering shoppers from the pavements. The heavens wept their choked tears – collective, but mainly his. Even the car wouldn't start – they sat there watching the wipers flick across the blurred screen. And, as he thought afterwards, grimly symbolic.

"Mum!" He was tugging at her elbow. "I'm in!"

"Sure, that's great news," she'd said without enthusiasm.

He picked up on it. "But I'm in."

She stopped what she was doing and threw him a brief smile. "I suppose there'll be more trips. Bound to be."

He went over and stuck a hand in the biscuit tin; a large, crumbly digestive which sent a shower of biscuit fragments over the floor. Bridy sighed. She had always resented him. Resented him ever since his unwarranted intrusion into the world. That night on Hadleigh Common had been the night of his conception. Too much wine and an inadequate picnic hamper. The stars had been so clear; the air fresh and heady with the scent of pine. She and David had spent one blissful night, till the early hours, then cycled precariously home for him to start the morning shift.

Daniel was on his way. Perhaps even then she knew he was destined to be a footballer by the ferocious kicking she'd had to endure. Easing her way back into work after a lengthy spell away had proved difficult. He'd spoilt that too for her. Then, of course, any social life went out the window. Fled, as if it were a bird on the wing. And she knew too that some of her friends were avoiding her.

For the first few years he'd squawked like a voracious gull. He'd not been an amenable child. Then both of them seemed to disappear from her sights as David said Daniel showed all the makings of being a footballer. They would vanish for hours on the common. Hours. Kicking a ball no doubt across the site of his conception. Then Daniel became old enough to go to matches. Weekends saw her watering solitary rose bushes, somehow a frail symbol of her own isolation. To give her something to do, she had the patio uprooted and stocked it with extra plants.

David had remonstrated. "But there's nowhere for the lad to play." She snarled at him. "He can use the park. Anyway, I'm not having him break my pots with that incessant thudding."

Slowly, they seemed to drift away as if relentless currents propelled them both in other directions.

"Are you sure there's nothing you want?"
Bridy looked blankly back. "What do I want?"
"From the shops," Sheila said.
Bridy shook her head. There was a long silence. The ball swivelled. It was mesmeric. It was as if the whole house was encapsulated in this one ball. The ball. Pride of place. How could she feel proud...ever?

"Dad, I'm in."

"That's great." And he lifted Daniel up and gave him a great big hug. He never hugged her like he hugged him. Either of them. It was as if Daniel knew he should instinctively shy away from her; from the tell-tale signs of smouldering resentment.

"Can we go out on the common?"

"Sure. What time's tea?"

"Six thirty," she lied, bringing it forward by nearly an hour.

"There's just time then. Let's take the bikes."

The front door slammed shut and in the ensuing silence she pressed the remote control to the opening theme of evening soaps. It was getting dark. They were late. Time slipped by on the common, as well she knew, like nowhere else. They would be apologetic. There would be an atmosphere, and she'd be bribed with a 'put your feet up', while the kitchen would chink and clang to the sounds of their ponderous washing-up and endless football banter. She was the lodger who cooked the meals. It was nice of them not to ask for any rent.

"It's great that he's in the team.' David said to her in bed that night. "Really great."

She nodded as he held her tight. The last words she remembered him saying before falling asleep were "oh, it's been a long day."

Of course they'd got him new kit and boots. The match was that Saturday.

"You are coming, love, aren't you?"

She wasn't sure. "I did say to…"

"He'd be so disappointed. Just this once." Something in his tone made it impossible to refuse. She'd postpone her visit to the garden centre in her quest for a suitable climber.

Daniel changed at home. He'd wanted to be seen by the neighbours getting into the car. He walked down the street three times to post letters and drew compliments. The red uniform enhanced his dark hair. He looked a bit like David when he was younger. The same dimpled chin. He looked grand.

They were driving to the ground against a background of non-stop chatter.

"Save your energy for the game," she'd told him. "You'll be worn out."

"The lad's excited," David said. "Looks great, doesn't he?"

The windswept field was full of little groups of mums and dads. The sky was overcast, grudging. Her mood mirrored the sky. Lombardy poplars swayed at the far end while lorries chugged into the hangars of the recycling centre. It was a soulless ground, she thought, but then this was not a time for thinking. The game had already started. Spectators billowing advice; cajoling, pleading, screaming.

She was wondering why the climbing rose was called Rambling Rector, whether it was because of excessive wordiness, when the cry went up. It was a solitary cry and the man next to her gave a gasp. David was out on the pitch. A small crowd had gathered round.

"What's happened?" she found herself asking, then realised, by looking at the other boys, that it was Daniel. Her legs were secured by heavy weights. Clouds flew overhead. She couldn't move. David was leaning over replica David and she heard the word ambulance.

She couldn't remember how long she stood there. There were people round her and someone was saying something to her, the mouth opening and closing like a fish in a tiny bowl. The siren jolted her back into action. She and David were in the ambulance. David kept stroking Daniel's forehead saying "it'll be all right."

They bumped over endless speed humps. The hospital swallowed them up; endless corridors, white coats. White everywhere. White the colour of amnesia.

He wasn't all right. Wasn't going to be. A kick to the side of the head. Complications. David explained it all to her after as she clenched the mug of lukewarm tea. The only thing they could do was go in each day and talk to him. He'd got time off work. Indefinitely. No, she didn't have to go in every day if she didn't want to. So long as someone was there.

The room became a little shrine. All it lacked were the candles. Scarves and banners draped around the bed. Football programmes in among the get-well cards. It went on for days, weeks, months.

One day, they had a special meeting with the consultant. "It was," he said, "for them.....for them to decide. Switch off. Disconnect. Unplug a life.

David buried his head in her. "I can't bear it," he said, "to see him like this. I can't bear…"

"I know," she said, and ran her hand through his hair.

That evening he decided. The drifts of rain. She nodded. Whatever he wanted. She wanted whatever he….

When Ralph came to take them to the hospital, it was a light, sunny morning. They weren't fit either of them to drive. They could put Daniel's things in Ralph's car. It was big enough. He'd make a second journey if necessary.

"No," David said. They'd sort out his things, give the others away.

A bright and sunny day. They sat in the back, Ralph's bald patch making him look like a proper chauffeur, only he'd be wearing a cap if he were. Ralph talked about the changeable weather, nearly mentioned Everton; changed tack.

There was a new receptionist on the hospital desk, she noticed, as they took their familiar walk. They started counting down the rooms till they came to D16. Sixteen. It never came to that.

David and Ralph were taking away bits and pieces. The room was sunlit and the curtain fluttered in the breeze. She was left alone with her silent son. She glanced up at the rows of cards. Sometimes she tried to count them. There was a humming in the corridor. A vacuum cleaner; an electric wheelchair perhaps. It was while she was listening to the sound...

Suddenly a hand reached up and grabbed her. His hand. His. For a moment she didn't know what it was and screamed. The room went whiter still, turning inwards. She knocked over a vase.

David and Ralph ran quickly back but all they could see was blood pouring from her arm and the broken fragments of glass. In an instant, the nurses were attending to her; stop the bleeding – words calming. She felt like she did on the football field when nothing in her moved. As the needle slid into her arm, she heard David saying to the nurse, "she's had a terrible ordeal....Only knows..."

The next morning they asked her if she wanted to go home. The curtains and the bandaged arm told her she was not at home.

"Daniel?" she asked David. "Daniel?"

"No," said David. "It's all over now. He's safe. He's where... Nothing's hurting him. They switched it off."

She drew herself up. "No!" she cried. "No! They can't have! No....."

As Sheila put down her cup and got up to go, Bridy remembered her words.

"In time. It'll all be behind you. You'll see."

"No," she screamed again. "Never!"

Stepping Out

His skin was pale under the shade of the green garden umbrella. Earlier she'd paid him a compliment as he was downing the last of his lemon barley.

"You still look young for your age," she said.

He smiled, noticing something in the bottom of the glass, and squeezed her hand. She turned away from her contemplation of shrubs.

"I'm worried about Gary," she murmured. "Do you think it'll do him good?"

"Course it will," Gerald said. "It's the gradual weaning process from home. Learn a bit of independence." He sighed. "Who knows, we might even get appreciated."

Annette put down her glass. "The water tastes funny," she replied. "What do they put in it?"

He shrugged. "I never drink it on its own. That's why."

She had her argumentative face on. "Couldn't your lot do something about it? Clean up their standards? Heaven knows we pay enough for it. And look at all those people in Cornwall nearly poisoned. All the company got was a measly fine."

Gerald smiled. Annette always referred to his lot as your lot. From day one they had never agreed on politics.

"Have a word with the Minister. Fine them. Renationalise them. I can't take to drinking lemon barley."

The earth was dry and dusty in the garden. The rhubarb had gone to seed, she noticed, sending out big frothy plumes above its slightly shrivelled leaves.

"That pig ate rhubarb in the film last night. What was it called?"

"The pig? I didn't see it."

"No, the film."… After a pause, "I suppose the good thing is that Gary might make some new friends. He spends far too much time in front of that computer."

And indeed, as she looked up, she could see a head bent in the upstairs window to confirm what she had just said. "It's a crime to be in on a day like this. So beautiful…."

"Sorry, darling, I didn't hear. What's a crime?"

Annette threw him a water-board look. "I suppose that's why you're in politics," she said. "The inability to listen."

"I'll make you a Pimm's," he offered, "and then take Coco."

She lay back in the chair. The sun was starting to disappear behind the rooftops opposite. The bowed head upstairs stood up, then sat down again. She would do some work when he was out, do some reports, but not now as the sun was still pleasantly warm and drowsy.

Gerald was looking for Coco, dangling the lead as bait. Annette smiled. It was amazing how daft even the most worldly-wise could appear when serenading their dogs. She heard the gate shut. The garden was still.

Gerald walked down the avenue, looking at the peeling bark of plane trees, a sniffing hyena tearing at the lead in front of him. He cut through the maze of neat back streets, then over the bridge to the station. The new-liveried train emerged in a few moments, a touch self-consciously, he thought, and he stepped alone into the front carriage.

A voice from Radio 3 announced a plethora of stations, but the next one would do. He enjoyed short train journeys, and in eight minutes he found himself alighting at the deserted station. It was a dismal affair, a stone hut harbouring a two-slatted seat next to a flaking timetable, though none of which really concerned him.

He wondered if Annette knew of his route, whether anyone had said to her that they had seen her husband and a dog boarding a train. But then they were hardly likely to, for like most inhabitants of Baltimore Avenue, they lived lives of splendid seclusion. And he was one of the faceless ones, wasn't he? Seldom seen, seldom heard, but adequate for the needs of the constituency.

The road he turned into now was a dead end, at the end of which was a mound and the beginning of woodland. He was still young for his age, he mused, in spite of... in spite of everything. It wouldn't make any difference if Gary came or went, but if the youngest Tom...

Coco was pulling hard at the lead and looking to perform acrobatics on the ground. The harsh, rubbery smell of fox piss was all around. This would do, he decided. Leaving Coco to the delectation of senses, he wound the lead swiftly round the tree and tied it.

"Good dog," he said, walking slowly away from him.

Coco lowered his nose to the ground as one well-heeled to a ritual. In the early days he had scuppered everything with his incessant barking. Subsequent deprivations of privilege and admonitions had caused Coco to think again.

A few strides uphill took him to the top of a mount, where he could survey all around him. For such a fine evening it appeared strangely deserted. Gerald wondered why that was. Perhaps there was football on the telly again, a curse even in the best of summer months, but no, he couldn't recall any.

Suddenly to the right, he could hear twigs breaking, and a little way off, he could see a white-haired figure with a potbelly. Gerald tutted inwardly. He was often here, roaming, the unofficial guardian of the blasted heath. The potbelly glanced around for a few moments, then walked slowly in the direction of the pond to ensconce himself on a neighbouring bench. He was sweeping, eyes sweeping. Gerald could hear a footfall behind him.

Behind a straggly line of hawthorn, he caught a flash of blue and white. He watched more closely, then started to follow. The hair was dark, the figure lithe and slim. This was altogether more promising, he thought and quickened his pursuit. The early evening walker vanished from view, then turned full circle, so that he came face to face unexpectedly with Gerald.

He was not disappointed. For a moment he seemed to fall into those dark eyes in appreciation, sensing too that the boy was a nice, comfortable height. His heart was beating quicker as the boy coolly and unflinchingly returned his gaze with the semblance of a smile. Then came the well-worn ritual, the bogus, aimless walk, ending in the seclusion of a bank of ivy that obscured them both from view. Gerald walked straight towards that smile and put his arms around him.

It was the best ever, it seemed to him later, as he laid his head appreciatively on the boy's shoulder to recover.

"Where are you from?" he asked him. The first fragment of dialogue.

"Purley," said the boy, doing up his trousers. "And you?"

"Kingston," lied Gerald.

The boy tucked in his shirt and tightened his belt. "I used to go to college there."

"Oh," said Gerald, affecting interest, but concentrating more on the near perfect orb of the boy's left cheek. "What's your name, by the way?"

"Kevin," he replied.

"James," he lied, extending an incongruous hand. Then, after a silence, "do you come here much?"

"I come plenty," the boy grinned, "but no, not that often. Just depends on the weather. If it's a nice afternoon..."

After a lengthy pause, Gerald said, "it'd be nice to meet again. Have you got a phone number I can reach you?"

Kevin scribbled something hastily on a piece of card, then handed it to him.

"I'll ring you," said Gerald, but Kevin was already making his retreat through the bushes. He raised a hand in farewell salutation.

For a while Gerald stood listening to the sounds and smells of the wood, then made one last trip to the top of the mound. There were no early evening walkers, and the sun was beginning to dip behind the far line of trees. Casting a final glimpse at the view, he turned back to retrieve Coco.

It took him five minutes to return to the spot, but when he got there it was with a sense of bewilderment. Coco was nowhere to be seen. Gerald looked again at the tree Coco had been tied to, then checked if he was on the right path. After getting his bearings right, he realised he was. There was even a mat of squashed grass where Coco's tummy had patiently waited and in all probability slept. But now...

Panic began to seize Gerald and he shouted urgent yells of Coco, Coco! He had never run off before, and if he had, would have made his way back no doubt to find him with his hands full of Kevin. Then a worse thought dawned on him. What was he going to tell Annette and the others? And how come he had gone off to a woodland spot seven miles away without telling her? The wood clouded over with uncertainty, which calls of "Coco" only served to reinforce rather than dispel.

Had Coco done this on purpose to show him up? The one occasion he had really enjoyed himself, really had a good time, and then this had to happen. But what if Coco had been helped? It couldn't have been Kevin because in all likelihood he didn't know about the dog. Or did he? Perhaps it was potbelly! The ever pervasive potbelly. And maybe too he had seen behind the ivy-screen, and it was a case of sour grapes.

"Coco! Coco! Coco!" he yelled.

In the unresponsive silence, the woodland yielded nothing. He began to walk the various paths swiftly, cursing potbelly, potbelly the prime suspect. How was he going to explain this? "Coco! Coco! Coco!"

Beyond the favoured rambling spot, the woods and heathland spread out for three or four miles more. Coco could be anywhere.

He rubbed the back of his neck in agitation. What was he going to do? What was he going to tell them? Why was there nobody around, just when you wanted them? Some days it was as overcrowded as a guppy tank, but now... just empty woodland and the light was beginning to go.

He sat down for a second on a solitary bench to gather his thoughts, and felt something dig him in his back pocket. Fumbling for a moment, he pulled out a piece of card. On it was the word Kevin and a telephone number. It jogged his memory, but now was not the time to think back to their brief encounter.

He stared at it again, then got up from the bench. It was a bit of a long shot but it might be worth it.

With a few parting Cocos, he made his way out of the woods and back to the direction of the railway station. On the corner of Shelduck Avenue, and still in its original red livery, was the obliging oblong of a phone box. Reaching in his pocket for coins, he spread them out above the phone, then dialled Kevin's number.

A woman's voice answered, framed against a backdrop of squawking TV.

"I don't think 'e's back yet," she said, "but 'e's comin' back for 'is tea, I'm sure."

"Okay, thanks," he muttered.

The phone box became an enclave of gloom. The next call would have to be. . .

"Hang on," she called suddenly. "I think I can 'ear a key."

There was a long interval of suspense, during which Gerald inserted another coin. Then suddenly a rasping voice was in his ear.

"Yes?"

"Kevin? Kevin, this is Gerald."

"Who?"

"We met in the woods a while back."

For a moment the phone went muffled and he could hear a voice saying "I'm going to take this upstairs."

For a further minute Gerald shuffled in the cubicle of uncertainty, till the phone was picked up again. With no TV for accompaniment Kevin's voice sounded clearer but more mocking.

"Who did you say you were?"

"Ger-ald. We met at the…. you know where."

"Sorry, mate. I think there's been some mistake. I met a geezer called James."

In a flash, Gerald realised his mistake. He had been undone by his customary duplicity.

"And who did you want to speak to?"

"Kevin," said Gerald, almost pleading with him. "You. Kevin."

"I think you've made another mistake," the voice said.

"But I…."

As the receiver went down on him, only to be followed by the engaged tone on his subsequent dialling, Gerald had heard another confusing noise.

At the same time that the voice had said 'mistake', he was sure, in the background, just very slightly, he had heard a solitary, mischievous and yet familiar bark.

Snowflakes

The plane touched down to muddled emotions. Emotions as scrambled as the raindrops on the taxi windscreen. What a flat place it was! Over fifty years!

Before the journey she had packed and repacked the suitcase, pushing down the springy jumpers. But each time they bobbed back and snagged on the zip. They refused to lie down so she flung the heavy dictionary on top of them, transferring the documents more prudently to her hand luggage.

"Are you sure you wouldn't like me to go with you?" Bernie had offered.

But Hannah shook her head. "You'd hate it. Be bored senseless."

A myriad of deflections, excuses.

"How do you know?" he started, but Hannah's expressionless face confirmed her resolve.

"You can always ring me," he said. "And I'll be over...Like a flash." He grinned.

Sitting in the taxi it was better alone; it was as if no other conversations existed than those of functions. It was not a social trip at all, and her grasp of the language, the language she had grown up with, was now like stepping on a highly polished floor.

"Here is the hotel."

The car that was poisoning half the bus queue drew up to a square fifties-style building. The word slab and slob combined as the taxi driver sat motionless, enthroned on his leather plinth and let her stagger out on to the raindrop steps.

"Why am I doing this?" she asked herself, as notes passed to the outstretched hand and she whirled her way through the hotel's revolving door. In the hotel lobby a young girl mirrored her mother's face. She remembered, and was reminded why.

"Remembered" seemed such an inappropriate word, she reflected later, sipping a late evening brandy in the hotel's closing dining room.

Everywhere long, drab net curtains to keep everything out; night, day, everything except memory, which fluttered back in under the long shrouds in the cocooned reception and lounge.

"If you want me over, just ring." Bernie's genial voice and grin. But this was no place for Bernie. His good humour and sense of fun was not for here. And tomorrow it would begin in earnest.

"Night, honey," she could hear him say, as she stepped onto the balcony, looking at the lights of the fading, twinkling city.

In the fridge's mini-bar the can of tonic had a dent in it. She decided against it, returning it to its lonely compartment. Pressing the light switch above the bed, she could hear the murmur of traffic from the street below. The room was still light from the street lamps. The whining of the fridge. It would be difficult to sleep at night, but even so, her body felt like a sack of potatoes.

The winter covered everything, a vast landscape of snow, she remembered, and that morning the first few flakes tumbled from the skies, a presage of the hard winter that flew in from the east.

"Nothing ever good comes in from the east," her taxi driver said that morning, as he drove her towards the town hall.

"Not much better from the west either," she thought, but this remained voiceless, constrained by the lack of sleep and voids in the accompanying language.

On the way through the long unending boulevards and grey slab buildings, she tried to re-remember words. Some slipped like little fish through the net, while others remained cumbersome and immovable like seaweed.

"Here we are," said the driver. Hannah alighted and paid him, then walked swiftly up the steps. She was diverted into various offices, went up and down the main staircase, along bleached corridors. At last she stood before the translucent door.

They couldn't quite comprehend why she was there, and they lost patience a little with her halting language, but eventually they gave her the information she needed. Before going to the land registry she would need her solicitor, and so she collected one who would also have the dual purpose of speaking the necessary language.

Bernie would be mowing the lawn, she thought, adding to the suburban chaos of machines, sitting down in his fold-up chair, pouring himself a bourbon. She could do with one too, but now her solicitor would have to be her only prop. Martin, tall, bespectacled and possibly a little hostile. Why had she come? Wasn't it better to...?

She put on her glasses as they surveyed the swathes of maps.

"I just want to know," she said, "you see?" as he looked at her, devoid of expression, but nonetheless polite, attentive.

"Do many people come back to see what happened?"

"I don't think so," replied Martin. "It is too complicated, especially when SRL is involved."

"SRL?"

"Land requisitioned by State. If that is so and some state building is on it, then it is difficult, well almost impossible."

"And private?"

"Private, well different, and if there is a case, of course you can claim."

They were driving out of the city into falling flakes, which now settled on the trees and scant hedgerows.

"In England," she said, "there were a lot of those, I remember. What is the word for them?"

Martin obliged.

"But not where I live now," she added.

The snow was settling, making a featureless landscape invisible. They were back in a small town, following a number 9 tram newly plastered in adverts.

"This must be a new thing," she said, pointing to the lurid letters of the cigarette makers.

"Yes," said Martin.

"A new kind of colonialism."

Martin did not return her wry smile, but looked puzzled, defensive. They stopped in front of a block of flats, where three sets of footprints had exited from the doorway. Again they consulted the map.

"Here is the railway," said Hannah, "then this must be the timber yard." Martin nodded in agreement.

"So this here is my grandfather's land, then?"

"Yes, yes."

"And this new building is also on the land?"

Martin followed the line her finger made.

"So that means I own this land now?"

"He paused as if finally making sure. "Yes, yes, you do."

She was tired that evening when she returned to the hotel. She was the only person eating in the faded dining room, and she could see they were eager to go home. The cabbage was lukewarm, the waitress disinterested. She hadn't the energy to complain, something she knew Bernie would berate her for. She drank a vodka to chase away the cold that had penetrated into her, and walked the dimly-lit staircase for bed.

"I'm afraid," she said to herself in the darkened room. "Bernie, I'm afraid." She went to the window, looking down at the bobbing lights of trams, the rows of chimneys belching smoke…and for a moment they reminded her…

She shuddered. She could have done with another "little water", a vodka. She could feel the dry, biting wind penetrating through the fallen putty of the window. In America they never had winds like this - such cold. She was enveloped in the icy wind of recollection and a lump seemed to bobble from her stomach into her throat, half-strangling her.

Martin was at the hotel promptly at half-past eight. He helped her down the steps, half swept with fallen slushy snow, and into the immaculate car.

"I have to do this," she said to herself. They were both silent for most of the journey.

As they came nearer to their last stop she asked, "What do they think about people coming back to claim their property?"

Martin paused for a moment as if memorising or rehearsing a speech. He scratched his nose as they waited behind a bus, "People here think, well…Maybe it's strange after such a long time. And as you know it is a difficult problem. It is not easy."

They drove for miles across white, treeless country. The wind buffeted the sides of the car. Hannah began to feel a sickly chill come over her as the road sign announced they were nearly there. It seemed so normal, traffic lights, bread shop on the corner, crossing. Why was she doing this? She could order him to turn round now and go back. Maybe this was the easiest solution. But the other Hannah, the one of reason, propelled her on. Not to know, not knowing, not ever knowing, would be far worse, of course. It was not much of a choice as they stopped opposite a garage.

"This is it?" she asked.

Martin nodded, and again they both consulted the map. Two coaches passed them and then a third. The word

Oswiecim was unfurling and unfolding in her head. They looked at the flimsy map then straight ahead at the preserved horror entrance as they both tried to get their bearings. As she looked down at the squiggly lines and squares her vision blurred, but she stared again, kept on looking.

"The boundary," she said. They traced it with their fingers.

"My grandfather's land then, too?"

"Here is the end," Martin pointed.

Silence. They both sat for a moment.

And then she knew. It was what her mother, the only survivor from her family, had kept all the time from her. Never wanted her to know.

She saw a party of schoolchildren alight from the coach. The teacher clapped his hands and vaguely, haphazardly, they gathered into a line.

"It was built on some of our land, then?" she said to him, and clasped her cheeks in horror.

Martin looked again; methodical, thoughtful. "It would seem so. Yes," he nodded.

She paused for breath. "What a terrible irony...terrible..." were her last words that seemed to fade into the air.

They sat in silence for a while, watching children playing, running beyond the fence.

Martin turned the car round. He would be responsible for any necessary paperwork, for carrying out her decisions.

She looked up. Snow was falling in ever thicker flakes across the windscreen.

The Right Sort

"George!" said Norma, sharply, "Come away from that window."

"Just a minute," replied George, curtain twitching, "I think they've arrived."

They both looked intently from either side of the window, half concealed by the curtains.

A well-dressed woman was walking up the path of the house next door. The neat, semi-detached had been empty for some while. They could see her fumbling with a key.

"You're right," said Norma. "I don't see anyone else though."

"No."

"She looks quite decent," Norma remarked. "Better than that man who worked for London Transport."

"He was alright," remonstrated George.

"Oh no, he wasn't. The language! And that bag he used to carry round with him. Made him look like the plumber."

George had no weapons to counter such irrefutable arguments, but he noticed that for the rest of the evening, Norma hummed around the house in an unusually good mood.

It was the next day when Norma met her new neighbour coming up the path. She was not alone. Her elegantly tinted hair met with her warm approval. As one elegant lady to another, Norma knew good taste when she saw it. She threw a radiant smile at the newcomer who reciprocated and pointed behind her.

"Hello," she said. "These are my four daughters. Christine, Marie, Sophie and Etienne."

Norma looked shyly at four very tall and attractive girls. They smiled together as a unit.

"And I am Constance Lamot," the new neighbour continued.

"Norma Wilkinson," said Norma. "Pleased to meet you." Then, recovering her inquisitiveness. "And Mr. Lamot?"

"Oh my dear," said Constance wistfully. "You'll hardly ever see him. He's so often away on business."

Norma nodded sympathetically.

The following morning, when they were eating their raspberries in front of the telly, they saw Mr. Lamot leave the house.

He was, as Norma imagined, a smart, well-dressed man with a trim beard and immaculate suit. He carried a long umbrella.

She hurried out into the front garden on the pretext of rescuing a punnet from underneath one of the bushes. As she went out she called over to him in her friendliest voice. At first he didn't appear to hear her, so Norma pursued him along the fence.

He turned around slightly apprehensively.

"Just moved in have you?" Norma cooed.

The man looked perplexed. From his position at the window, George saw him smile frequently and shake his head. But soon Norma came back into the house dejectedly.

"He doesn't speak any English!" she wailed.

"Dear me, how could he!" replied George. "By the way, is there any more cream?"

The following weeks passed fairly pleasantly and uneventfully with the new neighbours, though it seemed to Norma that next door's bell was always ringing.

"She's a bit strict," Norma remarked. "She doesn't even give her daughters a key."

The next day saw a lorry pull up outside the house. A batch of small garden canes was being delivered. "George." She nudged him from his newspaper. "It looks like they plan on making a go of the garden. That means you'll have to get out in ours more often."

"Yes." said George.

A day or so later, when she was out in the garden making plans for the cabbage patch, she heard a dreadful screeching coming from next door.

She stood bolt upright, secateurs in hand. A window was opened. Then there was the sound of heated voices and of something being knocked over. To her surprise, she saw a pair of trousers come flying out the window. They landed on top of the rhubarb in her garden.

"Ugh!" groaned Norma.

Then came a shirt and two socks, followed by a blonde wig. The wailing grew louder. Terrified, she ran back inside the house, clutching her secateurs, and firmly bolted the back door. She quivered nervously from her kitchen window, but everything was quiet now. Birds were beginning to appear on the lawn.

When George came back that evening she told him about everything that had gone on. But in his usual dismissive way he said calmly, "They're foreign dear, and a bit more excitable than we are. That's all."

Norma remained unconvinced. "What shall we do about the trousers? We can't have them in our garden."

"Take them back," he suggested. "They look quite an expensive pair." Norma thought for a moment. "No George. I think it would be better if you took them back. Supposing somebody spotted me. What would they think?"

"Put them in a bag," he volunteered. However Norma had decided.

"Where are they?" he mumbled grudgingly.

"In the garden by the rhubarb. On the other hand maybe you should wait until it gets dark."

So George waited until the onset of darkness, and at a little after half past nine, he stole across the lawn, hoping that at that moment no one was looking out of their bedroom window.

To his surprise, however, the disreputable pair of trousers had disappeared. Instead all he could see lying on the ground was a small white card. It bore the name Henrik van Eyck, architect.

George and Norma were mystified by the whole thing. The sudden disappearance of the trousers was as uncanny as the revelation of the white card.

Nearly a week later, Norma learned that the Lamots had suddenly moved, although a number of distinguished looking gentlemen kept calling at the house.

It was her task, if the ringing persisted for too long, to send them away with the sad news that the Lamots had indeed moved.

On one occasion she even used an old Japanese phrase book she had bought in a jumble sale.

"I knew they were no good," she said one evening when George was listening to Stars on Sunday.

"How's that?" said George, "I thought you said they were decent people."

"Maybe," said Norma. "Maybe," putting away the Japanese book. "But they never did do the garden, did they? And after ordering all those bamboo canes."

"It's typical," she continued, as George turned up the radio to a volume that ensured privacy. "It's all show."

From the Door

She awakes now. The room is there. In slow motion it adjusts itself and reveals itself as the sombre, heavily furnished room, letting in winter light. She gets out of bed, groggy, half-drunk, the cold floor serving as a reminder that it is all over now.

From the other side of the bed, the side where Mark has lain, she sees the crumpled pattern of sheets. Anna draws back the curtain fully, and now her feet are fast becoming colder. She welcomes it, though not the ensuing numbness. Snow falls on the other side of the window. The dream recedes, has gone. Daybreak.

It's a long way to the nearest store, but Anna will have to drive there later, only she hopes the snow will not set in, adding more time to the winding, tortuous roads.

The kettle sings on the stove, sending its warmth across the kitchen. It's a good companion in winter; its ever readiness to heat a soup, accommodate a kettle. Through the window, the flakes are subsiding, only a thin covering on this late October day. But there will more to come, this being the harbinger of winter.

"Hi, honey!" Mark comes in from his wood-logging, his face ruddy from the cold, his nose like something a clown would wear. "Is there tea on?"

She nods. She doesn't tell him about the dream as he would only worry, but she hopes he doesn't notice that she is still recovering, for the dream takes its toll. Like a bad drug whose effects take hours to wear off.

"You going to the store?"

She nods. "What do you need?"

In half an hour, he is away again – the surrounding woods provide an endless source of work, and now the days are shorter, he must get up early to profit from the daylight hours.

The key is in the ignition, the car chokes and starts. In her mind's eye, she can see them, surrounded by them.

She judders like the engine and in a moment is sailing slowly down the hill, as if sailing can ever describe a journey by car. Almost soundlessly, the car slides down the everlasting hill. For two and a half miles she will not have to use a drop of petrol as the road curves and turns. She smiles. Her grandfather would approve, seeing as he was thrift personified.

In the store they haven't much, but she makes the most of what they have. She'll cook something from her Hungarian cookbook, with lashings of paprika.

"Someone likes their food spicy," the woman says in the shop.

"Winter's coming," Anna says. "Why not?"

She puts her provisions in the boot and heads back for home. So far no more snow, but as the weather can turn very suddenly in this hilly region, she wastes no time.

The woman waves. "See you next week."

Back in the cabin she prepares the ingredients. In no time at all, it's gone again. Mark is ravenous from the chilly air and eats three bowls of paprikaš. He falls asleep in the chair in front of the Aga while Anna reads a book.

"You'd better turn in," she says.

"You coming?" he murmurs.

"I won't be long. Just five more pages."

Again he's asleep when she enters the room. As she falls into bed, she pleads silently for a moment. "Please don't let it come again. Please let it be a calm night."

The temperatures falls and they sleep like ones who have hibernated. Anna awakes refreshed from a dreamless sleep. Mark is already up. In the night there was a heavy fall of snow.

The air is silent now, no wind, and the woods are covered in a wrap of wool. Anna works inside the house and, after the midday soup, she leaves the cabin to take a walk.

The air is still with the threat of more snow and even though her breath unfurls in little balls of cloud, it does not feel that cold. She takes a detour from her usual path, where the trees are more tightly packed together, some deciduous mixed in with pine. She goes right down to the bottom, across the frozen stream, now covered in a deep, white blanket.

She begins the ascent, the steep slope, the snow in heavy drifts.

Suddenly she gives a start. To her right, in a thicker clump of trees, she can see the eyes of some wild animal looking at her. Anna stops, frozen to the ground. She is in the dream now, but there is only one of them. She must try and run through the thick snow.

All at once there is a tearing sound, a cracking – a deep, heavy thud. Blood rushes to her head and the wood goes very dark.

She awakes now in another white place. There is something attached to her arm. She is unable to move. A white figure, a sort of angel floats towards her.

"Would you like to see your husband now?"

Anna nods, still not comprehending where she is. Mark comes in with a small bunch of flowers – where did he get them this time of year? He sits beside her.

"You gave me quite a fright," he says.

"What happened?" she asks.

"A branch came down on you in the snow. It was with the weight. You were in quite a state."

Silence. Bright flowers.

"How long am I going to have to be here?"

"A few more days. You took a nasty blow. Do you remember anything?"

"Yes, I remember it all, except getting here."

When he leaves, he gives he a kiss.

"See you tomorrow."

It's not nice, she thinks, to be alone in bed. She misses his warm body, the way he curves into her at night.

"Only a few more days," she tells herself.

Next day there is a party at her bedside. The expressions are serious, no joviality, no false banter.

"Mrs Kerr," says the surgeon, "I'm afraid you'll have to be here a little longer."

She feels anxious, her prison term extended.

"When we did our examination," he says softly, "we found a growth."

The room goes white and cold. She is lying out in the snow.

"It'll mean more tests."

The afternoon is an age. A grey cold view from her window. She waits for Mark, and wants to cry, but she can only do this when he's there. She misses the cabin and the warm stove in the hills and the tap-tapping of trees being felled in the woods. The ride to the store on her grandfather's petrol, and she wants to be rid of the painful drip in her arm.

Mark comes. She cries. He holds her. The visitors disperse. He stays late, draws the curtains round the bed and holds her to the latest hour. At last she falls asleep, whereupon he leaves, to return tomorrow.

From her window she can see the next day is warmer. There's a fine, grey drizzle in the air which gives way to rain. It'll melt the snow, she thinks, and already the view from the large ward window is admitting streaks of grey and brown, leading towards the slushy avenues.

When she stayed at her grandparents', she used to love the rain at night. She slept in a small bedroom under the roof and the rain dripped down the gutters and splashed onto the pipes. They lived near a wood too, a smallholding at the end of a lane which led nowhere. It was nice because no traffic flew past, only bikers and walkers in thick socks and clumpy waterproof boots. Her grandfather was always in the garden, always growing things.

One morning, after as spring shower, whose soothing rain had sent her back to sleep, she found him planting lettuces in the large border.

"Elsie disapproves, but I likes to use the space."

The dibber made another hole. He stood up to face her, to smile at his favourite granddaughter.

"All helps to keep the wolf from the door, he grinned.

She looked back at the swaying flowers, uncomprehending. The wolf?

Anna could see herself standing in that garden, long, long before she ever came to Canada.

She lay very still for a moment, the snow outside the window receding. Her grandfather's words, words, those dreams….. And finally she understood it all.

The predatory shapes that haunted her, relentlessly, persistently, were now unmasked.

The ward seemed much clearer, vivid even. The male nurse, who came to ask her if she wanted anything, had beautiful eyes.

She felt her left breast gingerly, wondering how much longer it would still be there. In two hours' time Mark would be on his way.

The wind tapped the window. The blood within her was bubbling, ready to fight falling trees, snow, the growth that had crept upon her slowly, stealthily….. Even the wolf.

Vegetable Plot

It seemed to her the back gardens were fast becoming like a market place. Eileen Wharton peered out of the living room at the assorted heads on either side of the fence. Wiping her breath away from the window, she gazed more intently upon the scene. Savoy cabbages were being held up for inspection, each one eliciting a soft murmur of approval. Little round marbles identified as cherry tomatoes; stubby shaped potatoes. What was happening out there? Were they going to set up a stall? Her garden, however, had little to offer on the vegetable side. There was some scraggy rhubarb, but that was about it. Otherwise, the drooping hollyhocks that bordered either side of the garden were her main exhibit.

"Come on," she called to the cat nestling at her ankles, luring it as it lazily plodded into the kitchen. It buried its head in a familiar bowl and there was an odd munching sound as she spied through the window again. Eileen was beginning to get nettled by the vegetable community. Sometimes they stood there gabbling for hours; each day produced a new lecture. She fell asleep in Stars on Sunday and afterwards wearily climbed the stairs to bed.

The next day dawned bright and sunny, and, in positive mood, Eileen decided to make overtures to the leguminous community. She would start a conversation with Mrs. Logan, whose ample backside hovered beneath apple tree and washing line. It seemed to be grazing like a giant bumble bee as it swayed from side to side. She stepped out into the garden to address its serene posture. "Lovely day," she began, as the sun slipped behind a cloud. The buttocks quivered but there was no answer. "Lovely, isn't it?" she repeated. There was still no reply. Having forgotten that Mavis Logan was rather deaf, she took the stubborn silence of the uncultured posterior to be some kind of snub. Going back inside, she gazed for a while out of the window. Washing now formed a barrier to the sun, blotting out sky and poplars alike. The battery of Logan long johns, vests and assorted knickers oppressed her. In the aftermath, she felt hurt and excluded.

A few days later, there was another assembly at the bottom of next-door's garden. Various fingers pointed to an object below the greenhouse, and there were exclamations of "Oh, how lovely!" and "Coming on nicely now." They all bent down simultaneously to examine the prize object. Mr. Logan, like some proud father, fished out his watering can and began to spray it. Gradually, they drifted back into the house, with the exception of Henry Logan, who stood wondrously admiring the invisible masterpiece.

Eileen thought she too would venture out into the garden, pick a few dahlias and satisfy her curiosity. Stepping out onto the lawn, she executed a couple of cursory snips and drew nearer to the greenhouse. She approached the fence, and, as if by chance, glanced over.

At first, she couldn't see anything, so she stared at the greenfly on one of the rosebuds and then turned round again. Lying heavily under a collection of dark green leaves, and with one yellow flower, was an enormous marrow. It looked like some kind of oxygen cylinder, green and sparkling with the water that had been sprinkled on it.

"Oh, splendid!" she beamed across to Henry Logan, who seemed lost in admiration. He glanced up. "Oh, hello... yes..."

"I wondered what you were all looking at..." she began.

There was the sound of a phone ringing from somewhere, whereupon Mr. Logan suddenly became attentive. "That'll be mine. Probably Sid from the allotment. Back in a minute."

He hurried towards the house, casting a fleeting glimpse back towards the marrow, and disappeared through the open windows. Eileen stood alone in the garden with only the dahlias and the marrow for company. A blackbird sang softly behind the fence, but she didn't hear it. Snipping a couple more plants, she waited a while and then went back inside.

"What was the point?" she muttered gloomily and settled down to watch TV.

During the evening, the marrow returned to haunt her. She saw Mr and Mrs Logan running back into the house. She hated that marrow. Even though she sat back in her chair and tried to ignore it, it kept reappearing at odd intervals. During a programme on U boats, she became convinced that what she was looking at was none other than a giant version of an underwater courgette. Hurriedly, she changed channels. "Zucchini," said a bucolic voice. It was too much. She switched off, her evening ruined. Unless....

It was some while later when she crept out again into the garden. The fence between hers and the next-door garden was low. She could easily climb it. As she landed in the adjoining garden, the pair of shears she was carrying momentarily brushed the soil. The moon lit up the glass panels of the greenhouse. It would be easy to locate that offensive vegetable. Something scuttled away beneath the shrubs as she stood in front of the impressive spread of marrow, then bent down, gripping the shears tightly in her hand.

One decisive snip and that was it. The marrow slid away from its stem, lying heavy and Zeppelin-like on top of its crushed leaves. Glaring at it for a moment, Eileen Wharton picked it up and hurled it furiously over the fence. It flew briefly through the air then plummeted. There was a deep splashing sound. It had landed either in the pond at the bottom of the garden or in the Thompson's cold-frame. The wildlife chattered away to itself indignantly, then all was quiet.

It was about midday when the theft was discovered. The police were called but they never thought to drain the pond. The marrow had vanished without trace.

For days a funereal silence hung over the adjacent gardens, punctuated only by the odd Logan expletive. Yet

Eileen noticed that if anything the kidnapping of the marrow only served to strengthen the vegetable community. There was an abiding feeling of vigilant solidarity and even after she'd been to confession for the third time, Eileen still admitted to a pervading sense of guilt. She felt as if they held her permanently under suspicion and, as a result of which, she seldom let the cat, which clung more assiduously than ever to her ankles, stray out alone at night.

Us

Now where was I? Oh, yes. Yes, you could look on it like this. A kind of... well privatization perhaps. Popular word that nowadays. All sorts of unlikely commodities ending up in single pockets. Did I say pockets? I meant hands. Even the gentle drops of dew from heaven – it's back in fashion, by the way – diverted into special companies, only to leak back through antiquated pipes into the lush soil.

I'm well read, you can see. But I digress. So the order came from... well, over there. Just follow my finger. It was costing far too much – too much to run. I know the leadership seemed new and dynamic to you, especially when they'd buried three old men on the trot. You felt you could do business with them – not my words, of course. But actually the idea came long before that.

Your other question. What were those fences keeping out? I prefer state boundary myself, but have it your way. Mostly the alarms were being set off by stray partridges and wood-pigeons, the occasional deer, or the odd East German. It was costing far too much. Can you imagine how much? Way over budget. Them, us, everybody.

So what we did, we thought we'd have a change of personnel. A revolution which was orchestrated to a simple theme. A spontaneous outpouring. And then, waiting in the wings when the ancient men had gone... You guessed it! Us! Made to look so logical and natural, but to tell you the truth we'd been waiting in those wings for far too long, so that we were getting old too.

White like beards you acquire at late evening bus stops in lonely suburbs, with not even a traffic jam to keep you company. Whereas, under us, the roads were empty; broad vistas sweeping away to vast monuments. The Avenue of this, the Boulevard of that....

So just when I was looking forward to having my name on the door, the whole thing went round again. Ha! It makes me laugh, but do you know what it used to say on the revolving door of the university library? Revolution for Academics. Quite droll that. And appropriate. Cosmetic, ineffectual. And that's what we planned to do. Just the same; merely change the names.

But then the bastards did it again. Wouldn't budge until our special selection was unfrocked. This, frankly, was quite unnerving; a second click of the cog. Now that's not supposed to happen. Is it? Is it? I should remind you, it's us who do the hi-jacking.

Thank you, Maria. Yes, could you put it over there? I won't be too long. Just tying up a few loose ends. And yes, I won't forget to drink it. Her concern for me is quite touching. I think she too was most upset by the second click of the wheel. Yes. Hails from the mountains where we had our second summer home.

Anyway, there we were. All new faces. Slightly younger perhaps, less serious, smiling even. But still they went on strike again. On strike! Said they didn't want any of our sort. Said they'd had too much of us for far too long. Well, we disagreed. Said you can't have too much of a good thing. And *we* knew best. From where we could see, yes, we knew best.

Momentarily, we were looking to use all our powers of persuasion – in the old days it would have been unthinkable – but now.... It never came to that... unlike in some places I could care to mention. After all, we have a tradition of reasonableness here.

So the strike booted us out. Put the mockers on the carefully laid plans.

The square was full to capacity. A sea of arms and voices. Something we'd taught them to do, but of course we tempered it with our icons. Every year the heroes of the parade grew younger. Miraculously, the ageing process was halted. Bald heads became a little more hairy; sagging jowls a shade more angular; bold eyes containing a braver, brighter vision.

Of course, you're right. I freely admit it. The idea came from the incense swingers. Everything was replicated. Same thing, same time of year even. Same but sweetly different.

Look now. The priests have no congregation. They've gone elsewhere; forced to live like monks in solitude. But then, what a waste! Why should we forgo life's little pleasures? After all, there's all my knowledge. A wealth of experience tempered by an experience of wealth. All stashed away, too. Don't forget, we were the ones who could travel. We made the rules, the boundaries... What else is there to do in Switzerland? I ask you! A land so clean that no one lives there. Cuckoo clocks and chocolate boxes. I made my trips to the Institute discreetly, quietly.

That cake was delicious, by the way. Pity you didn't get some. Yum!

Second click of the cog.

I then had to make my way alone.... And very nicely I'm doing, too. I've got my own little concern; my money-spinner; financed by some appropriate and appropriated funds. I gather you've had the same thing too. All your various commodities: gas, water, telephone; the lot. So here I am. I'm back in business. Look upon it as if I never went away.

We're all here in fact, in one form or another. They dare not touch us. We know too much....

Fully privatised yet individual now. We all are.

And that's the way it is. Yes, we'll show you – the way, that is – we'll show you. You can rely on us. It'll be our pleasure.

Buoyant

I am heavier in the morning, I know. As I move from the bumpy springs of my bed, I sense I am scattered on the surf of another day. The curtains drawn back reveal a pale yard lit in sun. The yard is full of dust, blown up from the farm.

Emmanuel is already in the field.

I have never told him. Easy, you would think, but not easy to confide in the one who knows you. I slink like a slug onto the cold, stone floor. The cold runs up through my ankles, supporting the rest of me and the cold pain gives way to comfort. Pain means I'm not alone, and as the farmhouse clock ticks eight o'clock, I am descending slowly the staircase of wood, listening to each incisive creak. Each creak is me, but when he stands on each polished stair, the noise is oh so different.

Breakfast takes place with a little party of friends assembled there to greet me. The china jug with the crack just below the spout. The neat row of cup, saucer, plates; the bread nestling coyly in its basket.

He's long had his, out on the fields to meet the varying light of day. He'll be back late, or maybe at lunch to meet me, except on this day I won't be there. He'll scratch his head and then say 'oh yes, the market.' He'll see me behind a barrow load of cheeses, the stale sex smell of the seafood stall, and the china junk table with everything priced....

But no, he won't see me.

At eleven o'clock I'll collect my coat, buttoning it gently round me, breathing in a second as I close the door behind me, listening to its soft, impersonal click, a click that says neither goodbye nor welcome. A click that is merely a click.

The bus will take me into town; from the square in the lonely bus shelter, I am the only passenger till we pass the library. But the library is shut today, I remember, and so my lone vigil goes on. A bus to myself, a multitude of seats with no one to squash against or feel their unspoken sighs, as I tilt in my ungainly way on my path to the soft leather.

The seat squishes as it heeds my contact, but for me there is more squish than most. Empty, all to myself the bus, the driver cocooned in his thug-proof cubicle, the solitary boatman to whom I've paid the fare.

There, I've thought about it again, just when I wasn't going to.

Emmanuel is on the field, looking up at the dwindling hedgerows. The neighbours pulled them out. They have no sense and no need of them, it seems. Ours were covered in stray birds for a while and then they were gone. The prairiefication had already started; fewer trees gave less space in which to hide myself. Those people came and didn't know the land. It was just a fat cow to be sucked dry. Dry!

And I'm sure they made the climate change. Slowly, very gradually. Emmanuel said I imagined it, but prairies are such cold places. Not like welcome spinneys on a warm, wet afternoon.

But I'm on the bus now, as I said, passing giant razors and golden butter.

I remembered a poem; a knife, golden gutter or butter, or perhaps it was the other way round.

My solitary chauffeur turns round to greet me. It is the end. Terminus, he says. Silly of me to have forgotten. 'And high above the golden gutter, a something knife sinks into something butter.' No it wasn't that word, I'm sure.

He has delivered me and already his arms are straining at the wheel. I catch a look at his eyes and think, he's not bad, but he won't have thought the same of me. What is there to wonder about a wobbly pear?

Slowly I step along the egg-box cobbles, done purposefully to trip you up. I negotiate each one carefully. I'm walking therefore on tiny mushrooms, upturned stone circles. I look up, but I can see no sun in this maze of interlocking streets. I'm still climbing, climbing, past the chapel at the bend in the road, and for a second I stare back, seeing all before me.

Emmanuel, if he's not gone home, will be sitting on a tree-trunk having his lunch. Idyllic really. I can see him among the reeds and whispering grasses.

I turn my eyes from the pictured sandwich, the sharp, white teeth with never a filling, and the golden apple plucked from one of our own espalier trees.

I can hear the murmur of an engine, and at the next bend my eyes are looking at water. Real water. I close them for a second, then look again.

The boats below look tiny, like little stranded moths skimming the water. And in their wake, their ruffled paths cause the driftwood to bob against the shore.

I'm out of breath as perhaps I told you. Or maybe I didn't. I could have held that back. Perhaps you won't want to see me, hot and bothered, little drops of sweat gathering round my eyes. And I am out of breath for I was climbing, climbing.

I'm sailing now, in a manner of speaking, past the chimneys of the town, the red characteristic pantiles, and, in the wake of the great lumbering turtle, who leaves no ripples, I can sense the eyes drifting on me, watching me, as they always have, with amusement….and derision.

I hold onto one side and step up on to a small stone plinth. From here my path will be easy. The breeze will cool my sweat, those little beads of dew and indignity that have gathered round. Gather round.

As I step out, the wind is blowing quite a gale, so that I reach out to clasp a girder to steady me on my way.

Ironic really that I should be so careful. After all….

Now the moths are below my ankles. I can see them, bobbing, swirling. Bobbing. I like that word.

The breeze blows, and I shall join them in a last descent. And as I slide through the air, I shall be feather-light, and this great cumbersome body will float upon the water, lighter than air.

Will bob and float upon the water….lighter, brighter than air.

The Silence

"**T**hey said he was even better than his old man," Bill had said to her one afternoon when she'd come back in from the garden. May looked blankly at him as he jerked a thumb in the direction of the radio. She had no idea what the music was, nor the name he had suddenly spouted.

As soon as the news came on, he turned the radio off, being his cue to come out and see what she'd done in the greenhouse.

"Bloody wars," he had said, "nothing but bloody wars!" Then looking at the rows of potted cuttings, "you done well, girl," and he'd invariably ruffle her hair like a schoolgirl and smile.

May shuddered. It was lonely now in the greenhouse, despite the late autumn sun. Lonely too in the house for that matter, ever since… She put down the secateurs and gave them a brief wipe. The soil that had accumulated on them fell as powder, and she spooned it up carefully with her hands to put it back into the sack.

"Compost never came cheap," Bill had said once, nodding sagely at the time.

Stepping into the kitchen, she could hear his voice saying, 'potting'. Potting without the t's and the g. Po'in', po'in', po'in'. May stood there for a moment. Going, going, gone, she sighed, locking the back door as he'd always told her to.

The room was silent, still frozen in time. It was the noise she missed most, for Bill was always listening to music, humming tunes. "You're eiver a hummer, or you're not," he'd said. "Some people sing and some don't."

"Yes, dear," she said, making the tea. Another wisp of wisdom, for she could scarcely remember the last time she had sung.

Guiltily now, she switched on the TV, and sat down with her tea and biscuits. It was a game show, her favourite, something Bill would never have liked or watched even. It had been Joan who had persuaded her to get the 'box'. "Bit of company," she said, "and now lots of programmes are in colour. You'd love it for the gardening. The last words had clinched it. The thrill of seeing all those fuchsias and bright red begonias. Never seen anything like it, and sometimes they went out to visit stately homes and gardens. Tours of herbaceous borders accompanied by solemn music. The kind Bill liked. And as for Last Night of the Proms....

The game show was breaking for adverts, so she got up and nipped to the loo. After all, that's what adverts are for, she'd told Joan in her first week of telly ownership. That's what them things are for.

It was damp the next morning when she awoke. Clouds of drizzle blew across the garden, so gazing out of the window, she decided she would have to change her plans. Of course it was tempting just to sit in front of the telly, but she'd made a rule, a sort of 'deal with 'im', who, if he could see her now...No viewing before 4 o'clock. Get out the house, girl, she'd said to herself. And she did.

The street was rainy, rained-on. Forty minutes would take her in to town, ten by bus, but she was in no hurry, and the air, for all its dampness, would do her good.

She walked down the tree-lined street, looking at the new green litter-bins with smiley faces. This was the bit of town with houses set back from the road, cars instead of plants in the front gardens. Then, at the roundabout, it all changed, as if the tree-lined avenue had been a mistake, an afterthought, and it all reverted to the original plan. The street began to narrow, flanked by boarded-up buildings. Then the odd pub on the corner with its creaking sign, a chippie, blousy take-away. Otherwise the shops she knew had gone.

The bus overtook her at the swimming pool, displaying a row of solemn heads in profile. She was pleased to have got so far, and to have saved the money. It could go towards a packet of seeds as she meant to stop by Eric the ironmonger's after she'd been to the library.

As she climbed the steps to both town hall and library, she noticed that the fountain was not playing that morning. She liked to listen to its splash of jets and sit on one of the benches arranged round it, but now the morning brought only damp drizzle, and there was hardly anyone around. Pushing at the revolving door, she was now in the vestibule of the library; an enormous bare entrance. The book she'd finished was given over to the assistant as she headed off in search of another. "You can take up to eight," they'd said to her once, but she shook her head. The one would do, besides she wouldn't know which one to start with.

At the 'out' counter she put her ticket down on top of the book and waited.

"It isn't the right one," the assistant said. "It's for the music library."

"Music library?" She looked again, and holding the card up she saw Bill's signature not hers.

"Where is the music library?" she asked and followed the direction of an outstretched finger. "Keep that book for me, will you?" as she made her way gingerly up the staircase to the music section.

Glancing through the large panes of glass, it looked quite nice, smaller than the main library and it had long blue curtains tapering down the windows. Tentatively, she pushed open the door. There was no one to disturb here, just an odour of wood and polished floors, a waft of cardboard sleeves containing vinyl. Then she detected another smell, as she looked around, a strangely familiar smell. It took her a few minutes to work out what it was as she walked over to the unattended counter. Bill's raincoat. That's what it was. A musty smell of raincoat.

As she looked again at his name on the ticket, she realised that he'd never once told her that he belonged to the music library. She'd often wondered why it took him so long to come back home from town, and now the answer lay in her hand, in the form of his frayed and worn out library card.

Why had he never bothered to tell her? She wondered, as her eyes alighted on three sets of tables with adjacent headphones. Perhaps he thought she'd make fun of him for listening to more stuff when he already listened to the radio at home.

"Does the headphones mean I can listen to it here?" she asked a tall, slim boy emerging from behind the counter. He nodded.

"And where do I choose the records?"

He pointed towards the window. "There's a catalogue over there. We've got cassettes now too."

May looked over again at the three seats and wondered which one was his – which would have been his favourite one. She judged it to be the one on the left.

"In his time they reckoned him better than his old man." She recalled his words and wondered who he was talking about. She'd like to listen to something that he'd listened to, but she couldn't remember any of the names.

"My 'usband used to come here," she said, straying back to the counter. "Did you know 'im?"

The boy smiled and shook his head. "Sorry, but I've not been here that long. Just a couple of weeks. What was the name?"

"Burton. William Burton."

"Maybe some of the other staff would know."

"I want to listen to something he might have listened to," May announced.

"Of course." He waited for her to volunteer more information.

"Someone who wrote music and whose dad did too."

The young man tried to restrain a smile and thought for a moment. "Well now, Scarlatti, Strauss, Mozart even and Bach."

"The last one," she said, as if suddenly jolted. "The Bach."

"The father or the son?"

"'E said he liked the son." She followed him over to the catalogue, neat rows of cards in wooden drawers.

"Well, take your pick," he said. "J.C, W.F, Emmanuel…"

"Emmanuel," she replied. "I'd like to listen to the Emmanuel."

As she took a seat she was none the wiser as to how to work the things. She sat hesitantly as the boy adjusted the headphones for her. He had nice eyes, she thought, as he bent down in front of her, and a nice, slim body just like…She smiled. There was a strange hissing sound in her ears, followed by a bang that made her jump.

"Too loud?" he asked, and twiddled a switch on the left. "Better now?" he mouthed, and May nodded.

Gazing at the lime tree beyond the window, she sat back to listen to the music. It went very fast but it had a good rhythm. Her foot began tapping away involuntarily even if it kept stopping and starting all the time. And some snatches of it even sounded familiar. Perhaps Bill had hummed it to her when they were sitting there in the kitchen. Now it went abruptly from fast to slow, and she sat back and closed her eyes.

She was coming in from the garden, the kettle was on, and he was waving time to the music. She spread her hand out as he came towards her, then held it, gently at first, very gently then clasped it brightly, tight…

Wilf

Every week she would go to the large department store in the centre of town. Every Wednesday, she stepped across plush carpets under the screeching drone of the air-conditioning to perform the same ritual.

In the yellow cubicle she would try on a dress and then hand it back to the assistant. This was accompanied by a wistful expression and a shaking of the head. Sometimes she would leave the store having purchased a towel or a box of tissues, but nothing more.

One day, when she was in the cubicle, she had a strange sensation, like a hand rubbing lightly against her shoulder. Glynis pulled at the hem of her dress and saw, quite clearly in the mirror, a hand. It was ownerless. She looked again and saw it was fondling the nape of her neck. Glynis breathed a little sigh. It seemed to have friendly intentions. Handing back the dress to the assistant, she decided to keep quiet about the hand. After all, who would have believed her?

Returning the following day, more out of curiosity, she experienced the same thing. Slipping off her shoes, she noticed a wayward palm massaging her leg with its long fingernails. It then slid up her leg and reappeared suddenly by her ear, being content to tickle her lobe.

Whether it was male or female hand, she couldn't really tell. Moreover, she neither cared, for it was a change nowadays to find a hand with a pleasant and friendly disposition. After all, it was really rather attentive. After it had massaged her neck and chased away any oncoming headaches, she handed back the dress to the assistant.

She made several pilgrimages to the store and experienced many pleasant moments with the hand, whom she now referred to as Wilf. At times she thought there was more than one hand there, but this was entirely due to Wilf's successful technique. The long fingernails brightened up many a dull, wet afternoon.

One day, however, she was called away unexpectedly to a soufflé conference in Bodmin. It was nearly six weeks before she returned.

When she walked back across the carpets of her favourite store, she found, to her horror, that everything had changed. The hanky counter had disappeared, and her own counter had been moved further round. At least, to her relief, the cubicle remained.

But when she moved a fraction closer, she found the door had been painted a different colour and a collecting box had been placed outside.

"What's this for?" she asked a bright-eyed woman sitting at a table.

"Changing fee. To cover overheads."

She felt in her pockets and pulled out a pound coin.

"Not enough."

"Not enough? What do you mean, not enough?"

"The fee is ten percent of all purchases made."

"But how do you know I'm going to buy anything?" she replied.

"I'm afraid that's not my problem, dear."

And Glynis sadly thought of the hand behind the door and went in search of other department stores, wondering at the same time if Wilf had been a willing accomplice to such artless exploitation.

Spring Awakening

Slowly, under the flat, mossy stone, a pair of arms gently stirred. Small gnarled fingers stretched tentatively into the cool spring air, while an even wartier body moved clumsily from under the stone. It was a toad.

It had been a cold winter. The snow in February had given way to rains and blustery winds of March. Frogs had quickly courted in the ponds and left. Now it was the turn of the toad.

Shuffling out of his domain, the sleepy toad felt the sun on his nose. His eyes blinked as he stood still for a moment, squatting like a piece of mud on the grass.

Then both eyes opened and the warty arms moved through the wet grass. They began to go purposefully now, but then, after these sudden exertions, the toad dived into an old hollow tree trunk and fell back to sleep.

Down in the town hall, Mr Riley was pointing at something to his colleague Tim.

"Every year 'undreds of them buggers get flattened. Just round 'ere."

Tim followed the knobbly finger on the map.

"So this year, to cut down the cost of clearing 'em, and it ain't pretty, we've produced this sign."

Tim looked at the prototype. A triangular piece of cardboard with the word Caution and a frog-like creature above it.

"I didn't know they were dangerous, sir."

"No, you idiot," said Mr. Riley. "It's to warn the motorists, thick head!"

"Oh."

"If they drive carefully, then perhaps they won't squash so many. Then at least the dustmen won't be out all morning."

"Good idea, sir." Tim thought for a moment. "I wonder why they decided to rush all at once... to the pond I mean."

"Wouldn't you if you'd spent ten months of the year abstaining?"

"I suppose so, sir," said Tim. "Maybe it's a bit like the January sales."

"Hmm," replied Mr. Riley doubtfully, failing to see the relevance of this remark.

The toad awoke again and this time it was a warm day. The sun began to dry the damp wood. A breeze blew and he began to scamper energetically through the long grass. His little warty legs took him instinctively and mechanically in the direction of the green slimy pond. The wet grass brushed his tough, dry skin. Small worms and beetles appeared in his path, but today they were ignored by the otherwise rapacious mouth. His fat belly flopped onto a tuft of grass. He was still a mile or so away from the pond, the same pond, incidentally, in which, for generations, toads had congregated for their annual ritual.

For in toad folk-lore there is a rule that requires every toad to mate at the same pond in which he first sees daylight.

He was approaching the road, less than half a mile away now. He stopped, then slipped under a stile, ignoring a woozy and slumbering grass snake. His wet toes crawled onto the dry tarmac. He paused for a minute, looking carefully around him. Beyond the stile the snake still basked.

Then, suddenly, in front of him, he saw a strange apparition. Watching him from the other side of the road was a huge toad, far bigger than any he had ever seen before. He stared at it for a moment, then again at the empty road. It was strangely deserted. Usually at this point, he crossed in convoy with a number of other toads, but then some years he'd arrived at the pond a little later than others.

He crawled closer to the toad which was magically suspended in mid air. Then he remembered his toadhood, when he wiggled in ponds as a tiny tadpole, there had been talk, yes, of an all powerful and all seeing toad.

And this year, of all years, it was appearing to him! He kept very still. He looked at it, as it calmly and serenely stared back at him. He was transfixed. It seemed to be smiling at him, shining down on him. For a moment he forgot the pond, forgot everything, even a faint, distant rumble. He lowered himself before the great Toad. He pressed his nose against the warm tarmac. The rumble grew.

Then abruptly, the Toad vanished from vision and everything grew dark.

"Would you say," Mr. Riley's boss asked, "that it's been a success this year?"

"A bit hard to say," came the reply. "I suppose you can never really persuade the motorists to slow down."

"Maybe not."

"We kept finding them at odd intervals in dribs and drabs throughout the spring and summer."

"Mmm."

Mr. Riley's boss nodded sympathetically.

"I suppose what it needs really is a few more signs."

Soft Touch

I hate Mondays, just as I hate all days. But particularly this day because I know it's all starting again. Five days of it. Five. Could be like a month sometimes when I look at it from the waning security of Sundays.

As I put down my trowel, a great, long, slithering globule trickles down my neck, my blouse, and I look up anxiously to see if it's a passing bird, but no, just a giant spot of rain. Clouds are gathering on the horizon and all because I thought of Monday.

Over near the park, Mr. Burns is walking his dog and I nod to him from the sanctum of my garden, as his overweight spaniel sideshuffles, like himself, past the telephone box.

"Nice evening. Looks like rain, though."

"Yes, " I say, putting down my trowel.

After our routine exchange, I step into the still red telephone box. There's a smell of pee and ash and sometimes cashew nuts. I call this cocktail 'panache', the very thing that's missing... A click. "Yes, hello Myra. Yes.....yes. Maybe you'd like to come next Sunday. I thought... Oh, you can't Oh well.... No, never mind. No, no. Oh, the money's running out. Hang on. Yes, I've got another one. Yes... No. No, I don't think you can on this box. They've changed it."

I put the phone down. I always phone Myra from a public phone box, because she talks too much. Spends half her life on the phone. And yet she never comes, to visit that is, because she's permanently perched on the wires between Bristol and Birmingham and Macclesfield and.... Can't say I didn't try. I take the long walk back, ruminating over Myra's words. Past the green, the church; lights on in the adjoining hall. Tea and coffee and iced cakes and its chiming clock makes time draw nearer. It's seven o'clock from the church tower clock, and flickering TV sets watch Songs of Praise or Stars on Sunday. The congregation of three leave the church, looking across the green as if uncertain which way to go. But there are no stars on Sunday, for behind the faintly glowing street lamps, the darkness stretches into Monday, Tuesday and beyond.

I'm having a boiled egg now. The walk round the green tired me out. And I remember the time when they said you should go to work on an egg. And we all laughed and said that's a funny form of transport. I'm sure it's more reliable, though, than those new slab-sided buses with no conductors and concertina doors. Mrs. Webb was stuck in them the other week and it took them an hour to get them open again. That's progress, but I'm slicing my egg and thinking of the little boy on the advert. Auntie, I wonder what's become of him, for it was auntie who was the provider of the boiled egg.

I clear the plates and now in front of the mirror. I don't like that face much, so I'll paint it up. Good and proper; redecorate. No wonder they call it war paint, for so many of us have to do battle. If Jim were here now, my fights would be over. I could tell him. He'd listen. So many of them don't now. I can feel his hands on my shoulders before he'd hug me, kiss me, run for his bus. He ran too fast one day and.... You see, that's why....

The wind's blowing up as I step outside. Momentarily, I bow into it and my eyes are covered with dust; my newly painted eyes, as I scurry towards the stop. Going past me, Mr. Jones in his bright red car. But he never stops to give a lift. Doesn't think like that. Doesn't think. His car, his terrain, his jam-jar. A foreign bottom crumpling his seats. Unthinkable. No, they don't think. I've noticed that. We're all too busy looking at the cracks in the pavement to notice each other.

I'm holding up the bus this morning because I can't find the right pass. The driver waits and holds me to ransom as I, in turn, hold them in the serenade of sighs and tutting. But all's well and we're on the move, carrying on into deepest, darkest Monday.

Outside the Corn Exchange, which will soon re-house the TV company, I get out and walk up the rained-on street. The building, the office, the turnstile gates, the security man brooding at his desk, the voiceless nod, the lift, the view from parapet and balcony.

He's not in yet and I breathe a sigh of relief. One Monday, the curtain-raiser lasted all day, and he didn't come in. By three, I knew I was in for a reprieve; suspense over as the wife rang in. Conference lasted another day, apparently. Henry too busy to phone me. Could I see to..? For a moment, I was listening to the doubt in her voice. I didn't say much. Her light, bright warble betraying....

I sit down carefully at my desk and slowly sift through the Classified Section, as I always do when he's not here. Daydreaming, I know, and as Myra says, not too many things going when you reach a certain time in life. Myra, halfway down the line to Birmingham; spirit of optimism and hope.

The lift whirrs. He's here. Outside. Outside the glass panels. Then there's a tap. A knock. No, not him. With him the door opens and a chill wind blows into the office.

"Could you sign here, please?" The delivery boy holds out a pen, despite my formidable armoury. For a moment, I thought he said "miss" and I'm wondering in what way I manage to look a miss. But he repeats, "no, here please," and points a finger that almost touches mine. Contact of the welcome kind and his eyes, dark and serious, give the flicker of a smile.

Eleven now. Eleven. The lift whirrs. Someone gets out. The breeze, the familiar step. It's him.

"Good morning, Ann."

"Good morning, Mr. Lawrence."

His immaculate suit and toothpaste stripes, sunken piggy eyes – not like the delivery boy's – and flabby, wobbling cheeks. From his lips there are traces of saliva which draw my eyes to them, and that sudden recollection of horror, when, after one long liquid lunch, he pressed them slobbering into mine. For one week after, I was the recipient of presents.

He has to touch, you see. Just as he touches everything that's female. Assembled objects on a mantelpiece of life. It's as if he's taking stock.

I wait for the errant hand to touch my shoulder, as he leans over to cast an eye on the state of my written competence. The hand will linger while he asks me anything; banalities, what I did on… Questions whose answers are never listened to. The solution, I've found, is to keep the talk as brief as possible, in the hope that the molesting fingers will go away. Monosyllables, however, are no use. They bring on the souciant charm.

"Everything okay? Sure?"

The hand squeezes my shoulder tighter, so that behind my inward shaking, I give light bubble answers.

"Had a good weekend?", as my eyes mist over the month's statistics.

Then, suddenly, my fingers are in revolt. The hand is between my neck and shoulders. The thick glass ashtray is light and pliable as a rubber ring. It sways and leaps into my hand. I jump up.

It only takes a few seconds but there's blood now, sliding down his face, like the cracked shell of a hard-boiled egg. Little streams. The fingers that were massaging my neck crumple and like a collapsible balloon, he's stretched out on the floor. He's motionless, apart from the air hissing from his mouth. There's a silence in the office. A relentless ticking of the clock.

"Yes, I had a good weekend," I say, as the fingers move further up and down, rubbing the shiny chain which hangs loosely, limply round my neck.

Poetic Licence

There were times when she had come close to strangling her, throttling her, garrotting her! When Doris announced she was coming on the October weekend too, Mildred could happily have done all three.

"It's a writing weekend, dear," she said. "And you're not a writer."

She hesitated for a moment, fearing that some long-lost forsaken manuscript had been concealed from her in an empty drawer or chamber pot and now awaited a chorus of approbation. This, fortunately, was not Doris's line of approach.

"It says you can bring guests," she mumbled, pointing to the leaflet in which a neo-timber-boarded hotel squatted over a babbling stream.

"Oh yes, so it does." Mildred remembered, cursing Mr. Pewsley's agitation for change at their last annual meeting. "You'd be bored silly," she soothed. "Really."

"Why?" Doris countered. "What makes you think that? And why go if you're bored? I mean how do you know I'll be bored, especially when you're always telling me how good the stuff is they keep churning out?"

Mildred was about to impale her sister-in-law on an imaginary railing, but instead conceded defeat. Ever since Harry had gone to the eternal snooker room in the sky, she had promised that she would look after Doris and keep in touch with Kitty.

Kitty had proved no problem and was even rumoured to be having what was termed a meaningful relationship with her postman, which was what caused Doris to descend on her.

"It's no good," she confided. "I'm in the way. I know it. And when I'm not, they keep going off to endless stamp exhibitions."

Her long weekend of being an 'evacuee' had slithered now into months and soon it was clear to 'Mildy', as 'Dor' invariably called her, that Doris was not going back.

At first it hadn't been too bad. Mildy retreated more frequently to the allotment club which met every Sunday afternoon, until Doris suddenly announced that she too had taken up an interest in gardening. That was when the first homicidal flicker involving a large pair of garden shears had taken place. Instead Mildred had diverted her frustrations on the sunken privet hedge behind the lily pond, and indulged in an unusual display of topiary. But now the writing weekend! That was really the last straw!

The taxi slid into the station car-park, a funereal bead against an early autumn sky.

"Do they always talk that much on the trains," Doris grumbled. "Thank you for this, thank you for that. There was a packet of crisps on the line, so we'll be delayed for…"

"Always," answered Mildred, who remembered that on Spanish trains they played flamenco music, and shuddered involuntarily.

"Those cows," said Doris, gesturing out of the taxi window. "There's something wrong with them."

"They're saddlebacks, "Mildred replied. "'They're meant to look like that."

At the hotel entrance, Mildred was fervently hoping that Doris would find fault with something, but now she was moving into enthused vein.

Down the hotel steps tripped Mr. Henry Pewsley in welcoming mode.

"Mildred, this must be the lovely sister-in-law you've told me about."

For a moment, Mildred was confused and looked around. Kitty, it must have been Kitty she'd told him about. But Doris... lovely?

"Welcome," he beamed, leaning forward to kiss Doris's outstretched hand.

She gave a kittenish nod of approval.

"He's got a partner," Mildred intoned later into her ear. "A retired librarian from Southsea."

Undaunted, the smile of eagerness still spread across her companion's face.

"Called George."

The smile dipped a little, then vanished rather like an expiring light bulb.

"You didn't tell me it was full of nancys."

"You never asked, dear."

That evening Mr. Pewsley was dispensing the "batting order" for the following day. "

"He gathers the subjects up and arranges who reads when," Mildred whispered, anticipating Doris's interruption of curiosity, but her "sister" was more interested in watching a grey heron paddling in the stream beyond the window.

It was when the meeting came to an end that consternation finally broke loose. Mr. Pewsley's bell, which was occasionally rung to silence the out of control ladies, had gone missing.

"I put it on the table when I came in," he wailed in agitation. "George bought it in..."

"Help us look for it, Doris," said Mildred, but instead she was addressing an empty chair, as the resident cuckoo was now walking briskly across the car park.

They searched well up to dinner, having little time to digest the sherry, and as they chewed forlornly over appropriately named minute steaks, it seemed a cloud had fallen over the assembly. Miss Albuquerque helped Mr.

Pewsley to his room. What was to become of them all? Without the means to silence the riotous ladies – although occasionally there was one token gentleman – only anarchy would prevail.

"Everyone's gone to bed early," Mildred moaned. "Very early. And all because of that missing bell."

"Bell," said Doris. "What bell?"

"Mr. Pewsley's instant rapier," replied Mildred. "He's very upset."

"Was it a little white china thing with a naked limbo dancer on the inside?"

Mildred was looking in horror at Doris. "You didn't!" she cried. "You've broken it!"

"Nothing of the sort," Doris replied. "I took it to reception. I thought it had got mislaid."

An instant vision of a room reduced to chaos, of various rheumatic knees crawling under tables, of cloths being carefully unwrapped leapt into her mind. And all for nothing. She knew Doris should never have come, knew it would be no good. But then, as she reflected, it was Henry's suggestion, after all, to bring along guests this year for their biggest and farewell bash.

"Why did you have to interfere?" she snapped. "They're probably searching half of Hertfordshire by now, and there it is lying in reception."

Doris was in no way contrite. "Well, if that's the thanks I get for trying to help, for being a responsible citizen, for wanting to play my part, then I'm off to bed. Sort yourself out!"

At that very moment, Mildred thought she heard a far-away waft of the Hallelujah Chorus, but when she stepped down into the bar ten minutes later, they were playing Georgie Fame. Oona Pookenberger, actress and radio star, who'd once made a guest appearance in The Archers, was sitting in front of her gin and tonic.

"Say, wasn't that bell thing a no-no? Everyone's gone to bed. Who could have run off with it? Have you written your story yet?"

"Oh yes," Mildred smiled, at the same time rummaging in her handbag. It was not until the third and final rummage was complete and she sat down again, listening to the ample cushion sigh beneath her, that the awful realisation set in. She was one story light. Had brought only one instead of the customary two.

The bubbles on Oona's drink looked flat.

"I'm off to write mine," Oona confessed. "You know me. It's usually a four in the morning job. Then I'm so knackered, I have to pinch myself to keep awake in the stories."

She downed the rest of her drink. "Goo' night, honey."

"Good night," said Mildred. She sat in glum realisation. Doris. It was Doris. She'd been so distracted by her coming on the weekend, that she'd forgotten her story entitled "Kiki the Parakeet". It was probably lying on the bedside table, pages curling up in the dry, residual heat of the bedroom, waiting for the audience it craved. But it was not to be.

"Would madame like e-something to drink?" A voice of consolation cooed in her ear. She looked up to see the red and white liveried barman collecting the empties. For a moment she was falling into those dark eyes, tumbling into a bottomless well...

"Yes, I would," she said.

"Yes, madame," he said, in a voice that was both attentive and subservient.

"What is your wish?"

"Well you, actually," thought Mildred, but instead was mouthing the platitudes "a sherry and...where are you from?"

"Barcelona."

"What's your name?" before he had even time to finish.

"Javier," he spluttered, "but no one can manage that name here, so when I work in Bakingstoke, they call me Darren."

"Cheers, Darren," said Mildred, feeling like she could run round the park.

"And have one yourself too."

It occurred to her afterwards that Darren may have misheard "have one" for "have fun", but as he was showing her the carpets in the servants' quarters after the bar closed, she was hardly going to complain.

As she crept smugly from his room at around four in the morning, she thought she could see a light on under Doris's door. Had she been waiting up?

Deftly, to avoid detection, she slunk silently across the carpets and clicked the door to. She would celebrate by drinking the contents of her mini-bar. But first, the matter for which she had come. The story.

Pen was gliding swiftly across paper. Inspired by Darren and his cocktail shaker, words flowed, poured even, and very faintly, in the distance, she thought she could hear the rhythmic tapping of Oona's typewriter.

The next morning, she staggered in to breakfast. Feeling some affinity with the scrambled egg that lay splattered on vast oval plates, she thought back with grateful weariness to the nocturnal antics. Two bursts of creativity. She had never done it before, as she smiled quietly to herself, whilst avoiding Doris's questioning gaze.

"I knocked on your door."

"I was writing my story."

But Doris continued to stare disbelievingly at Mildred's wrecked appearance.

"Finished it?"

"Oh yes," Mildred nodded.

As usual that lunchtime, they were across the road in the pub, looking wistfully at the jugged hare casserole that would sabotage and confuse appetites for the hotel evening meal.

"Did you finish your story?" Oona P. asked.

"Yes," said Mildred.

"I'm doing my second one tonight. By the way, where's your sister?"

"That's a point," said Mildred, who had happily forgotten her. Perhaps the thought of having to buy a drink had left her languishing in the sanctuary of the hotel.

It was during the prawn salad that Mildred, anticipating an attack of wind, declined a second drink and slipped back across the road to the hotel. Feeling mildly guilty as she passed the hotel reception with beery breath, she looked in at the bar. Alas, no Darren as yet and no Doris either.

She ascended the staircase and took out the absurdly large room key. The bed was made up, the pillaged contents of the fridge shipped away, and there, to one side, was a note on the table. It was then that Mildred turned half-anxiously to the new manuscript perched on a bedside chair.

"I read your story," Doris had written, "and I was incensed. I know of course that literature acts as some kind of confession, but if that's the sort of thing that happens on your weekends, then I wish to have no further association with it. You should be ashamed of yourself. At your age! And with a Spaniard too!"

"Catalan, actually," thought Mildred, in a pedantic moment that would have done Doris proud.

"I've decided I'm going to move back home rather than run the risk of being resident in a brothel. In fact, I shall probably contact St. Martin's convent and enquire about late vocations. Yours, in great disapproval, 'Doris'.

This time the room took on a golden glow. The writing weekend had worked like none other. She would buy Mr. Pewsley a stack of hand bells. She could hug him. She would make over half her house to Darren, who was wanting to give her Spanish lessons. And she would write all her stories well into the night now.

All this, she thought, as in the distance, building up to a giant crescendo, came a massive Hallelujah chorus.

Stumbling in the Dark

I look on Charlie as my enlightener, my unofficial Minister of Culture. Usually, about Wednesday, the phone rings and he's offering his latest suggestion. He's into foreign films at present, studying for some French and Spanish exams.

"Bunuel," I say, anticipating his current trend. We've seen 'That Obscure Object of Desire' and 'The Diary of a Chambermaid.' Generally his choices don't disappoint.

"No," he says. "Maur-ice." The stress is on the second syllable, which makes me think it's French.

"Maurice?"

"No, Maur-ice." Second syllable again.

"Is it foreign?" I seem to see the hills of southern France, a swarthy, dark-haired urchin misunderstood by his peers. It could be me, in fact.

There's hesitation as if he's having a puff from a surreptitious ciggy, but which I know can't be true after he puked on a spliff at Fiona's party. Luckily I managed to open the back door in time. "No, I don't think so," he says.

We're not far from the entrance of the Bald Faced Stag, a whacking great corner pub we've yet to enter. It's full of my ancestors' relations supping copious pints of Guinness. As we climb the cinema steps, ducking out of a northerly wind, I catch sight of the poster of what we're about to see; the name of the director whose films are like staring at rolls of Laura Ashley wallpaper and I groan inwardly.

"Dave said it was good," says Charlie as if guessing my thoughts.

Dave is another guru, an oracle on films. He specialises in one word critiques. He generally goes to the cinema on his own, chooses the matinees, which do not interfere with his drinking habits. Twice if he likes it. He seems to have some sort of arrangement with the local management.

"Oh well, then."

The sarcasm is lost on Charlie, slim, fair, good-looking and amiable. I decide that he's not unlike James Dean, a dimple on his chin, but much taller. In fact, it was Charlie who pointed out how short in fact actors were. Small people compensating for lost ambitions. I had better not say any more. I have no wish to offend anyone...

Charlie is wearing his tight fitting jeans; holes worn away where his bony knees project. At least I'm told they're bony because whenever we have a lift in Greg's car, Sarah, the extra and possibly illegal passenger, always opts to sit on Charlie's knee. At times I envy her position, her privilege as she flicks her long hair from side to side, flopping away like rabbits' ears.

We sit in our usual part of the cinema. Charlie prefers the end of a row. This is to allow his legs to drift off into the aisle in moments of feeling cramped, of boredom possibly, or even both. Occasionally, his feet wander out beyond the rows of seats and he unwittingly trips up groping latecomers stumbling in the dark.

The film is slow. It's some sort of costume drama, one of Charlie's, and incidentally Dave's, pet hates. I fidget, find my attention's wandering and feel a momentary regret at the lack of subtitles. But Charlie is watching, eyes glued to the reliable and familiar consort of players. For my part, I like the ones with unknown actors; people in their own right. That way I can't determine whether they're playing themselves or...

My eyelids are heavy. It's warm in here. They're succumbing to the gentle force of gravity, lowering like a cow's in the fields. My leg slides out towards Charlie's and stays there. After a moment or two, I feel the warmth of his thighs seeping through my trousers and a reaction follows. I gaze at him in profile, observe him watching the film, see the flickering lights of the big screen throw shadows onto his fair hair, cast reflections in his eyes. The darkness hides my trouser pyramid, already stuck on a steep incline. I adjust myself as I'm caught uncomfortably, whereupon a voice behind me hisses, 'Stop fidgeting!'

"I'm not!"

"Yes, you are. You're in my eye-line."

There's a stut from the row behind and I'm beginning to regret not having sat in the back. I fumble around for a moment or so – there's another stut – and I take a tangerine from my pocket. It sends out its scented waft as I pierce the warty skin; a zest to distract a few studious, contemplative noses gazing in front of me. I flick the pips between my fingers and I see someone clasp the back of their neck as if they've been stung by a midge.

"Stop it!" says Charlie.

"Stop what?"

"You know." He sends a corrective fist against my thigh and I adjust to the shock of a forthcoming bruise. I wonder if my pyramid is visible in the alternating lights and decide to slide my sweater across me.

I find the subject of the film surprising. It's a love story, a homosexual one. Repressed and unrequited love. Why has Charlie chosen this? I move to one side and sense the simultaneous disapproval behind me. The film meanders on. I find I don't really care; lack empathy. Am only aware of the hardness of the cinema seat, the stiffness in my… It's just the repressed upper classes of a non-tactile society. I think about the sentence again and quite like it. I must remember it for some essays. I'm also of the opinion that the two leads are not attractive enough; they seem overly wholesome, far too clean.

But suddenly and quite unexpectedly, the film changes. A new character enters the stage. He's a Mr Scudder, of lowly class and not from the prevailing refined mould. He shows resourcefulness. Now he's cunningly placing a ladder against Sir's window, mounts the ladder, climbs through the window… and then mounts Sir. I'm quite enjoying Scudder and his boldness, regretting only his lack of height. He's not like Charlie to look at, whose long legs have to drift into the aisle for space. We witness Scudder's tender intimacies. I glance across and see that Charlie's legs are actually cramped up. He's watching avidly, screen lights dancing across his face.

Back to Scudder now. He's underneath the blankets, blowing away collected years of bedroom dust as well as Sir…

We stumble out into the dark. The film was too long; too late now to go for a pint. Charlie asks me for my opinion and I give it. He taps me gently on the shoulder as we part, like a bishop to an archdeacon perhaps. He is my film educator, my mentor in the world of celluloid, and to him I'm more than grateful. I see him turning down the lane, disappearing into darkness.

And in my mind's eye, as I walk home along the frosted streets, I see him clambering up the ladder whilst I am softly stirring in my sleep. The wind blows away the curtains to reveal his entry, triumphant and knowing. There's even a fanfare of trumpets. All conquering.

All Things

"I'm so pleased to see so many of you at the meeting!" The Dean beamed at the assembly wilting in the heat.

"I'm afraid Miss Rushforth won't be here," said Geoffrey eager to impart the news. "She sends her apologies, though."

The Dean appeared a little pained at the sudden interruption. His preference was for a longer, unpunctuated prologue.

"And I was wondering also if Any Other Business could be brought forward in the order of things," pleaded Celia. "So often we run out of time and it tends to get squeezed out."

The Dean gazed round at the more inactive members of the group. "Does anyone have any objections to Celia Robinson's request?"

As inactive members they remained silent, although one or two were gently shaking their heads.

Geoffrey was meditating on the aforementioned word 'squeezed'. It was a judicious selection that somehow encapsulated the essence of democracy, or what he called 'Barchester' democracy, where the platform for free expression and new ideas would mysteriously evaporate and vanish. His gaze wandered through the deanery window where a large bovine was shading itself under a spreading chestnut tree. As the bovine relieved itself of an assortment of selected grasses, Geoffrey wondered where the adjective 'spreading' may have come from. It was a poem he had read a long time ago, but not about a cow – something else. Now what was it?

"So we've agreed the new colour of the litter bins in the Close is to be a striking yellow," summarised the Dean.

Had they voted? Had he missed the chance to raise an assenting hand?

"Good!"

"Why are we changing the colour of the litter bins?" enquired Geoffrey in the briefly designated coffee break.

"Well," said Celia. "I wasn't exactly sure myself but some of the more short-sighted members of the congregation find the current green shade acts as a kind of camouflage against the colours of the lawns and the yew hedges."

"Oh," said Geoffrey. He wasn't aware that the congregation went round with huge deposits of litter to place in the provided refuse bins. Surely it was the tourists and visitors, and as they were much younger they would have no problems with colour distinction?

"Can I welcome you back from your tea and coffee?" invited the Dean.

Celia wolfed down the remains of her Eccles cake. As Dean Worsthall glanced briefly out of the window, the occupant of the chestnut tree shadow relieved itself vastly. Geoffrey noticed this seemed to happen more frequently when the Dean was about and almost as clockwork if the same member of clergy happened to pass by.

"Now to an issue which I'd like to present before you."

The assembly wiped away the traces of Garibaldis, Morning Coffees – although it was afternoon – and stray currants from the aptly named rock cakes. Celia took a last gulp of tea to ease a putty-like object that seemed to have got wedged in her gullet. The Dean gave her an unpleasant look.

"It has been felt that it is now time to vacate the Lawrence field of animals. The field in question is, as you know, opposite the deanery and the one you are able to see from out of the window."

Almost as if instructed by a tour guide, the group glanced as one out of the deanery window.

"It would enable people, such as yourselves, to take in the splendour of the lime trees and the horse chestnuts!"

On a point of order, Geoffrey noted that they were actually sweet chestnuts but felt it might be unwise to interrupt.

"But there have *always* been animals in the field," protested Marjorie. "*Always!* It's part of our rural tradition. Our heritage."

"Maybe," continued the Dean, "but I think the persistent odours may be offensive to some."

"What odours are you referring to?" ventured Geoffrey.

The Dean pursed his lips, grabbed the edge of his cassock but did not accord the questioner the dignity of a reply.

"And who are the *some?*" insisted Marjorie.

"I'm not sure our visitors appreciate the things that we take for granted," replied the Dean.

The tourists, thought Geoffrey. He's only interested in the travelling populous that augment the cathedral coffers.

"Not only the odours," continued the Dean, "but I have had a number of complaints about the animals' behaviour."

Complaints, thought Geoffrey? Behaviour? It sounded like an end of term report. Not only that but it seemed they were living in a country accountable to customers!

"You mean we should issue a code of conduct to the animals?"

The Dean afforded Geoffrey the same muted reply he gave earlier.

"What *kind* of behaviour?" enquired Marjorie.

Celia blushed at her colleague's question. There had been one or two problems with the donkey at the bottom of the field, which prompted some of the passing children to ask awkward questions of their parents. There was also the incident of the pony, believed to be called Douglas, mounting a sheep.

"The Chapter have agreed that this is something we should operate for a while at least," continued the Dean.

"But what's the point of having a field with no animals?" persisted Marjorie.

"Will it be a wildflower meadow?" asked Celia hopefully.

"And if there are no animals, will it be open to members of the public?"

Geoffrey shuddered. He had a sudden vision of half-naked, wildly inebriated, large-bellied men lying in various comatose positions across the field.

"Certainly not!" snapped the Dean. "The barriers will remain!"

"I see," said Marjorie. "So the unoccupied field is to be a small paradigm of paradise?"

The Dean appeared not to hear her.

"But there are horses on the city badge!" pointed out Geoffrey, feeling that a historical approach might be more successful.

The Dean winced in irritable fashion, glanced out of the window, where the inevitable happened, and then at the clock.

"Any Other Business?" chimed Celia hopefully.

But the Dean had removed his glasses and was packing up, shifting folders around as if they were destined for some invisible cupboard. "Thank you all for coming, everyone. Our next meeting will be…"

"The twenty-fifth," piped up an otherwise silent Emily.

The Dean beamed. He would probably appreciate a meeting packed full of Emilys and her kind. "Thank you," he repeated. He was out the door.

The following Sunday the Alexander hymn was sung at the morning service; 'All things bright and beautiful'. As Geoffrey put on his glasses to scrutinise the words, he noticed that Marjorie was singing more vociferously than usual. She was directly opposite the ornately dressed figure of the Dean. Oddly though, beneath the clouds of incense, he did not reciprocate her enthusiasm.

The Wife of Bath

They told her how she'd be feeling – how she *would* feel – describing a range of emotions which read like a shopping list. They knew, of course. 'Trust me, I've been there," each of them said.

She had met Henry at a cricket match. It was over on the sports ground which has now been turned into a supermarket. He was tall and lean and kitted out in baggy cricket whites. She had been helping her cousin Theresa with the tea – a mixture of cucumber and egg sandwiches and a collection of gently perspiring fairy cakes. They took tea at ten past four.

She was slicing the cucumber to Theresa's exact specifications, placing them on a dish to be liberally sprinkled with salt. "Takes off the excess water," Theresa explained. "Mind you, these are beauties. My Tom grew 'em."

Jean was cutting away the hard skin, removing the unsightly bumps and truncated spikes. She had never seen cucumbers like this before.

"They may look unappealing," Theresa had explained. "But when you eat 'em, they just melt in yer mouth."

Jean was sampling a slice when Henry strolled in. He only said one word, 'My!' and walked out again.

After the game, in the bar – despite tasting the bitter vinegar of defeat – he was more loquacious. He praised the sandwiches, the spread, the rock cakes even!

"I was only doing what Theresa said," Jean explained in an attempt to demystify the process.

Thereafter, she was at most games, a willing accomplice to the labours of Theresa, chopping, arranging, slicing, stacking… At the end of each game, Henry would come and chat with her – tall, lean, earnest but with the occasional smile.

When the season was over, after a total of several hundred cucumber sandwiches, he proposed to her. To her surprise, she accepted, though it later occurred to her that they had never really been out together. Romance lay confined to the cricket field on either side of its prescribed boundaries, the wooden clubhouse and the paraffin-lit bar.

"Where would you like to go, then?" he asked.

Jean remembered that most couples went to the pictures and sat in the back row.

They stepped into the over-illuminated cinema foyer, as light as the clubhouse was dark and gloomy, with a pair of adjacent clocks foretelling their future. 'If you come in now,' said one, 'You will leave at ten past ten,' advised the other.

There was something in the reluctance of Henry's wallet, a wince at the price of the Upper Circle that should have told her something. But Jean was still basking in the radiance of the foyer, the sense of expectation and the art nouveau decor – or was it art deco? – to pay too much attention. In the interval she asked for an ice lolly. Again the wallet hesitated for a second.

It was only after they had tied the knot, honeymooning in Hastings, that Jean realised the full extent of Henry's slavish devotion to sport. It was not just confined to cricket. There was also the football season, which seemed to go on for much longer. In May, when the two overlapped, Henry was faced with an agony of indecision. Fortunately, however, he did not play football, content instead to be an enthusiastic listener and spectator.

"I was never quite quick enough," he confided to her.

He followed it mainly on the wireless. To Jean it sounded more histrionic than cricket, which was more akin to the relaxed nature of cucumbers. The reporters on the radio, or whatever they were called, used to shriek and let out a series of blood-curdling cries, a shrill litany of ejaculation. Then Henry turned his sports attention to ice-hockey and horse racing.

During these periods when he was loath to be disturbed, Jean read in the upstairs room.

There was plenty of time for reading now and in her frequent visits to the library she forged an enlightening literary relationship with Mr Appleton, the deputy librarian. He appeared to know something about almost every book that lay on the shelves. From historical romances, Jean glided to the sleuthing worlds of Marjorie Allingham and Raymond Chandler.

"I prefer the dialogue to plot," she confided one evening in the library. Mr Appleton nodded. "I particularly like the line 'she was the kind of woman to make a bishop stick his foot through a stained glass window.' Or something like that."

She recited it to Henry later but on reflection her timing was bad. Wolverhampton Wanderers had just been routed five-nil. "Does that mean they don't have a home ground?" she asked him one day, trying to show a friendly interest. Henry merely grunted then made an urgent 'Shush!' sign and turned back to the radio.

Jean found herself longing for the comparative freedom of cricket; the late spring and summer days that gradually melted into autumn. She liked the pleasing sight of boys in cricket whites, some barely in their teens. And then no sooner had the season started than it appeared to be over. She noticed the dew collecting on the heavy roller behind the sightscreen, the gradual fading of the light and a damp mist which crept over the hedgerows.

Dreading the claustrophobic atmosphere of the shorter days, the radio, the football and winter, she had it in her mind to leave Henry. He probably wouldn't have noticed other than his breakfast was not on the table. She could have lumbered out with heavy suitcases while he was listening to those interminable rugby results.

However, her contemplation of departure was unexpectedly derailed. Much to her surprise, she fell pregnant in her late thirties. How could it have happened she asked? How? But then she remembered there had been a four-hour power cut halfway through the World Cup. Rosie's entry into the world effectively blocked off any escape.

Although it was never actually said, Henry seemed disappointed with Rosie, preferring perhaps a male heir, a kindred spirit to accompany him to all his sporting ventures. But the time with Rosie was like a return to summer. Henry coming back home late in the evenings would only see her at weekends, his devotion and preoccupation with her more similar to a passing train.

Rosie grew up fast. In her early teens there were boyfriends purring like tomcats at the garden gate. At the earliest opportunity Rosie met a handsome sailor and quickly fled the nest.

Jean was left with Henry…and the radio. She continued with her reading. Mr Appleton was still at the library.

"I think it's time to go in another direction," she said to her literary adviser one day. She found herself enjoying novels with sex in them. Some even had positions she'd never tried with Henry. Just like in cricket, he always fielded in the same 'position', which she later learned was 'gulley,' although she had been intrigued by the oddly named 'silly mid-off.'

Why silly? Perhaps that was for her. For falling for Henry and not moving on. She had been caught in mid-flow on the square leg boundary and had never really weighed up the alternatives.

"I'd like to try the classics," she said to Mr. Appleton one morning, moving onto another shelf in the library. She scrutinised a selection of books she had gathered.

"Ah, Chaucer," said Mr Appleton, peering at the small print.

He was more attractive when he removed his glasses. Rugged almost. She couldn't imagine him on the cricket field, though. More in the pavilion making the fish-paste sandwiches.

"The language is a little difficult but you'll find there's a glossary at the back." He thumbed through the pages to show her then read the first line of the Prologue in what sounded like a type of Brummie twang. "The dialect of the East Midlands," he intoned solemnly.

But Birmingham was surely west, Jean thought. She ploughed heroically through the Prologue with the help of Cuthbert Appleton. Then came the characters themselves, a diverse collection of folk. She found herself particularly liking the dialogues and exchanges when a tale or a prologue had finished and in this she especially admired the Wife of Bath.

"It's all right if you can understand the words," grumbled Henry when he saw the book.

"I do," she replied smugly.

He turned the book over and gazed at the back cover. "Ninety-five pence!" He put it down immediately. She omitted to tell him that her own copy, over which she could freely scribble, had been generously paid for by Mr Appleton.

What price literature? What price enjoyment or enlightenment? It took pride of place firstly on her dressing table and then on the sparse bookshelves in the sitting room. Perhaps her excess of 'extravagance' and devotion to the Wife of Bath – the world's first literary feminist, as Mr Appleton had called her – had given Henry the idea of buying a telly.

"We've got enough put by."

She was sure there was a fortune put by but was unable to estimate how much.

"It'll be good for the sport," he reassured her, forgetting that she was a bystander rather than a spectator.

Henry's impending retirement meant that he could spend most of the day in front of what was called 'the box.' Cricket, inexplicably punctuated by horse racing and athletics,

Wimbledon fortnight, Saturday football in the evening and mid-week soccer matches. The list was endless.

Jean was wondering about taking a degree with the Open University but Henry was disparaging.

"Studying is for youngsters when they leave school. Not for sixty-three year olds."

"That's why it's an Open University," she wanted to say but Henry had returned to the confines of his newspaper.

She got the syllabus from Mr Appleton in the library.

"It's quite comprehensive," she said looking at the list of books.

"You've probably read most of them," he replied.

"And there's Chaucer too. And poetry."

One evening she came back from her library visit noticing that Henry lay fast asleep on the sofa. The TV was still flickering. She went upstairs to shut the bedroom window, which was still open in the breeze, when she spied the Wife of Bath lying on the floor. Bending down she picked up the book and saw that one or two pages had worked loose. She ran a finger over them to smooth them down. Only when she peered more closely did she realise that *two* pages were in fact missing. Just by the fold in the book there were now jagged edges where the sheets had been removed.

Who could have done it? Who would want to do such a thing? There could only be one culprit! The grandchildren had not been visiting that week and the house had not entertained another guest. She ran quickly down to the sleeping bulk of Henry.

"What is the meaning of this?" she cried, turning off the telly and holding up the book with its violated shreds.

Henry stirred, grunted and gazed up in surprise. It took him a few minutes before he understood what she'd said. "Oh, that," he said. "That dirty thing!"

"It's *my* book!"

"You don't want to be bothered with that kind of nonsense. I looked up two or three of those words in the back."

"But you *never* read my books!"

"No, dear. But when the content is…"

"When the content is *what*?" She realised she had never really yelled at him before.

"Filth! Debauchery! Nothing more. I'm not having it! Not having it in *my* house!"

My house? *My* house? Two people had lived here and once it had been her. So who was she then? The lodger, the sandwich lady, the cucumber slicer?

Henry got up quickly and put the telly back on, its increased volume barring any discussion.

It was two weeks before conversation reverted to normal, an obligatory period perhaps for a statutory sulk. But not on her part. Henry studiously ignored her, averting his eyes and steadfastly refusing to return to the subject. The appropriate sentence, the apposite punishment had been meted out. The book had been dealt with accordingly and it was a mark of his magnanimity that it had not been confined to the dustbin or chucked into the incinerator. But somehow the 'normal' was never fully regained. A kind of Cold War fluttered through the house and all because she had questioned his judgement; for having protested and indulged in what *he* saw as literary filth and pornography.

Perhaps it was an ironic revenge on the Wife of Bath herself, she wondered. For had not the self-same lady removed a page or two out of her husband's book which had been derogatory towards women. Was it possible that Henry knew more than he let on and had attempted to level the scores?

She found him early one afternoon. At first she thought he'd fallen asleep during the racing results – something he often did. But his posture was different this time, his mouth was open and he was gazing…

They told her, both at the church and the W.I, her other two former places of refuge besides the library. They explained to her how she was feeling and how she *would* feel. There were various stages, they said. They listed them.

Jean had never been fully committed to the W.I, regarding her attempts at jam and lemon curd making as woefully below the approved standard. From time to time she trundled out the home products expected of her but little more. They called in on her, invited her to functions, said they would put any of their surplus flowers over by Henry's headstone.

Jean was walking through the churchyard one morning when she saw a container squatting there. A vase of orange and pink chrysanthemums in front of the dedication to Henry. The clouds lifted for a moment and the churchyard was bathed in bright sunlight. The momentary illumination seemed to her symbolic.

It was a sudden gesture on her part, a descending arm that plucked the blooms from the pot. A similar movement perhaps that had also rearranged the pages of the Wife of Bath. She clutched them tightly to her for a second, noticed their musty scent. If she wasn't mistaken there was an essay on these very same flowers by D.H. Lawrence.

At the bottom of her basket were a few spare pages of newspaper. Carefully wrapping the flowers in the grubby paper, she left the silent churchyard and headed out into the lane. There were daisies swaying in the breeze as she strode quickly and ever more purposefully, towards Mr Appleton and the library.

Lamentation.

There, that's better. I'll just sit down for a moment. It's been a busy day. Oh dear! I have to be careful not to sit on me sting, otherwise it can be most unfortunate.

Me sting? Well, everyone has one. It's an ovipositor, actually, only something went wrong. Aunty Doris blames it on 'evolution'. Evolution! It sounds like a cold. So now all the child-bearing has become a monopoly. Gladys, the egg-layer's called. Breeds like rabbits. ..

I'm a bit of a republican at heart so I shan't call her the Queen.

Then there's the colours. Shocking really. A little garish, I know. Bit like a traffic warden's or a ticket collector's. I'm not entirely sure which came first. You'd better ask Doris the evolution expert.

And now to the most pressing thing. Some will call it behavioural patterns but I feel I must speak up for our much maligned breed!

In't beginning we were all tee-total. Truly, we were! But, you know, wi'out word of a lie, and I speak from the bottom of my vespic heart, somebody laced all them apples! Spiked 'em! All those Coxes, Golden Nobles, Beauty of Baths… So we all became pissed as parrots. Drunk as judges…

It's worse down South, apparently. The abundance of fruit. Orchards. And the behaviour, honestly! Always had it better down there, they have.

What to do then, you say? Well, I'm sure it could be sorted out. There must be an ovipositor place somewhere where they can sort your ovipositor out. I'm told it's a bit like a vasectomy – only for girls – and in reverse. And if that were to happen we'd all be layin' eggs instead of stinging folk.

Do you know what I heard on the back of a Ramsbottom bus one morning? I was a little tipsy and had fallen in through the window. There was this man – he'd had a few like me – talking about reincarnation.

'If I come back,' he says, 'I want to come back as a wasp and sting everyone who stung me!'

I were speechless! It were a number 27 bus.

This Sceptred Isle

The elderly King sat on his throne and said, "Know that we have in three divided this kingdom."

There was a brief pause, a moment of reflection.

"Is that a good idea, daddy? You know, a little divisive? We're actually quite happy as we are, aren't we Regan?"

"Absolutely, Goneril. Have another think, daddy!"

The King gazed at his three loving daughters, threw a quick look at the stars and then returned to his affectionate brood. "I'm a little disappointed, my dears. In the interests of essential tragedy, not to mention the requirements of plot, or the inevitable appeal to Tudor audiences, who will have been more than familiar with the strife and division of Civil War which preceded this glorious reign, I feel we should persist with the disharmony theme and my foolish if not erroneous decision. What say you, Cordelia?"

"I'm with my sisters, daddy. Although I cannot exactly heave my heart into my mouth – it would interfere with my medication – I think they're absolutely right. They are as wise and beautiful as their names. After all, we don't want you wandering about on a blasted heath at night in the company of madmen, disinherited dukes and dubious bastards. In all likelihood you'll catch a chill and who'll have to look after you then?"

"Well I will," grumbled the Fool. "And I've already booked a holiday in Bongor Regis."

"It's Bognor, you Fool!" they all said.

"And daddy," continued Goneril, "as you said yourself, to divide this splendid kingdom into three would be an erroneous decision. If you were to disregard and deny that inherent knowledge and telling insight, in spite of your advancing years, it would be sheer folly indeed.

"I see," replied the King. "Well I must say I don't really fancy a blasted heath at this time of year. That gardening I did yesterday has given me a touch of lumbago. Someone should really do something about that bindweed. And I'm greatly touched by all your concern. All of you."

"He that hath a little tiny wit…"

"Thank you, Fool," they all said.

"So we'll call it off then, daddy?" chirped Regan.

"I think so. For the time being," replied the King. "Now how about a nice glass of mead everyone?"

A Gesture of Brotherhood

"They should be coming about three," Beryl announced.

Henry Rowley looked up. He had little enthusiasm for these kinds of occasions although he accepted the idea in principle, a gesture of brotherhood, a communal holding of hands.

"By train?" he asked.

"Yes, from Dover, I believe."

He wondered what sort of crossing they would have. He had once gone over the Channel on a catamaran, a kind of flimsy construction that flipped from side to side. He had deposited the full contents of an early breakfast just in front of a litter bin in Calais.

"Councillor Moke will be coming with me to meet them," Beryl informed him.

"Very good," said Henry. He returned to his logbook of statistics. He would take a look at the crossword when Beryl had departed.

At the station forecourt the indicator board gave the unhelpful information 'Train delayed. Listen for further announcements.'

"It's not a great start," said Beryl shivering in the breeze. If she moved slightly to one side, the ample girth of Councillor Arthur Moke would take off some of the wind chill.

"Whenever I go by train," Arthur said, "and it's not very often, the trains are always held up."

Half an hour later the train unapologetically sidled in to platform two. There had been no further announcements as promised and the nature of the delay had been mysteriously concealed.

"I can see them," said Beryl waving to a trio of slightly confused passengers.

"What are their names again?" asked Councillor Moke quickly.

Beryl peered in her diary. She had had the presence of mind to jot down the information beforehand.

"There's Ivanka…"

"From…?"

"A town that nobody can pronounce."

"Oh."

"And Ernesto from Lucca."

"That'll be Italy, then."

"And Maximillian from…Oh dear, it looks like Luderholz something…"

"Beckerbrau. That's the place Henry calls Ludicrous Beefburger."

"Well, really!" protested Beryl.

"Guten dag," said a voice behind her. Beryl was gazing up at the tallest member of the trio and surmised it must be Maximillian. His straw-blond hair flopped over a large pair of glasses. Next to Max was a slightly shorter dark-haired man, quite handsome, and not unlike Tony her neighbour, who ran an ice cream round. She immediately berated herself for reflecting on stereotypes. It seemed to go against the twinning ethos. Behind him was a small pale-faced woman who looked as if she had just woken up.

"The train was late," complained Max. "Is this normal, I imagine?"

"Where I live," said Ernesto, "the train is always late."

Beryl thought for a moment. Her experience of Italy, rather like the concerts there, was that they never started on time. Consequently, she never missed a train either. She rather liked it.

"British trains," mumbled Maximillian.

"Partly," Councillor Moke felt obliged to intervene. "I think this one might be run by your comrades, Deutsche Bahn. Privatised the bloody lot, they did. Then state-owned railways from abroad come over here and run them…"

"I think we should be going," suggested Beryl, keen that any wisp of controversy should have no time to prosper. "Would you like a trip round the town or…?"

"It's better hotel," said Ivanka. "We are all a little tired."

"Just as you like," Beryl replied. "I think Henry was going to book a table for later."

"A table?" queried Max. "It is very good but we must entspannen."

Entspannen, thought Beryl. What on earth was that? However, given the rather weary nature of the group, she decided not to push it. She pictured Henry's delight at being able to wriggle out of yet another obligation.

"A taxi will pick you up tomorrow and then we'll take you on a tour of the Council Offices. Herbert Williamson from the Twinning Committee will be formally welcoming you. Then we can show you our beautifully proportioned town."

Councillor Moke glanced over at Ivanka. She seemed beautifully proportioned too although on the verge of falling asleep.

"I would also very much like to see one of your rural villages," announced Maximillian. "I make the studies of such small places."

"Oh," replied Beryl somewhat wrong-footed. "Well, I'm sure we can arrange something."

"They want to see a village," she informed Henry next day. "Something about rural development and community."

"Do they?" said Henry, pleased at having been given the previous evening off. "Well let's take them, then!"

"Oh." Beryl was mildly surprised at his willingness. "But there's not much to see in any of them."

"Take them to the pub. They generally like that."

"Aren't you coming?" she pleaded.

"I was down for last night."

"But they cancelled. Went to bed or something."

"I'm not down for any more," insisted Henry. "Take 'em to Hopton. They've got the Queen's Head…"

"But isn't that the one with grumpy Sid? His rudeness is legendary."

"All half-decent pubs have miserable landlords. It's one of the great mysteries of life. And there's a bakery, too. Beer and bread. Present it as celebration of the yeast. They'll like that."

When the morning tour, address and canapes, had finished, Beryl took them off shortly after one o'clock to see the requested village.

"Most pretty, these small trees," Ivanka pointed out as they set off down some winding lanes.

"Hedges," said Beryl. "Excellent for wildlife."

"I think they were part of the Enclosures Act," remarked Maximillian. "When much land was stolen from the peasants."

"Ah," said Beryl. History was her Achilles heel. If only Henry were here.

They drove slowly into the village and parked near the pond. A number of geese and ducks waddled indignantly towards the water.

"I love these birds!" thrilled Ivanka. "It sounds as if they are always laughing."

"Be-yoot-iful, this one!" Ernesto was pointing at a ruddy duck, its flattened bill looking as if a mishap had befallen it.

"There are two ponds," enthused Beryl as she locked the car.

"By the way," said Ernesto, "when we took Tube I saw a poster."

"Oh yes," said Ivanka. "Most strange. It had a happy woman and under this was written New Fares."

"In fact," added Ernesto, "the price go up and yet she is happy."

"The home of capitalism," observed Max.

"Incredible! But somebody write under New Fares…"

"Oh yes," breathed Ivanka. "Some motto. New Fares, Same Old Bollocks!"

"Pardon?" As with history, Beryl was quite unprepared.

"I thought it very strange to mention cow. It is type of cow."

"I wouldn't know," responded Beryl, reddening. "Perhaps it was bullocks."

"Definitely bollocks," insisted Ivanka.

"I think if we hurry," said Beryl, "the bakery might still be open. They do a lovely range of traditional loaves."

She hurried across the green and in the direction of the shop but Ivanka had got something caught in her shoe. Ernesto and Max lagged behind with her.

Beryl peered through the steamy glass of the bakery window but it seemed strangely empty. Then as she stared further into the gloom she thought she could make out a horizontal foot. Further inspection revealed it to be attached to something pink. She shielded her hand against the pane and immediately froze. The leg had given way to another naked leg. Standing over the pair of pale pink legs, which may or may not have been subjected to a dusting of flour, was a tall man dressed only in boxer shorts. The shorts were hastily discarded as he descended on the pair of legs.

Beryl turned round in horror to find the trio immediately behind her. "So sorry!" she gasped. "It appears the bakery is closed." There was a sudden shriek from within the shop.

"Such pity," commiserated Ivanka. "Especially when is so traditional."

"Should we try the door?" suggested the ever resourceful Maximillian, placing his fingers on the handle. There came a second cry from within.

"No, no!" pleaded Beryl. "I think they must be hard at it… baking."

"It's an unusual time to bake," said Ernesto. "My grandfather had a bakery in Uvopopolo."

Beryl wondered for a moment if the performing baker and his assistant were aware of the conversation and the intense speculation outside. Across the green the pub sign squeaked forlornly. It was a welcome distraction.

"The pub!" shouted Beryl. "We'll go there! A nice glass of local ale! Or there's cider if you prefer. They serve it out of wooden barrels."

"How exciting!" replied Ernesto.

"One moment," said Ivanka, lingering ominously near the bread shop window. "I still have problem with shoe."

While Ernesto attended to the discomfort of Ivanka's heel, massaging it a little, Max sat down on one of the bird-limed benches.

"I'll just go and have a look," said Beryl. "Reserve a table."

"Good idea," said Max.

Please be open, thought Beryl, cursing whoever's idea it was to visit one of these villages. And if you are, please do not subject us to anything remotely like the bakery…

As she approached the pub she noticed that the car park was empty. There were no lights on as she stepped into the small back garden. Just beneath the inn sign was a large board with something written on it. No doubt the specials of the day, the times of food. She took out a pair of glasses and looked at the sign. Instead of advertising bar snacks and evening meals there was a terse valedictory inscription. She looked again in disbelief. 'The fat **** has gone at last!'

She gave a gasp. It was the noun that was the problem, although the adjective was hardly flattering. Turning round in horror, she could see Max striding over to meet her, leaving Ernesto to the ministrations of Ivanka's foot. Beryl had not had a particularly dynamic or worldly life but she was unfortunately familiar with the painted expletive. Hastily taking a stick of dark lipstick from her bag she surreptitiously inserted a circular vowel after the C.

"It is not open?" Max asked.

"We're not having much luck," pleaded Beryl.

"Maybe we should go back to the town and find some refreshment there."

"Oh yes," agreed Beryl, grateful for his resourcefulness, although he was still staring intently at the valedictory sign.

They joined Ernesto and Ivanka, who was slowly hobbling back to the car.

"I suppose it is evidence of the pervading system of class," said Max. "The continuing struggle of the underdogs."

Beryl was unlocking the car, grateful for the chance to flee rural life. "Very likely," she said.

The car was momentarily in the wrong gear and it protested noisily. She thought of Henry sitting comfortably and lazily in the office, head bent over the crossword. Glancing in the mirror, she noticed Ernesto and Ivanka were sitting more closely together. Max was sliding his seat belt on.

"It is pity about your bakery and pub," commiserated Ivanka.

"All the same," insisted Max. "I would have liked to have spoken to the Count. Tried to reason with him. The inequalities of your social system. Maybe over a glass of your deeply traditional beer."

"Yes, perhaps," said Beryl.

The car lunged quickly down the controversially hedgerowed lane.

About the Author

D ominic O'Sullivan grew up in Muswell Hill, North London, but has spent much of his time in East Anglia. He studied German at university in Norwich under the guidance of Dr W G 'Max' Sebald.

A number of his short stories have also been performed as monologues at the ADC Theatre in Cambridge including *Birdsong, New Wave, A Dash of Soda, Undercover* and *The Open Window*. His plays *Stray Paths* and *Forbidden Fruit* have also been performed as part of the First Stage season of new writing.

In 2017 *Portal* and *Dreams* were both performed at the Boathouse Theatre, Cambridge.

ISBN 978-1-912505-08-1

#0013 - 110618 - C0 - 210/148/18 - PB - 9781912505081